Eric Wilder

Of Love and Magic

Gondwana Press

Edmond, Oklahoma

Other books by Eric Wilder

Gondwana Press
1802 Canyon Park Cir. Ste C
Edmond, OK 73013

Front Cover by Gondwana Graphics

ISBN: 978-1-946576-23-1

Acknowledgments

Thanks to the many beta readers who gave the author detailed and valuable feedback.

for Marilyn and Anne

**"Love makes your soul crawl out from its
hiding place."**

— Zora Neale Hurston

Of Love and Magic

A novel by
Eric Wilder

Chapter 1

On a gray afternoon in Oklahoma, snow began
to fall before sunset. Cynthia Warren didn't
notice as she sorted through rows of expensive
clothes draped together in her walk-in closet. Young
and attractive, she was also a klutz, bumping into a
stool after picking out a pale blue gown.

"Dammit!" she said.

After rubbing her leg, she rushed to her dressing
table, colliding with her husband and knocking the
drink from his hand. Dan Warren, tall and thin with
dark, wavy hair, dabbed at the wet spot on his tuxedo
pants, hardly noticing as he read the newspaper in his
hand.

"Will you hurry?" Cynthia said. "The sitter will be
here any minute."

Getting no reaction, she glanced at her husband in the mirror.

"Jake Thompson died last night," he said.

Slipping the dress over her head, she sat on the edge of the bed to straighten her hose.

"Who's that?"

"Dad's best friend," he said, smoothing thick brown hair with his long fingers. "War buddies."

"Have you told him?"

Dan shook his head, a fleeting expression of pain flickering behind his pale blue eyes.

"I can't speak to him anymore. He sits around in that old chair, staring out the window."

"Don't be so hard on him," she said. "He's just lonely."

"Senile's more like it. I may as well tell him about Jake and break the news about Crestview."

Standing in front of the bathroom mirror, Cynthia frantically brushed her hair.

"I'm still not sure we're doing the right thing. Can't it wait till tomorrow?"

Dan poured another drink from the scotch bottle on the dresser before heading upstairs to his father's room.

"I've already put this off long enough," he said.

Cynthia stopped brushing her hair and stared at her husband as he went upstairs, a look of determination on his face. Knocking on the old man's door, not expecting a response, he walked in without waiting for one. His father sat in an Afghan-draped rocking chair, gazing listlessly out the window. The pale skin on the old man's neck blended with the faded orange Afghan.

"Dad, we need to talk." When the older man didn't respond or even turn around, Dan pressed on. "Mom passed away three years ago. The girls will start school next year, and Cyn is doing more charity work. My workload at the firm has increased, and I'm on track for a partnership this year. Do you understand what I'm trying to say?"

The older man spoke in a low, nearly inaudible voice. "I'm proud of you. If your mother were still alive, I know she'd also feel proud."

Dan took a deep breath, nearly choking on his frustration. Instead, he lowered his head, clenched his teeth, and fiddled with a stray strand of hair. When the book in the old man's hand fell to the floor, neither father nor son noticed the dull thud it made upon striking the carpet. Dan opened his eyes and continued speaking in measured tones.

"That's not what I mean."

As if in a trance, the older man appeared oblivious to the severity of his son's tone, continuing to gaze out the window at the gently falling snow. It was more than Dan could bear. Grabbing the chair, he violently wheeled it around.

"Damn it! Look at me while I'm talking to you."

Pressing even harder against the Afghan, the old man briefly thought his angry son might hit him.

His voice cracked when he said, "I'm sorry, Son."

Dan let go of the chair again and tried to breathe deeply. His efforts only kept the veins of erupting redness from leaving his face. Pacing to the opposite wall, he struck his hand against it and tossed the newspaper, crumpled like a club, onto the floor. This time, a paperback Western from the nightstand beside the bed fell to the carpet. Dan kicked it under the bed.

"Cynthia and I want you to be around people your age. You've been stuck in this room since you broke your hip. You don't talk. You don't come downstairs to eat; honestly, I'm fed up with your nonsense." He touched his throat to emphasize how fed up he was and added, "Come Monday, like it or not, we're taking you to Crestview."

"Son . . ."

"No! That's it. Damn it to hell! I'm so angry right now I can't think straight. You're going on Monday, and that's final."

Dan Warren dropped a third book to the floor as he left his father, backed out the door, and slammed it shut behind him.

When he returned to the bedroom, Cynthia said, "Is he all right?"

"Yeah," he mumbled, still frowning as he buttoned his shirt.

"Is who all right, Mama?"

Trish and Emily, identical twins, entered the room already dressed for bed. As beautiful as their mother, both little girls had blue eyes and raven hair. Unlike their mother's close-cropped, sophisticated cut, long dark braids tied with bright red bows framed their lovely faces.

Cynthia had trouble distinguishing them. Dan couldn't. Sparky, their ever-present cocker puppy, padded along behind them. Like the girls, his fur was also black, and he sported a red bow tied jauntily around his neck. Emily handed the puppy to her mother, and it promptly licked a warm swath across her nose.

Insistently, Trish asked, "Is who all right?"

"No one, dear," Cynthia said, rushing to the dressing table to repair her make-up. "Is Julie here yet?"

"She helped us with our pajamas," Emily said. "We came to kiss you goodnight."

After hugging and kissing their mother, the two little girls wriggled away from her and seized Dan's elbows, pulling his arm until he bent down to return their hugs.

"Goodnight, you two rug rats."

"Sorry, Mrs. Warren," the sitter said, poking her head into the room.

"No problem, Julie. We'll be home late if it's okay with you."

"I'll be fine. Come on, girls. Let's go say goodnight to Grandpa."

Cynthia continued combing her hair until the combined stairway clatter of dogs and little girls dissipated, and then she glanced apprehensively at Dan.

"Sure about this?"

Grabbing her elbow, he pulled her toward the door. "The only thing I'm sure about, my dear, is we're late."

❦

Trish and Emily rushed into their grandfather's room unannounced just as their parents hurried out the front door. They found the old man kneeling, staring at the paper that Dan had tossed to the floor. Trish handed him the wriggling puppy, which immediately licked a warm streak across his mouth.

"What you doing, Grandpa?"

"Reading the paper, Trishy," he said, petting the dog.

"How do you know I'm not Emily?"

"Cause grandpas know everything."

"We came to say goodnight," Emily said, joining them.

John Warren dropped the paper to the floor, placed the wiggling puppy beside it, and hugged the two little girls.

"Pleasant dreams, my sweethearts."

Emily wiped her hand across his craggy face. "Grandpa, are you crying?"

"No, Emily. It's just something in my eye."

Turning away, he rubbed his eyes with his shirt sleeve before turning back and kissing them.

"Sleep well, my pretties."

"Please tell us a bedtime story before we go to sleep," Emily pleaded. "Please?"

With a nod, he shrugged his scrawny shoulders, smiled, and said, "Old men like their arms twisted."

5

Both little girls grabbed his arms, squealed, and said, "Please, please."

"Okay, then. Go to your room and get ready. I'll be along to tell you a short one."

"Please hurry. We'll be waiting."

They didn't bother to shut the door behind them. Silence engulfed the dark little room once their scurrying footsteps faded down the hallway. John pulled himself stiffly to his feet using the bedpost and, for a long moment, stood staring at the newspaper he had retrieved from the floor.

"Jake Thompson, you old gutter-snipe," he said, shaking his head.

Jutting out from his craggy cheeks and sloping sharply downward, John's prominent nose dominated his face. This and his closely spaced eyes made him resemble a hawk or perhaps a bald eagle. His feathery gray hair enhanced this illusion. He was also tall and slender like his son, making the family resemblance instantly noticeable.

Wiping another tear from his nose, he shuffled through the clothes in his dresser drawer, searching for a hidden bottle of bourbon. Upon finding it, he tipped the container up and drank until amber liquid dribbled from his thin lips down the loose skin of his neck.

"Here's to you, Jake."

After taking another long swig from the bottle, he grabbed an overnight bag from the upper shelf of the closet and started packing it with clothes from the dresser. Before closing the bag, he took his wife's picture from his nightstand and set it on the clothes. Once finished, he limped down the hall to his granddaughters' bedroom, where he found the babysitter waiting at the door.

"I'll be downstairs if you need me," she said.

"Thanks, Julie," he said, subconsciously resentful of her implication, though he knew she meant well.

Already in bed, the two little girls waited anxiously while John sat in the chair. He couldn't help but smile at their eager anticipation.

"What story do you want to hear tonight?"

"A new one," Emily said.

"Something we haven't heard," Trish said.

Scratching his head, he paused for a moment. "I have a new story. It's about an otter and a salamander. Would you like to hear it?"

"Yes," both little girls shouted.

Dreamily staring at the ceiling, he leaned back in the chair and began, "Once upon a time, an otter lived in a small pond in the woods. The otter was old, like your grandfather, and his children were grown. In fact, he was so old that almost all his friends, except for his best friend Salamander, had passed away. Mr. Salamander's children had moved him far away to a much smaller pond. The otter missed their chess games and storytelling, but Salamander kept in touch. They talked every day on the wildlife telephone. One day, Salamander didn't call."

Trish asked, "What happened?"

"Stop squirming, young lady, and I'll tell you," he said with a wink. "Otter was worried about his friend. He wanted to call but had caught his toe in a trap the previous spring. Otter was old, and the sore toe didn't heal as quickly as it used to. Feeling sorry for himself because of his loneliness, he somehow blamed everyone else. When he learned that his old friend had passed away, he felt very, very sad."

"What did he do?" the twins caroled.

"As I mentioned, Otter was old but not too old. He left the pond for one final trip: to visit the Magic Fountain before he passed away."

Trish asked, "What's that?" He raised his hand toward the ceiling. "The Magic Fountain exists in our minds. Crystal water flows from its mouth, revitalizing both body and spirit. Otter had visited it once in his youth. Now, on a whim, he decided to go there one last time. Packing his otter luggage, he set out on an odyssey."

"Grandpa, what's an odyssey?"

John smiled while gently brushing Emily's long hair from her sleepy eyes and explained.

"It's a journey to a faraway place that isn't easy to reach. But Otter had a kind heart and a strong desire. He left the pond in search of the fountain."

"Did he find it?"

After kissing both little girls, he tucked the covers around their necks. "Tell you next time. Just remember," he said, pausing on his way out the door. "It's not always so important that we find the Magic Fountain; only that we never stop looking."

With that, he turned off the lights and closed the door behind him. Rock music vibrated through the hallway walls as he made his way back to his room. After a frustrating moment spent searching his closet, he realized he no longer had a heavy coat. After looking at the crumpled newspaper lying on the bed, he switched off the lights and quietly crept to the hall closet.

Cynthia and Dan were both avid skiers, and they had all the expensive gear that came with the sport. John had once tried on his son's goose-down ski jacket.

"Sorry, Dan," he said, slipping the jacket over his bony shoulders.

John tightened the hood around his neck. With a stubborn smile and a quick backward glance, he stepped into the snowstorm, trudging down the icy sidewalk toward the inviting glimmer of distant streetlights.

Chapter 2

Snow fell in damp white clumps as John walked out of the kitchen door, having no idea where he was headed, yet intent on getting there. Unexpected spring snow left the streets in the upscale Tulsa neighborhood deserted. Two blocks from home, the sounds of tires slipping on ice and snow caught his attention. When he rounded the corner, he found a large recreational vehicle stuck on the curb, one rear wheel spinning uselessly. He tapped on the driver's window, which was misted with condensation.

When a woman's head appeared, he said, "Need help?"

"Sure do. Do you have a couple of big, strong sons? Or the number of a good wrecker service?"

John chuckled. "Don't have either, but I can get you off the curb if you'd like."

Taking her foot off the gas, she gave him a slow appraisal. "Don't know what horse you rode in on, but I'll bite."

"Do you have a tire iron on that bus?" he asked, disregarding her sarcasm.

"Yes, I have a tire iron, and no, this isn't a bus. It's a recreational vehicle."

"Maybe that's your problem."

"What's that supposed to mean?"

"You'd probably be better off in a National Park than a snowed-in Tulsa subdivision. But don't worry. Bring me that tire iron, and I'll get you off the curb."

9

Closing the window with an annoyed grumble, she disappeared into the RV, returning shortly with a tire iron. With a skeptical glance, she handed him the tool.

He smiled and pointed his thumb skyward. "Turn on the engine and wait for my signal before giving it a little gas."

She watched as he positioned the tire iron beneath the large rear tire. After maneuvering it a bit, he raised his finger. As she pressed the gas, he wiggled the tire iron. With a brief lurch, the long RV slid easily off the curb. Driving it to the center of the snow-covered road, she stopped and opened the window when he raised the tool.

"Don't forget your tire iron."

Winking and smiling again, he waited for her to take the tool and drive away. Instead, she sat there, staring at him with a quizzical expression.

"Thanks. I was just about to panic. Can I give you a ride somewhere?"

"Don't know. Where are you headed?"

Smiling for the first time, she said, "Depends on where I am. I've been driving in circles in this crazy neighborhood for nearly an hour."

"61st Street is just around the corner," he said.

"Is there a filling station close by? I'm almost out of gas."

"Turn right on 61st. There's a station at the intersection."

The nearby thoroughfare was busy with passing cars, tires crunching through patches of snow. The neighbor's dog began barking and hushing when it recognized John.

"You didn't answer my question about the ride."

"You didn't say where you're going," he said.

"The filling station, if I don't get lost again. Show me the way, and I'll drop you off afterward."

"Deal," he said, offering his hand as he entered the RV. "My name's John Warren."

"Attie Johnson. Buckle up. Never know when we might wind up in the ditch."

John fastened his seat belt, stealing glances at the attractive woman behind the wheel as he leaned back in the high-backed, comfortable seat. When she turned around and caught him staring, he grinned playfully. Attie Johnson was youthful, with large dark eyes, gray-streaked braided hair, and classically high cheekbones. He guessed she might be in her fifties, but suspected she could easily be older.

They followed the snow-covered street to a brightly lit gas station. While waiting for the attendant, she turned on an overhead light, took a map from the side pocket, and spread it out on the console between them.

"I'm headed to play Indian bingo at Red Rock. Can you tell me how to get to the Cimarron Turnpike from here?"

"You bet," he said, taking the map and pointing out the route with his finger.

When the tanks were full, she started the engine and backed onto the street, slipping in the icy slush but never really losing control.

"It's better if you let me off here," he said.

"We came from the other direction."

"I'm not going home. I'm heading to Hot Springs."

"Surely you aren't on foot."

"Yes, I am. I'll hitch a ride on the Interstate," he said.

Attie suddenly slammed on the brakes, skidding to a stop in the snow. "In a hurry?" she asked, her dark-eyed gaze immediately making him uncomfortable.

"Not really."

"Neither am I. I could use a cup of hot coffee. Let's park this thing, and I'll brew us up a pot."

When Attie parked across the street in a nearly empty shopping center parking lot, John settled in as the aroma of brewing coffee filled the dry air in the RV.

When the last sputter of coffee came through the spout, Attie placed their cups on the built-in table.

"Now, tell me what a man your age is doing out on a night like this, hitchhiking to Hot Springs."

John chuckled as he sipped his coffee. "It sounds silly, even to me. I guess you could say I'm running away from home."

"You're right. It does sound silly. Why?"

"I don't want my son to know where I am."

"That's irrational, not childish. Maybe you'd better explain."

John slumped back against the bench seat. "My wife died three years ago, around the time I fell and broke my hip. I moved in with my son and his wife. Now I realize I started acting like an invalid, and they began treating me that way."

"Is that all?"

He slowly shook his head and eased back against the couch. "No. Sometimes, you just let things happen because it's easier than taking action. You know what I mean?"

"Maybe. Tell me anyway."

"After Martha died, I just blanked out for a while. Between Martha's death and my broken hip, I didn't feel like explaining my feelings to anyone. Not that they would have understood. My son interpreted my reticence as senility."

"You sound cognizant to me," Attie said.

"Thanks. Never felt more aware in my life."

"So what happened?"

"Dan, my son, is an attorney. He had me declared incompetent. It's partly my own fault because I knowingly allowed him to do it. On Monday, he's putting me in a nursing home. If I end up there, that is."

"Just explain to him you're not incompetent. Move back to your own house."

"He sold it and liquidated my assets."

"Have him give them back."

"I don't care about the house and money. Right now, I only want to go to Hot Springs."

Staring straight at him with dark, piercing eyes, she said, "To die?"

Shaking his head, he grinned. "Not to die. I want to live, at least as long as I can."

Attie leaned across the table and touched his hand. "It's no fun playing bingo alone. Why don't you detour with me to Red Rock?"

Dan and Cynthia came home from the party to find the twins tucked in bed and Julie asleep on the couch. Trish and Emily allowed them to sleep soundly until late the following day. Unable to hold back, they pushed open the bedroom door and stepped in, creating a clatter of noisy heels against the hardwood floor.

"Take us to the park, Daddy."

"I'm sleeping," he said.

"You promised we could go on Saturday. It's Saturday."

Dan sat up in bed, licked his salty lips, unhinged his glue-encrusted eyelids, and ran his hand over the dark stubble on his face. His stomach churned, and pain reverberated through his temples. Without responding to the little girl, he lifted himself out of bed and dashed to the bathroom.

"I don't think Daddy feels well," Cynthia said. "I'll take you to the park after I dress."

"But Daddy promised," Emily pouted.

"Next Saturday," he said, returning from the bathroom. "Now go outside and play until your mother's ready."

Cynthia cast him a dirty look as the two little girls rushed from the room. "I don't feel much better than you, Tarzan. Why can't you take Trish and Emily to the park occasionally and let me stay in bed?"

"I'm working on a big case and brought some things home that I need to finish," he said, glancing at his watch. "If I don't hurry, I'll miss the ball game."

Cynthia threw her hands in the air as she went to the bathroom. "Heaven help us!"

She dressed and joined him at the breakfast table, where he sipped coffee while reading the morning paper. Billie, the cook and housekeeper, poured her a cup as soon as she sat down.

"Would you like bacon and eggs, Ms. Warren?"

"Yes, thank you, Billie."

"Old Mr. Warren didn't eat this morning," she said, scraping the food from a plate into the disposal."

Dan glanced up from his paper. "Is that unusual?"

"Yes, sir," she replied. "The old man, I mean Mr. Warren, typically eats like a dog pulling a sled."

"Humph!" he allowed, burying his head into the paper. "I didn't realize he ate that much."

"I know. You wouldn't think a skinny man like that could put away so much food."

"Maybe you should check on him," Cynthia said.

He shook his head. "I'm sure he's fine. You couldn't injure the old bat with a lead-weighted club."

"That's not very nice to say about your father."

"But true. The old bird will probably outlive us both."

With a sudden clatter of tiny heels on the polished wood floor of the living room, Trish and Emily, followed by the panting cocker puppy, emerged from around the corner.

"Mommy, Mommy, Grandpa's not in his room."

"Whoa," Dan said, holding up his hand. "Didn't I tell you not to run in the living room? You know it'll scratch the floor."

"Daddy, Grandpa's gone," Emily said.

Again, he buried his head in the paper. "Probably just down the hall."

"Does he move around the house during the day?" Cynthia asked.

Billie shook her head. "He sticks mostly to his room."

"Dan," Cynthia said. "Check on your father." He continued staring stoically at the paper. "Dan!"

Dan's stubborn glare was his only response. Frowning, she went upstairs, closely followed by Trish, Emily, and Sparky. He slapped the unfinished paper on the kitchen table and started after them. When they reached the old man's bedroom, they nudged the door and stood looking at his tidy living space.

"Dan, he's not here."

"Where the hell is he?" he said.

Trish and Emily hung on their mother's legs, looking worried. Even the usually frenetic puppy crouched against Cynthia's foot.

"Don't know," she said. "Maybe you should call the police."

"That's ridiculous. He has to be somewhere in the house. Let's go find him."

Cynthia called Billie, and they began to search the large house methodically. After twenty unsuccessful minutes, they returned to the old man's room.

Genuinely worried, Cynthia frowned and said, "Where could he have gone?"

Something on the bed caught Dan's attention. Spotting the newspaper he had left on the floor the night before, he quickly reached for the phone.

"Maybe you're right, Cyn. I think I'd better call the police."

Chapter 3

When Vince Blakeman arrived, he found Cynthia sitting on a couch, twiddling her thumbs as her husband paced wider circles around the living room floor. She kept staring at the detective's tweed sports coat and mismatched tie. Sitting beside her, he took out a notepad from his jacket. Likely in his mid-thirties, Blakeman had the earnest yet unremarkable appearance of a hard-working man with tousled hair, a small mustache, and brown eyes that didn't miss much.

"Sorry, Lieutenant Blakeman," Dan said. "I genuinely have no idea where he could have gone."

"Has he ever done this before?"

"No,"

"Yes," Cynthia said, interrupting.

"Ma'am?"

Dan glared at his wife and then resumed pacing. "Once, after my mother passed away, he visited a friend in Oklahoma City and didn't return when expected."

"Where was he?"

"Police found him in a bar," Cynthia said.

Blakeman noted the frown on Dan Warren's face. "A bar?"

"He and his friend had too much to drink," Cynthia explained. "The owner of the bar called the police."

"Is he an alcoholic?"

"Course not," Dan said. "He's a doctor, for God's sake."

"You mean a medical doctor?"

"Yes, a medical doctor."

"Was he on any prescription medication such as Valium or anything?"

Dan stopped pacing and glared at the detective. "What are you getting at?"

"He may have had a stroke, an allergic reaction to a drug, or maybe an insulin seizure if he's diabetic."

"He isn't," Dan said.

Cynthia frowned at her husband and then looked away. "Would you like more coffee?" she asked, picking up Blakeman's empty cup. "We can provide you with his medical records if that would help."

"Big help," he said.

Glaring at her husband again, she left the room with the empty coffee cup.

"Mr. Warren, why don't you take a seat and relax? We won't get to the bottom of this unless you cooperate."

"My father could freeze on the side of the road while I'm answering questions."

"My men have covered every foot in a ten-mile radius around your house. An old man couldn't have walked any farther than that."

"Maybe he's not on foot," Cynthia said, returning with fresh coffee.

When Dan frowned at her insinuation, Blakeman wrote something on his notepad, pretending not to notice.

"We're exploring that option. State Police are searching for hitchhikers and questioning motorists they encounter."

"Damn it!" Dan said, slapping the wall. "This is so frustrating."

"Maybe he's with a friend somewhere in town," Blakeman said, ignoring the outburst. "A list of his friends and acquaintances would help us a bunch"

"Certainly, Detective," Cynthia said. "We'll take care of it right away."

"Good. We're checking hospitals and emergency rooms. Does your father have any illnesses you're aware of?"

"He's healthy as a horse," Dan said.

Again, Vince Blakeman caught Cynthia's worried expression. "Mrs. Warren?"

"He has some heart problems, although nothing serious."

"Any indication of Alzheimer's? At first, it's hard to notice."

"Look here," Dan said. "His mind's like a steel trap."

"I'm not trying to be negative; he may be a little forgetful."

"You've told me many times that you think your father sometimes has memory lapses," Cynthia said.

"I wasn't serious," Dan replied, miffed at the suggestion.

"Considering his age, a stroke isn't out of the question."

Scratching through the last note, Blakeman sat back against the couch and sipped his coffee, hoping the young couple would relax.

"We're so worried," Cynthia said. "What else can we do?"

"TV's already picked up the story. You could post a reward. That sometimes helps."

"This is being blown out of proportion," Dan said. "How far could an old man have gone? I don't like all this adverse publicity."

This time, both Cynthia and Blakeman frowned at his insensitive statement.

"You're not running for governor, and he is your father?" she said.

After folding his notepad and returning it to his jacket, Blakeman draped the overcoat over his arm and started for the door.

"Thanks for your help. We'll find him in no time. I'll stay in touch until then."

Cynthia walked him to the front door as her husband frowned and paced, ignoring the detective's departure. Twin sets of running feet greeted her, with Sparky right behind.

"Girls, remember what your father said about running on the living room floor."

Trish asked, "They found Grandpa yet?"

"Not yet. Very soon now."

Emily said, "Will he be all right?"

Cynthia smiled and pointed toward the door. "He'll be fine. Why don't you take Sparky into the backyard?"

The twins vanished out the door as quickly as they had appeared, Sparky's nails scraping against the wood as he followed closely behind. By this point, Dan had stopped pacing. Cynthia found him leaning against the wall, frowning as he stared out the picture window with a vacant expression.

"They'll find him," she said, touching his shoulder.

After shooting Cynthia a sour look, Dan walked away in silence.

ꡳ꜂ꜗꝭ

When sunlight awoke him the following day, John didn't remember where he was. Pulling the window shade aside, he squinted over the parking lot, bustling with Saturday morning shoppers. Rising, he bumped his head on a cabinet above the couch. His eyes finally focused on an attractive woman in an old flannel robe. She was cooking something on a small stove, and the rich aroma of brewing coffee sparked his memory.

"Morning, John," Attie said, handing him a cup. "Sleep well?"

"Like a ton of bricks," he said, rubbing his back.

She chuckled. "Sorry about that. It was either the couch or the floor."

He reached down and patted the floor. "It couldn't be much worse."

"You'll feel better after breakfast. Bathroom's in back," she said. "When we finish eating, you can shower and shave. I have an extra razor and toothbrush."

"How about an extra change of clothes? I left my suitcase on the sidewalk while helping you off the curb."

"We could go back for it."

"No."

"Then you'll have to make do until we get you some more."

"Look, I . . ."

"Attie," she said.

"Look, Attie. Maybe this isn't such a good idea."

She paused, stirring the eggs, and asked, "Are you coming to Red Rock with me, or are you heading home?"

He sipped his coffee before replying. "Even though I already miss my two granddaughters, I'm not returning there."

"You have granddaughters?"

Fishing through his coat pocket, he found a picture and handed it to Attie.

"Wow, identical twins. How old are they?"

"Five going on twenty."

"They're gorgeous. But so young."

He glanced up into her brown eyes. "I look that old?"

"No," she said.

"I was well into my forties when I married."

Grinning, she patted his shoulder. "I didn't mean to pry. Let's eat. You can decide what you want to do when we're done."

After breakfast, John closed the door to the RV's tiny bathroom. Attie had already showered and dressed before him, and her nightgown hung on a hook. A sensual, almost forgotten sensation surged from his finger to his brain when he touched the soft material. The secretly shared intimacy embarrassed him, so he returned to finish dressing, trying not to dwell on his suddenly confusing feelings.

Alone, he examined some of Attie's belongings. Next to her bed, a small picture of a man and a boy piqued his interest. The boy, about ten years old, had dark hair and eyes with a bronze complexion. Like the man in the picture, he shared the regal curve of a Native American nose. The man's long black hair and dignified presence reminded him of powerful chiefs from a bygone era. Posed as if they were father and son, they seemed suspended in another time.

Staring at the picture, John wondered about the two people, though snooping into the personal life of someone he barely knew filled him with guilt. Trying to forget his voyeurism, he finished dressing and joined Attie. She had already put everything away and opened the flower-print curtains to greet the sunlight. Shielding his eyes from the glare of the melting snow, he found her waiting in the driver's seat, studying a map.

Without looking up to acknowledge his presence, she asked, "Feeling better?"

"Much better."

"Decide what you're going to do?"

John finished buttoning his shirt sleeves before replying. "Attie, I appreciate the bunk for the night, the breakfast, and all your hospitality. I don't feel right intruding on you any more than I already have."

"If you have someplace else to go, I'll understand, though I assure you, you aren't intruding. Still thinking about Hot Springs?" When he nodded, she said, "Told you I'd take you there after I play bingo."

"You don't mind if I tag along?"

"I'm just a lonely old woman. I welcome the company."

"You're not old. I have to have at least twenty years on you. Where did you say you are going?"

"Red Rock to play bingo, then Oklahoma City to gamble on the horses. After that, I'm heading back to Arkansas. We can detour through Hot Springs if you like."

He scratched his chin, remembering a nearly forgotten memory, and smiled. "I haven't played bingo since I was a boy."

"Won't be any children playing bingo in Red Rock. It's big business. They give away about a quarter of a million dollars a week," she said.

"You mean two hundred and fifty thousand dollars? Are you kidding?"

"It's the wildest thing this side of Vegas. On an Indian reservation and exempt from state taxes."

"Bet that makes our bureaucrats happy."

Attie nodded, agreeing. "They don't like it one little bit. The place is a gold mine. Saturday night, there will be people pouring in from six states."

John's eyebrows arched. "I knew there was gambling involved, but I had no idea."

"You're in for a treat," she said. "I've been twice, though never alone."

"You like to gamble?"

Shrugging, she said, "An old woman's vice."

"Attie, stop saying that. You're not old."

Patting the seat beside her, she said, "Neither are you. Now, help me navigate. Don't want to get lost again."

"Tulsa is the easiest town in the world to find your way around," he said with a knowing grin. "Streets are all numbered or else in alphabetical order."

"Someone could have told me that last night."

"Not to worry. You have me to guide you now."

Reaching across the console, she gave his knee a friendly pat. He felt an immediate warmth reminiscent of the moment he'd touched her nightgown. She started the engine after lowering the visor to shield against the harsh glare of the bright morning sunlight.

"Just get me out of town. Tonight, we'll break the bank in Red Rock."

Grinning with satisfaction, he crossed his arms and leaned back against the seat. As he did, a wave of exciting anticipation surged through his veins for the first time in several years.

Chapter 4

Cynthia entered the house through the back door, closely followed by the twins and their black cocker spaniel. She grabbed a canister from the cabinet and set a kettle on the stove before taking off her coat. Not waiting for their hot chocolate, Trish and Emily tossed their coats onto the kitchen table and dashed into the hall.

"Whoa! Wait just a minute," Cynthia called after them. "Don't leave your jackets on the table. Where are you going in such a hurry?"

"To see if Grandpa is back yet," Trish said.

"Hang your jackets in the closet, and then go see about Grandpa. Hurry back. I'm fixing hot chocolate."

Screeching to a halt, Trish and Emily grabbed the jackets and raced from the kitchen. Cynthia grinned and went to the living room, finding Dan sulking by the fireplace.

"We're back from the park," she said, kissing him. "Anything new on Grandpa?"

"Nothing," he said, mumbling the word.

Cynthia touched Dan's shoulder and reacted to his frown, pulling her hand back. He stared sullenly out the window, ignoring her question until she took his hand and squeezed it.

"They'll find him. He'll be fine."

Dark crescents shadowed his eyes, and his face was red and puffy. With a subdued tone, he finally spoke. "I haven't had a moment's rest all day. The phone keeps ringing. Everyone wants to know what happened."

Cynthia traced gentle arcs across Dan's unshaven face with her finger and said, "That's wonderful."

Wrenching away, he angrily slapped the wall. Startled by his sudden outburst, she pulled her hand back once more.

"No, it's humiliating," he said, narrowing his eyes. "Thanks to the radio and noon news, every redneck this side of Wewoka knows my father wandered off in the middle of the night."

When she reached for his shoulders, he pulled away. "You have nothing to be ashamed of. No one is blaming you."

"Blame me? No. Laugh at me? Yes," he said. "How will I feel in court Monday morning with everyone talking behind my back, knowing they're pointing fingers at the son of the senile old man who walked out of the house in the middle of a snowstorm? What do you think they'll say at the office?"

She clenched a tight, desperate fist. Loosening it with a frustrated frown, she leaned closer and ran her fingers through his hair.

"Who cares, and what reflection does it have on you?"

His face grew even redder. Now, his voice sounded shrill. "He's done this to me my whole life—grabbing the spotlight and embarrassing me in front of my friends. I can't stand it."

Little voices and running feet approaching from behind startled her. She stopped the twins at the living room door, pivoting and raising her hand.

"Girls, your father and I are having a private conversation. Please go to the kitchen and wait for me there."

Trish and Emily exchanged knowing glances, did an about-face, and exited the room.

"Forget Grandpa. Isn't there a ball game on television?"

"To hell with the ball game!"

She glanced around at the open door and said, "Get a grip. This isn't your fault or your father's. There's a logical explanation for what has happened, and Detective Blakeman will uncover it."

When he didn't respond, Cynthia frowned and followed the twins into the kitchen, turning around when she reached the door. Dan had returned to his previous posture by the fireplace, staring lethargically out the window. She found Trish and Emily at the kitchen table. They looked up with troubled little eyes when she entered the room.

"We're worried about Grandpa. Have they found him yet?"

When Cynthia opened her mouth to respond, she noticed her lips were trembling, and her hands were shaking. She poured a glass of water from the tap and drank it before speaking.

"Not yet."

Cynthia took the kettle off the stove, made the twins cups of hot chocolate, and then poured herself some coffee from the pot into a cup. Feeling a bit more steady, she sat down at the table.

"Did Grandpa say anything unusual to you last night before you went to bed?"

Trish said, "Like what?"

Cynthia paused and closed her eyes. "I don't know?"

In unison, they said, "He told us a bedtime story."

Suddenly sensing another presence in the room, she turned around. It was Dan standing by the door, listening to their conversation. Ignoring her gaze, he poured coffee from the pot and joined them at the table.

"I may be grasping at straws," Cynthia said defensively. "Still, it can't hurt to ask."

"What story did Grandpa tell you?" he said, not waiting for her to raise the question.

"Otter and the Salamander."

When Cynthia glanced at Dan, he motioned her to remain silent. "Never heard that one," he said, clutching Trish's hand. "Can you tell it to us?"

"Otter's friend, Mr. Salamander, died, and Otter went away to find the magic fountain," Trish said.

"Magic fountain?"

"Grandpa said it was far away and not easy to reach. Otter wanted to revisit it before he died," Emily said.

Pushing away her husband's arm and bending closer to the little girl, Cynthia said, "He told you he'd been there?"

"Once when he was young," they said.

Again, Cynthia glanced at Dan. "Has he ever told you this story before?"

"No," Emily said.

"Did he tell you where the magic fountain is located?" Dan asked.

"Yes," Trish said.

"Where?" he asked, grabbing the little girl's shoulders.

"In our minds," she said in a high-pitched voice.

As John and Attie left Tulsa, a warm southerly breeze quickly melted the snow from the night before. Patches of ice lingered on either side of the road, though they were no longer threatening enough to deceive hungry birds or budding blackjack trees. West of Tulsa, the countryside grew less urban, with gently rolling terrain. Like an emerald mackinaw, vegetation had begun to cover the weathered hills. It was spring in Oklahoma, and John wanted the world to know.

"This is wonderful. I can't remember anything so beautiful."

"Yes, it's beautiful. I love these hills."

Leaning back and resting his head in his hands, he said, "I'd almost forgotten."

Attie briefly shifted her gaze from the winding blacktop and looked at him curiously. "How could you forget something so lovely?"

Smiling contentedly, he said, "Too much time indoors, worrying about yesterday, I suppose."

When she didn't reply, he observed her golden complexion, radiant in the sunlight reflecting through the windshield. Braided hair, dark eyes, turquoise earrings, and a silver squash blossom necklace framed her sculpted cheeks.

"You're an Indian, aren't you?"

"It's Oklahoma. Aren't we all?"

"Good point. I'm part Cherokee myself, though not enough for head rights."

"Is that a curse or a blessing?"

He chuckled. "You're not from Tulsa, are you?"

"Born in Tahlequah, though I haven't lived there for years."

"Where are you from?"

"I live on a farm in the Ozarks near Eureka Springs, Arkansas."

As if recalling a pleasant memory, his eyes grew dreamy. "Little Switzerland. I haven't visited in twenty years."

"It hasn't changed much."

"Don't suppose it would," he said. "Why did you move to Arkansas?"

"My husband had an art gallery there."

"Had?"

"I sold it when he died."

"I'm sorry, Attie."

She reached across the console, smiled, and patted his knee while keeping her eyes on the winding road. "It's been a while. Are you from Tulsa?"

"I've lived here all my life except for eighteen months or so during the war."

"Thought so," she said.

"Where in the world did you get this bus?" he asked, thumping the armrest and changing the subject.

"Roland bought it to tour the country. He died before we ever used it, and it sat behind the house, collecting dust. One day, out of curiosity more than anything else, I drove it to town and thought, this isn't so hard. I've been taking trips in Ol' Nellie ever since," she said, giving the dashboard an affectionate tap.

Basking in their friendly camaraderie, he grinned and pinched his arm to ensure he was awake.

"Martha and I traveled some when I retired. I haven't gone two blocks from my son's house in three years."

"Well, it's high time you did."

"I love to travel. I do have one small problem."

"And what would that be?" she said, eyebrows raised.

"I didn't plan to leave when I did, although it had been on my mind. I haven't needed money for several years, and now I'm left with not a penny to my name."

A smile of relief spread rapidly across her attractive face. "Is that all? I'll grubstake you."

"Can't let you do that."

"Why not? You have an honest face."

Feeling his honest face burning with embarrassment, he pivoted in his seat and glanced out the window at passing scenery.

"I don't know," he said.

"Do you have problems borrowing money from a woman?"

"I have a problem borrowing from anyone if I can't pay it back."

"I'll tell you what. I'll lend you five hundred dollars. If you break the bank at Red Rock, we'll split it fifty-fifty. If not, I'll write it off as a bad bet."

John smiled at Attie's proposal. "Mighty kind, but you don't have to lend me money."

"I know I don't have to. I want to."

29

Still staring out the passenger window, John turned around and faced her, a grin on his craggy lips.

"Guess if you're so determined, I'll just have to break the bank at Red Rock."

She patted his knee again, smiling. "That's the spirit."

Basking in the warmth of her touch, he reclined against the leather bucket seat, watching the rugged scenery of northeast Oklahoma pass by the window. They left the main highway and continued along an old road lined with rolling pastures, slow-pumping oil wells, and white-blooming dogwood trees.

"We'll reach Red Rock before long," he said. "It's still only ten in the morning. What will we do until bingo starts?"

"Find an RV camp, park this bus, fix a bite to eat and relax. Games start at five, and we can catch a shuttle or walk over from the camp."

"Bus?" he said with a smile.

"You know what I mean. Do something useful and check the map. Let me know where to turn before we end up in Ponca City.

John looked at the map and gave her directions. Unable to contain his curiosity any longer, he asked, "Is that a picture of Roland and your son in the bedroom?"

Attie's friendly smile faded instantly.

Realizing he had touched a sensitive nerve, he said, "I'm sorry. Please forgive me for getting too personal."

Attie's frown softened, and she said, "I'm glad you decided to come along. My friend Beth had to cancel at the last minute, and I detest traveling alone."

Feeling somehow vindicated by her remark, he said, "If you don't mind traveling with a nosy old man, I certainly don't mind traveling with the most attractive woman in northeast Oklahoma."

Attie's neck flushed bright red as she stifled a smile to hide her satisfaction with his unexpected compliment. Wrapped in the warm comfort of each other's company, they continued in silence along the lonely country road.

Chapter 5

As John and Attie arrived in Red Rock, a slow spring rain replaced the brief stint of morning sunshine. Ice melting in the ditches signaled that the week-long cold front had finally retreated. Attie left the main highway and followed a side street into town.

"Better buy you some clothes," she said. "Can't let you break the bank wearing a pair of bedroom slippers."

He glanced at his feet. "An old man can't think of everything," he said.

"Let's hope there's a store here. Don't want to drive to Ponca City."

He mentally counted Red Rock's six stores and said, "If there is, it shouldn't be hard to find one."

Carved with a dull knife from hilly terrain, the small northern Oklahoma town occupied no more than a square mile. Scrub oaks surrounded four blocks of frame houses, along with a business district dominated by a clapboard gas station and a general store made of crumbling brick.

Attie parked in front of the store and said, "Maybe we won't have to drive to Ponca City after all."

Shrill bells announced their entry into the store. A nostalgic nod to the fifties, groceries and canned goods filled half the building, while sundries and dry goods occupied the rest. A young woman in a bright printed dress arranged clothes on a rack as a man in a white smock stacked cereal boxes nearby. Smiling warmly, the woman welcomed them as they approached the racks of miscellaneous clothing.

She said with a friendly country drawl, "Do you folks need help?"

Pointing to the trousers and smiling in return, Attie said, "Just browsing."

"My name's Jane. Need me, I'll be in back." Her starched skirt rustled as she returned to the rack of clothes.

"These are nice," Attie said, holding up a pair of dark gray trousers.

Glancing at the tag, John said, "Too big. My waist is thirty-two inches."

Attie wiggled her shoulders and fluttered her eyelashes. "Sorry. I didn't mean to insult you."

Ignoring her levity, he found another pair of dark pants. "Think these might suit me?"

Nodding her approval, she said, "Try them on. And take these with you."

She handed him a pair of khaki pants, and he walked to the small dressing room at the back. While she waited, she browsed the clothing racks, choosing several sets of socks and underwear. He came back with both pairs of pants draped over his arm.

"Well?"

"Fit like a charm," he said.

She stopped him as he started to hang the khaki pants back on the rack. "Then let's get both. I like the khakis."

Hesitating briefly, he draped the brown pants over his arm and said, "It's your pocketbook."

"I also found some shirts while you tried on the pants."

She showed him a light blue pinstripe, a white dress shirt, and a Hawaiian print and measured one against his chest.

"I'm the white shirt type," he said.

"I like the others better. Since it's my pocketbook and not yours, I'll buy the other two instead."

"You're getting carried away."

"Stop it," she said. "Don't spoil my fun."

John grimaced as he trailed Attie to the back of the store counter. They discovered Jane deeply engaged in conversation with the man in the white smock. Their arrival interrupted the discussion.

"Have any shoes?" Attie said, pretending not to notice their discourse.

The man's smile became a frozen mask. "You bet. In the corner, by the flashlights."

Casting a worried glance at Attie, John accompanied her to the shoe department.

"You folks from around here?" Jane asked.

"No. Arkansas," Attie said.

"Here for bingo?"

When Attie nodded hesitantly, Jane said, "I knew it. We have buses arriving on weekends from Dallas and Kansas City. Ralph and I even played once or twice ourselves."

Attie remained silent, and the curious young woman started ringing up the purchases on the mechanical cash register. Once she was done, she put the clothes into a large sack.

"Ninety-four dollars," Jane said.

Attie handed her a hundred-dollar bill.

"Knocked the heck out of that Benji," Jane quipped as she returned Attie's change.

"Money well spent," Attie said.

"Where are you folks planning to stay?" Ralph, the salesman in the smock, asked.

Once again, John glanced at Attie, who replied, "I don't know yet. On our way to Wichita, we considered playing bingo. I'm so tired and unsure if I'm up to it."

John clasped the package to his chest. He grabbed Attie's elbow and said, "Better be on our way."

Ralph said, "What'd you folks say your name was?"

"Jones," John said, pulling Attie toward the door. "Sam and Prudence Jones."

Once they were back inside the RV, Attie said, "Prudence?"

"The only thing I could think of at the moment," he said with a grin.

"Do I look like Prudence?"

"If you do, she must certainly be an attractive woman."

Accepting his compliment with a muted headshake, she started the engine. "Let's find a place to park this bus."

John consulted the map and directed her to the Indian reservation.

"You think those people recognized me?"

"Don't know. They acted suspicious."

"I noticed," he said.

"When we reach the RV Park, we'll hook up the antenna and watch the news on TV."

Finding the park just outside the reservation gates, John waited while Attie went into the office to rent their space for the night. During his wait, several camping vans and RVs arrived. He could see that the park was already nearly full.

"Just in time," she said when she returned. "They only had four spaces left."

"I didn't realize bingo was so popular," he said.

"It is tonight. Final game's worth fifty-thousand dollars."

John signaled Attie, standing behind the RV and waving her arms, as she carefully backed the tricky vehicle into the tight spot. Once parked, he connected the water and electricity and emptied the holding tanks. When he entered the RV, he saw Attie making sandwiches.

"The couple at the store upset me, and I forgot to buy groceries. We'll have to eat bologna sandwiches. I hope you don't mind."

"I've endured more than my fair share of bologna in seventy-odd years," he said with a dead-pan smirk.

"Quite the jokester, aren't you? Everything hooked up?"

"We're in business, Madam," he said.

Attie flipped a switch on the wall, producing a whirring rattle. She opened a cabinet, pulled out a tiny television set, and turned it on.

"Maybe we can get the noonday news."

They listened intently. John felt despair when he discovered his disappearance was the top news story. Police speculated everything from suicide to kidnapping. A reward was offered, and the broadcast included an old photograph of him. After noticing Ralph and Jane's suspicious behavior, he paced increasingly wider circles around the RV.

"I have to go back to Tulsa," he said as Attie switched off the TV. "I know my son and daughter-in-law are worried sick, not to mention my granddaughters."

Attie touched his elbow and said, "Do you think returning to Tulsa will solve anything? They might just put you in a rest home instead."

"At least they'll know I'm safe and won't have to worry about me. I don't know if I can live with the guilt."

"So, you've made up your mind?"

He nodded. "I saw a pay phone outside the park office. Maybe I'll walk down and give them a call. My son can come and get me."

He started slowly toward the door.

"John, wait until tomorrow. Spending one night in town before going home won't hurt."

Seriously considering her gentle proposal, he paused before responding. "I kind of had my heart set on playing bingo tonight."

She handed him the bologna sandwich, her face flushed and tears streaming down her dark eyes.

"What's the matter?" he asked, confused.

Turning away, Attie wiped her face with her sleeve. Her voice choked with emotion as she said, "I'm just a foolish old woman. Even though I've known you for less than twenty-four hours, I will miss you when you're gone."

Spring sunshine faded into a chilly evening as Vince pulled his collar around his neck, waiting impatiently on Dan Warren's front porch. After hearing footsteps on the parquet floor, he felt a rush of warm air as Cynthia opened the door and welcomed him inside.

"Detective Blakeman, come in," she said, leading him into the foyer. "Let me take your overcoat."

"Thanks, Mrs. Warren."

"Like a cup of coffee?" she asked as she hung his coat in the hall closet.

"Don't mind if I do. Is your husband around?"

With strikingly expressive eyes, she winked and nodded toward the couch in the living room. "Have a seat. I'll get him and the coffee." He settled onto the sofa, admiring the antique furniture and luxurious carpets. Hearing a ruckus in the hall, he looked up as twin little girls and a black cocker spaniel approached him. Fearlessly, they placed the squirming puppy in his lap.

"Are you a policeman?" Trish asked.

"Yep," he said, trying to avoid the puppy's long tongue. "Who are you?"

"Trish. This is Emily and Sparky."

"How do people tell you apart?"

"They don't, except Mama and Grandpa," Emily said

Before he could field another question, Cynthia returned with the coffee and her husband. Looking at the twins and apologetically at Vince, she said, "Girls, take Sparky and get ready for bed."

"Oh, Mama, we want to hear about Grandpa," Trish said, her lower lip protruding in a sullen pout.

"If there's any news, I'll tell you tomorrow. Now scoot."

Emily grabbed the wiggling puppy and hurried from the room.

"Do you have news, Detective?" Dan asked.

"Please sit," Vince said.

Dan frowned and leaned against Cynthia's chair. Folding his arms tightly, he showed his apparent dislike for the tone in the detective's voice.

Vince dismissed his frown. "We've checked every hospital within a hundred miles. None has admitted anyone matching your father's description in the last twenty-four hours." After pausing to sip his coffee, he added, "Unfortunately, most of your father's friends have passed away. We've contacted everyone who is still alive."

"Look, Detective Blakeman, why are you here if you have nothing new?" Cynthia winced and replied, "Don't be so nasty. Detective Blakeman is doing everything he can."

Vince gave Dan his coldest stare until he began to fidget.

"You didn't let me finish."

Cynthia also stared intently at her husband. She grabbed Vince's nearly empty cup and said, "Let me warm up your coffee, and you can finish telling us about Grandpa."

"As I was saying," he continued when Cynthia returned. "We were all convinced your father left home of his own accord when we found his suitcase down the block. He either caught a ride with someone or was abducted."

Vince paused for Dan and Cynthia to absorb this tidbit of information before continuing, "The fact that he left the suitcase on the sidewalk suggests the latter, but we tend to believe the former."

"How can you be so sure?" Cynthia asked.

"Your reward offer has borne fruit. There's an unverified report of your father being here in Oklahoma."

"Where?" Dan asked.

Savoring the rapt attention following his unexpected announcement, Vince sipped his coffee before explaining. Raising his voice slightly for dramatic effect, he said, "Someone spotted him in a store in Red Rock. He was buying clothes, and he wasn't alone."

Chapter 6

Attie shook John's shoulder until he opened his eyes. Once he did, he blinked several times, not immediately recalling where he was. She waited until he sat up and shook the cobwebs from his fuzzy brain before handing him a glass of water. He drank half and smiled, noticing her quizzical gaze.

"Never could take naps in the middle of the day," he said. "It always makes me feel like my head is stuffed with wet cotton."

Attie grinned and retrieved the glass. "Sometimes you remind me so very much of Victor."

John rolled his feet to the floor, stood up slowly, and stretched his arms toward the ceiling. "I thought your husband's name was Roland."

"Not my husband," she said, chuckling. "A basset hound I once had."

John blinked, his cheek muscles twitching as his lips curled into a smile. He lifted his chin toward the ceiling slowly and let out a howl.

Patting his cheek playfully, she said, "Just like Victor. If you play bingo the way you howl, we're in for a big night."

She went to the back of the RV and shut the door behind her. A moment later, she opened it a crack and glanced out, grinning. "I'm getting dressed, Wolf Man. When I finish, you can use the bathroom."

Just before five, John and Attie left the RV and walked the short distance to the bingo building. A dozen chartered buses crowded the lot beside the giant prefab structure. A throng of people milled around outside, chatting and enjoying the warm weather. Attie grabbed John's elbow and stopped him. "I better give you this," she said, handing him five one-hundred-dollar bills. Turning away and looking at the ground, he shook his head and replied, "Why don't I just watch you play."

Staring into his faded eyes, she grabbed his hand, gently unfolded his fingers, and placed the bills into his palm.

"Let's have just one night before you go. Remember?"

Understanding her meaning, he smiled and said, "All right, one night it is."

They waited in line for five minutes before reaching the door, and each paid $100 for special game packages. "We're all set, High Roller, unless you can play ten games simultaneously. In that case, we'll buy you another game package," she said. "One is probably too many." He followed her into the large, open room crowded with people. When she spotted a gaming window, she grabbed his elbow.

"Let's buy some scratch cards," she said, steering him toward the window.

His eyebrows lifted as they walked through the spacious open room to the enclosed booth. She gave the cashier ten dollars, and the woman behind the counter counted out ten brightly colored cardboard pieces and placed them in Attie's hand.

"Your turn, big boy," she said.

Smiling at the ticket seller, he held up all ten fingers. Attie nodded approval, and he followed her to a less-than-crowded corner of the building.

"Now what?" he asked, glancing dubiously at his purchase.

"Scratch off the coating. Find out what you won."

He watched as she took a penny from her coin purse and proceeded to scratch away the black coating on each of her ten cards. When she finished, she shook her head and frowned.

"Shoot! I've never won a nickel with these things."

"Then why keep trying?"

"Because it's fun."

John kept a single card from his stack, handing her the rest. "Take some of mine."

Without bothering to thank him for his generosity, she greedily took the cards and scratched off the coating with the same results.

"Try yours," she said, tossing the worthless cardboard into a nearby trashcan.

After scratching the coating from his remaining card, his eyes opened wide, and then his mouth.

"What is it? What did you get?" When she reached for the card, he pulled it away. "John, did you win something, or are you just fooling around?"

Turning the card so she could see, he said, "Fifty bucks. Tonight's my lucky night."

After a spontaneous hug, she returned him to the counter to cash in the ticket. "You might drive home in a new Cadillac with your luck."

"The way my luck usually runs, the back of a cattle truck is more likely," he said.

Grasping his hand, Attie pulled him through the nervous bingo players to a long table with two adjacent empty seats.

"You call that bad luck? I'd love to know where I can get a double dose. You'd better find a seat. The first game starts in fifteen minutes."

From their vantage point, they could easily see the elevated platform, enclosed by four short walls, at the front of the open room. A woman's upper torso was visible behind a crane-neck microphone, and a plastic box filled with brightly colored, numbered balls floated inside on a cushion of air. TV monitors were located near the ceiling in every corner of the building.

John asked, "Why the enclosed platform?"

"They don't want to make it easy for a would-be robber," she explained.

He glanced around the room and noticed several security guards positioned by the doors and near the booth where they had purchased the pull-tabs.

"Guess that's a consideration."

"You bet," she said. "Seventy-five thousand dollars will change hands tonight."

"I can hardly believe it."

"Look around," she said. "There are probably five or six hundred people here tonight. Playing the mini-games costs a dollar each, and at least three hundred people play every time. Each game lasts less than two minutes, allowing forty games an hour."

"Twelve thousand dollars an hour," he calculated.

She nodded. "And that doesn't include what they win from scratch cards. Most of these players are experienced and buy several cards each game. Some even play five at once. I suspect the house takes around a quarter of a million dollars on a good night."

"Amazing!"

Opening their game packages, they spread the contents in front of them. John held up a red marker.

"What's this?"

"It's an ink dauber. If you have the number they call, daub it with a red mark."

"No corn?"

"Except for you, old man," she said, straight-faced.

Ignoring her humor, John said, "Which of these cards do we play first?"

"Blue one," she said.

Puzzled, he held up the blue rectangular game board. "There are five games on this card. Which one do we play?"

"All of them. You can't win by getting a bingo on a single card. You need two winners and sometimes three or more."

43

"And you say a game takes less than two minutes?"

Attie leaned back in her chair and smiled knowingly. "That's right. They draw a ball from the box and place it in front of the television camera. You can see the call even if you can't hear it on screen."

Within minutes, the tables began to fill with eager players excited to start the game. The couple next to John appeared to be at least ten years older. As he glanced around the crowded hall, he suddenly felt young again and smiled at the pleasant-looking, white-haired older woman beside him.

"First time?" she asked.

"How can you tell?"

Casting a nodding glance at the red dauber still resting on the table before him, she said, "The game's about to start."

Picking up the dauber, he waited as a man with a leather folder crossed the elevated enclosure. After tapping the woman on the shoulder, he whispered something in her ear before leaving the stage. With a smile, the woman blew into the chrome microphone, the resulting whistle blasting from the wall speakers. Suddenly, the hall fell deathly quiet.

"We're about ready to start the first game, folks," the caller said. "Card is blue and has number thirty-four in the upper right-hand corner."

Seeing John's confusion, Attie pulled the blue card from the pile and handed it to him. "Watch the card, and I'll watch the monitor."

"Everyone ready?" the woman in the enclosure asked.

"Yes," the crowd roared.

"Okay," she said. "The first game is for twenty-five dollars, and you need two bingos to win. When you bingo, please hold your sheet above your head and yell so the spotters can see you."

Her tinny voice echoed through the large room's bare metal walls like a cheap speaker. John glanced around and noticed several men in suits standing in the aisles between rows of tables.

"If everyone's ready, let's do it," she said, pressing a button and retrieving a ball from a slot in the floating box. "B-13," she announced.

As the caller set the ball on a rack, its image appeared instantly on the television screen.

"Oh, five," she said, continuing rapidly.

Attie reached across with her dauber and made a red mark on John's colored card.

"Pay attention," she said.

"Gee seven."

The game proceeded at a blazingly fast pace. "Bingo!" someone behind them shouted.

One of the spotters snatched the card and rushed it to a man behind a teller-like window.

Immediately, the second game began.

"Red card number fifteen," the woman announced. "Eye twelve," she called.

John tried to keep up with the game's pace but fell hopelessly behind. The nice white-haired woman reached across him and marked four spots on his card.

"You got a bingo," she said, elbowing him in the ribs.

Attie grabbed his arm and nudged him until he stood. "Say it, John. Hurry!"

"Bingo," he yelled.

Attie cheered enthusiastically and hugged him when he took a seat. A bulky spotter grabbed his card and hurried off to the window cage, coming back with twenty-five dollars in cash that he quickly stuffed into his shirt pocket and focused on the next game. No matter how hard he tried, he couldn't keep up with the game's pace. Eventually, he dropped the dauber, crossed his arms, and leaned back in the chair, frustrated, as the white-haired woman beside him chirped and shook her head.

Attie never missed a beat, marking her cards and then his. Yet, five more games passed without either of them achieving another bingo. After fifty minutes, the woman in the enclosure called for a short break. Like a wave crashing to shore during a hurricane, the noise in the room instantly surged. Attie grabbed his hand and squeezed, her excited smile so infectious that it made him grin.

"Oh, John, I hope you're having fun."

When she kept holding his hand against her breast, a warm flush spread across his neck and face. The sensation made him happy, though it was uncomfortable.

"I don't quite have the hang of it yet. I'm getting there," he said. "How about a cold drink or something to eat?"

"I could go for an iced tea."

Reluctantly pulling away from her grip, John got out of his chair. Attie's smile was so warm that he could feel the heat three feet away. Feeling slightly foolish, he broke their locked gaze and stepped away from her chair.

"Be right back," he said with a wink. "Unless there's a team of mules I don't know about."

"I'm waiting," she replied.

Blowing her a kiss before turning into the crowd, he felt as foolish as he ever had at sixteen.

Chapter 7

When the caller announced the break, everyone shared the same idea as John. Almost in unison, the crowd rose from their seats and headed for the restrooms and concessions. Anticipating the rush, he hurried forward, finding himself in a shoulder-to-shoulder crowd, with people so close that he could barely see his feet for their bodies. Standing still for five minutes, his neck flushed from the heat. Finally, he glanced at the fluorescent lights and suddenly felt dizzy. A man beside him grabbed his shoulder.

"You all right, Mac?"

John nodded and smiled weakly. "Yes, thank you. I'm just a bit lightheaded. Must have stood up too fast."

Releasing his arm, the man tapped his shoulder. "Take it easy, old-timer."

John thanked him, and the man melted into the crowd. Feeling sick to his stomach, he touched his forehead and massaged his right temple, which suddenly began pounding like a rusty piston. When the crowd moved forward, he went to the bathroom and sponged his face with a wet paper towel, breathing deeply to calm his erratic heart before attempting to return to the concession stand. Still dizzy and disoriented, he bought two large iced teas and looked around desperately for their table. With his chest aching and head pounding, he slowly made his way toward the center of the large room.

"Are you all right?" Attie asked when he handed her the tea.

John nodded without responding. The older couple sitting next to them listened in with concern. "Take one of these," the white-haired man said, handing John a small pill. He glanced at the pill before placing it under his tongue.

"Thanks," he said.

"What did you give him?" Attie asked.

"Nitroglycerin," the man said.

Attie glared at the older man and then shifted her gaze to John. "You took that pill without asking what it was."

Avoiding her question, he glanced in the direction of the bathroom.

"I'm still feeling queasy. Mind if I step outside for some air?"

Her expression dissolved into a worried mask. "I'll go you."

"I'm fine now. Please play my cards for me while I'm gone."

Attie grabbed his hand and squeezed it, releasing it after a moment. "Are you sure?"

Feeling her concern, he bent down and kissed her forehead, managing a grin as he patted her cheek.

"I'm okay."

Before turning for the door, he stopped to whisper something in the white-haired man's ear.

"Thanks," he said.

After patting the old man's shoulder, he hurried to the main door and found the well-lit parking lot deserted. Drawing a deep breath, he leaned against the building for support. He wasn't alone; a man in a wheelchair was watching from the shadows.

"Feel okay?"

"I have a little trouble once in a while."

"Better see a doctor about that," the man advised.

John smiled. "It's nothing serious. Why aren't you inside playing bingo with everyone else?"

"I get bored after a few games," he said.

John took another deep breath and sat beside him on a concrete retaining wall. "John Warren," he said, offering his hand.

"Name's Scooter Bates. I seen you on TV."

Scooter had a full head of brown hair and an infectious grin. John glanced away into the darkness, not knowing what to say.

"It's all right," Scooter said. "Ain't going to turn you in. Think I know why you skedaddled."

John faced him again. "You do?"

"Shore I do. Kin can drive you up a tree if you let 'em."

"You're right about that. Still, I'm going back tomorrow."

"Run out of money?"

"It's not that. I miss my granddaughters and don't want them worrying about me anymore."

Scooter lowered his chin and gazed at John over his gold-rimmed glasses. "Weren't them made you run away though, was they?"

John didn't immediately answer. "No," he finally said. "I left because I decided I was too young to die and too old to live with my son any longer, at least without being able to spank him."

Scooter grinned knowingly. "Same here," he said, slapping his right thigh. "Ain't always been like this. I was a policeman in Tulsa. I worked part-time as a security guard after I retired. Got shot in a robbery and paralyzed from the waist down."

"Sorry," John said.

Scooter held up a palm and shook his head. "Don't feel sorry for me. Felt sorry enough on my own after it happened. My wife passed away about ten years ago, and I was used to seeing for myself. Still, took me a while to adjust."

"I can imagine," John said.

"I moved in with my boy down in Oklahoma City. Things was fine for a while, but we commenced to get

49

on each other's nerves before long. When I couldn't take it no more, I moved to Dallas to live with Cassie, my daughter. After a spell, we was at each other's throats, too."

"What did you do?"

"Moved out and went back home to Tulsa. Figured I was too old and set in my ways to live with my kids."

"I know the feeling. What are you doing here if you don't like bingo?"

"Sue, my girlfriend, can't get enough of it. I play once in a while. Mostly I just sit out here and people watch."

"It is a bit crowded in there," John said.

"Can I give you a piece of advice?"

"I'm not too old to listen to advice."

"Don't go back. You love your family, and they love you, but you can't live their lives, and they sure as hell can't live yours. The best way to make them happy is to be happy yourself."

Slumping forward, John stared at the ground. "My son wants to put me in a nursing home. That's not the issue. I can't bear to put them through the agony of not knowing where I am or what happened to me."

"Long as you don't turn up dead in a ditch somewhere, they'll always believe you're okay. I know how families of people who disappear act. I was a cop."

"I'm not so sure."

"How old are your granddaughters?"

"Trish and Emily are twins, both five."

"I'll say it again. Don't go back. Trish and Emily will understand. You can contact them when you're settled someplace."

John shook Scooter's hand again. "Don't know what I'm going to do, but you gave me some grist for the mill. I thank you."

Scooter smiled and raised his thumb. "Hang in there," he said. "I'm pulling for you."

As John reentered the bingo palace, the crowd hummed excitedly as the time drew near for the big money game. Appearing relieved, Attie smiled and hugged him when he returned to the table. One of his cards had won another twenty-five-dollar game. He decided to forget about tomorrow and have fun with Attie until then.

Minutes later, a tap on his shoulder interrupted his concentration. Behind him in the wheelchair, Scooter Bates looked worried.

"You got to get out of here. Quick."

Attie turned around to see who was talking to him.

"Attie, this is Scooter Bates."

"Pleased to meet you," Scooter said. "There are cops all over the parking lot. They's looking for you."

Again worried, Attie asked, "How do you know that?"

"Hell, I know a cop when I see one. Besides, one showed me a picture and asked if I'd seen you. I told him I hadn't."

Attie cast a questioning glance at John and said, "You ready to go back, old man?"

John's frowning face flushed bright red, and he slowly shook his head. "In my own time. I won't let them drag me out of here like a common thief. Besides, we have a date for the races in Oklahoma City."

"That's my man," Scooter said, slapping his shoulder. "What are you going to do?"

"I'm taking your wheelchair if you'll let me," John said.

A big grin enveloped Scooter's face. "Hot damn! Good idea."

John helped Scooter into his vacated seat. After taking his place in the wheelchair, he draped Attie's shawl over his legs.

"Put these on," Scooter said, handing him a pair of dark sunglasses and an old misshapen baseball cap.

John winked, slipped on the glasses and pulled the cap down over his eyes. "Attie will return your wheelchair."

"Take your time. I'll just occupy myself playing your bingo cards."

Putting her hands on his shoulders, she kissed his forehead. "Thanks. We owe you one."

John leaned back in the chair as Attie pushed him up the crowded aisle toward the door. Before they reached it, they noticed several uniformed policemen and men dressed for something other than bingo. Despite their two nervous stomachs, they made it out the door without a sideways glance from the police. However, when they reached the parking lot, their luck ran out.

"Ma'am, wait," a man called to Attie.

When she dug her fingernails into John's shoulders, he didn't need to see her face to sense her anxiety. A man in a blue suit stepped in front of the wheelchair, raising his hand. Attie froze, and John held his breath as he scrutinized them from head to toe. Silently, the man shifted his gaze to Attie.

"Seen this person?" he asked, handing her a snapshot.

John fidgeted as Attie studied the photo. "He does look familiar."

"Well?" the man prompted.

"Afraid I haven't. Is there trouble?"

"No trouble, ma'am," he said. "Thanks for your help."

Attie embraced him as they hurried back toward the building, trembling as she did so. After five minutes, she arrived at the RV park and paused in the doorway.

"Sit here a minute. I'll see if anyone is watching."

John waited until she returned and opened the RV's door. She didn't switch on the lights. After lowering all the curtains, she said, "Grab that contraption and come inside."

She shut the door behind him. When their anxiety subsided, she giggled and gave him a quick kiss.

"Slick as a whistle," she said. "We should have been spies."

"Not out of here yet. Someone's probably guarding the front gate."

"I'm going to return Scooter's wheelchair," she said. "We'll worry about leaving the front gate when I return."

Relaxing on the couch, he waited for thirty nervous minutes. When she returned, she wasn't alone. Scooter accompanied her, and they both laughed as he opened the door. They kept laughing while John helped Scooter into the RV.

"Scooter won the fifty thousand dollars," Attie said.

"You're kidding! Why, that's fantastic," John said. "Congratulations."

"Congratulations to you. It was your card."

"I gave them to you. You won the money and it's rightfully yours."

"Maybe," Scooter said. "But I ain't keeping it."

John shook his head. "Neither am I. Not after what you did for me."

"You don't want it, I'll give it to Attie," Scooter said.

Attie touched his shoulder and said, "You're the sweetest man. I can't take it either."

Scooter's smile disappeared, and he glanced at the door. "I feel like I've known you two forever. I don't treat my friends that way. If neither of you ain't going to take the money, I'm flat going to give it back to Red Rock."

Attie studied John with a look of concern. "Don't you dare give that money back, Scooter Bates," she said. "We earned it fair and square."

"You said it, Attie. You earned it. I didn't help you two out cause of money," he said.

John scratched his wispy-thin hair and began to smile. "We're partners. We split it fifty-fifty."

Attie grinned, and so did Scooter. John shook Scooter's hand.

"Wish we at least had a beer to celebrate with," John said. "Guess we'll have to make do with iced tea."

"No way," Scooter said, reaching into the backpack attached to the wheelchair and pulling out three cans of cold beer.

"Here's to all of us," John said, holding up a bottle. "Now if we could just get out the front gate."

Scooter drained his beer in one long draw, belched loudly, and excused himself with a grin. "Easy," he said. "There's an exit behind the building. The man on the gate is Sue's brother-in-law."

An hour later, John sat in the RV's front seat, gazing at the passing light posts on Interstate 35. Neither he nor Attie had spoken since leaving the compound. He observed as her shoulders finally relaxed, and she slumped in her seat. When she noticed him looking, she smiled.

"We made it, old man. Think we did the right thing?"

Shrugging, he said, "Don't know. It'll take someone older and wiser than me to answer that question."

Chapter 8

Against his better judgment, Detective Vince Blakeman waited on a downtown park bench for an unanticipated meeting with Cynthia Warren. Still suffering from winter malaise, he studied the cracks in his shoes while occasionally glancing at lunchtime strollers, relishing the beautiful weather.

His nerves were shot from too much precinct coffee. Anticipating his meeting with Cynthia, he fussed with his hair, which was tousled by the gusting Tulsa wind. It felt even thinner than the week before, and his efforts did little to boost his self-confidence. He attempted to smooth out the wrinkles in his corduroy suit with similar results.

Cynthia appeared, hurrying up the walkway toward him. When she reached him, breathless, she shook his hand.

"Sorry, I'm late, Vince."

He tried to appear stern, expressing displeasure at having waited forty-five minutes. His expression was about as menacing as a sleeping hound; the attempt failed, as her infectious smile overpowered his pent-up grumpiness.

"No problem, Mrs. Warren," he said, animosity wafting upward like the pretty lady's beguiling perfume. "Please, have a seat."

Cynthia dismissed his suggestion with a roll of her large greenish-blue eyes and a synchronized movement of her short black hair.

Pointing at the pathway, she said, "Let's walk. Please."

He could only nod and follow her like an obedient puppy. Wearing stylish high heels, she seemed to tower over him. Her confident beauty and expensive dress made him feel even more uncomfortable.

"Eaten yet?" she asked.

Vince glanced at his belt as a horn from a passing pickup blared in the street beside them. "I was thinking about skipping lunch. I need to get a handle on my waistline."

Cynthia licked her glossy lips as if suddenly struck by an idea. "There's a restaurant that overlooks the ice arena across the street." When she noticed him briefly touch his wallet, she added, "My treat."

"You don't have to do that, Mrs. Warren."

"Nonsense, this is my first trip downtown all year without the girls. I insist."

She hurried along the path lined with trees, not waiting for a negative reply, with Vince following close behind. He trailed her across the street and up the escalator to the second floor of the multi-story shopping complex, where restaurants, shops, and other establishments surrounded a large skating rink. She guided them to a restaurant on the top floor, where a glass-enclosed, fern-draped atrium offered a view of the ice rink. Her smile secured them a coveted table in a dimly lit corner. Before the waiter could speak, she ordered a champagne cocktail.

"Light draw, please," he said when the waiter asked what he was having.

When their drinks arrived, Cynthia sipped hers and stared at him with hypnotic eyes that appeared to shift colors with the changing light. Leaning toward him, she took his hand before he could pull it away.

"Although it seems odd to meet like this, I wanted to speak with you privately."

Vince twisted his mustache between his fingers and looked around to see if anyone was watching.

"No problem," he said, unable or unwilling to free his hand.

Pretending not to notice his discomfort, she smiled and said, "Dan is very sensitive about his father's disappearance. He thinks everyone blames him."

"Sorry, Mrs. Warren. Afraid I don't understand."

"He's acting moody and has sulked around the house since Friday. It's beginning to affect his work."

"And?"

"I'd like him to move past the incident and forget the investigation as much as he can. I'd appreciate it if you could confer with me about it from now on rather than with him."

Vince cleared his throat, gently pulling his hand away from her grasp. He didn't respond to her concern until the waiter returned to take their orders, and he waited until the young man had left before answering her.

"Maybe your husband needs professional help, perhaps counseling."

She leaned back in her chair, stroking her dark bangs with anxious fingers. Her finely manicured nails, smooth and shiny with polish that matched her lips, glimmered in the dim light. Vince also noticed a flicker of agitation in her striking eyes.

"Dan would never go for that."

"Nothing to be ashamed of."

"I know," she said, lowering her eyes. "Nothing is wrong with Dan. His father was a prominent local physician, and his mother was a well-known socialite. Dan is an only child. I'm afraid he received very little attention when he was young and still resents it. I think he somehow feels that his neglect may have resulted in Grandpa's disappearance. The guilt is consuming him."

"Look, Mrs. Warren . . ."

"Please, call me Cynthia."

"We're doing everything we can to locate your father-in-law. We have some promising leads. See if you can persuade your husband to speak to a therapist. I'll keep you updated directly until we find Mr. Warren."

"Thanks, Vince."

Once again, the waiter interrupted their conversation, bringing Cynthia's salad and Vince's club sandwich. After taking a few small bites, she set her fork down on the table, leaned back in her chair, and took a sip of her drink.

"Tell me about the positive leads you have."

Though he toyed with the sandwich out of desire, he realized she preferred to talk rather than eat. Setting it back on the plate, he said, "We checked out the Indian bingo tip." Below them, on the ice rink, a girl dressed in pink pirouetted, touching the tip of her outstretched toe as she balanced on one foot while skating.

"And?"

"A couple was spotted. They eluded my people. The man fit your father-in-law's description."

Cynthia nibbled on a piece of lettuce. "He was with someone?"

The girl in pink leaned against the railing as a Zamboni smoothed the ice. Vince felt his collar had suddenly become unbearably tight. After loosening it with his finger, he took a small bite of the sandwich.

"An attractive older woman, mid-fifties to early sixties. They were playing bingo together."

"Who identified them?"

The detective's stomach growled in disapproval when he pushed the sandwich aside.

"An elderly couple playing beside them at the bingo table. The picture you gave us is several years old. Still, they made a positive identification."

Cynthia leaned back in her chair. "How did you miss them?"

"Mr. Warren borrowed a wheelchair from someone he met playing bingo. His female companion pushed him out the door, past our officers."

She finished her cocktail before replying. "Then he did run away on purpose."

"That's what it looks like."

Again, she touched his hand. "I'm glad we talked in private. This will be our little secret."

She saw something in his eyes. Something he'd left unsaid.

"What's wrong?"

"The old couple that identified your father-in-law told us he had a problem."

She squeezed her nails into his hand. "What problem?"

"They thought he might have had a minor heart attack."

❧✦❧

Soft filtered light poured through the yellow RV curtains, waking John the following day. He sat on the short couch, slowly straightened his long legs, and painfully rotated his sore neck. Attie was already up, wearing her white terry cloth robe and pouring coffee from the pot. She smiled upon noticing him moving around and brought him a cup.

"Morning, John. I won't ask how you slept."

He grumbled, "You don't want to know."

After placing their cups on the coffee table, she stood behind him and massaged his shoulders.

"Oh!" he moaned. "Don't stop."

Though she continued rubbing, her smile faded. "I hardly slept last night, worrying about your heart."

"I'm fine. I have a preexisting condition."

"And your medicine was in the bag you left on the street?"

Nodding, he replied, "I'll take care of it when we get to Oklahoma City."

"How?"

"I'll think of something."

59

After finishing breakfast in silence, he showered and put on a fresh shirt and pants. Before continuing their drive to Oklahoma City, they walked around the roadside park to stretch their legs. A flock of Canadian geese flew in formation overhead, heading north. A trucker speeding by on the freeway honked his horn and waved.

When they returned to the RV, the sun had fully risen, and the temperature was comfortably in the mid-sixties. Feeling recharged, they headed south on the freeway toward Oklahoma City. Upon arriving in the sprawling prairie town, John spotted a pay phone and signaled Attie to pull over.

"A friend of my son is a doctor in town. I'll call and have him phone in a prescription for me."

"Good," she said. "We'll skip the races and go straight to Hot Springs."

"No way. You have your heart set on watching the ponies."

"But the doctor will report you to the police."

"Maybe he will, maybe not."

"If you want to go back . . ."

Clutching her hand, he said, "I can't remember when I've had so much fun. I've already made up my mind. I've no intention of returning to Tulsa."

Attie waited in the RV while he made his call. A receptionist answered on the second ring.

"May I speak with Doctor Watson?"

"Who may I say is calling?"

"John Warren. Doctor John Warren."

A young man's voice replaced tinny elevator music pouring from the receiver. "Doctor Warren! Where are you?"

"Oklahoma City, Tim. Do a favor for me. My heart condition has flared up again."

"You okay?"

"I'm fine. Same old problem. I need you to call in a prescription for me. The medicine you prescribed last summer worked just fine."

"Everyone is looking for you. Tell me where you are, and I'll pick you up."

"Unnecessary. I'm not lost."

"But Sir, your family . . ."

"Tim, please. I can't explain now. I'm fine. I'm not going back to Tulsa just yet."

"But . . ."

"Tim, you remember when you finished pre-med and weren't accepted at OU medical school on your first try?"

John waited through a pause before the doctor answered.

"You know I haven't forgotten, Doctor Warren."

"I called in some chits for you," he said, not letting him finish. "Now I need your help."

Doctor Tim Watson paused again. When he finally spoke, he sounded like the boy John remembered playing cowboys and Indians with his son in his backyard in Tulsa.

"Sir, if something happens to you, I won't be able to look Dan in the eye."

"You two spent so much time together growing up. I still think of you as my second son. I want you to call and tell him you helped me, but not until tomorrow."

"Doctor Warren . . ."

"Please, Tim. Will you do it for me?"

A resigned sigh followed another pause. "All right then. Where are you?" After John told him, Tim said, "There's a pharmacy on the corner. I'll give them a call."

"Thanks, Tim."

"Doctor Warren?"

"Yes?"

"I'm not sure what's going on here. Please take care."

John hung up the phone and returned to the RV. "There's a pharmacy across the street," he said, pointing.

Attie pulled away from the curb without speaking. When they reached the parking lot, she said, "I'm going with you. If the police are waiting inside, I want to be with you."

They entered the drugstore hand in hand, like nervous lovers. When they reached the pharmacy in the back, they looked around warily for signs of the police.

He asked the lady pharmacist, "Is there a call-in for John Warren?"

Nodding, she said, "Doctor Watson just called. We'll have it ready in about ten minutes."

Attie frowned and squeezed his hand.

"We'll do some shopping and return to pick it up," he said.

Attie's nervous expression failed to camouflage her anxiety as they strolled through the drugstore, even though John acted nonchalantly, patting her hand to calm her.

"Tim won't call the police."

"How can you be so sure?"

John kissed Attie's forehead, not thinking about the intimacy until he pulled away, his face red, and he felt foolish.

"Because I practically raised him. He and Dan were best friends, almost inseparable. When Dan wasn't at Tim's house, Tim was at ours. He's like my second son."

Attie blinked and feigned innocence to the red flush on his neck and forehead. They wandered through the drugstore, browsing magazines and examining vaporizers until ten minutes had elapsed.

John's theory about Tim's loyalty was proven right. When they returned to the pharmacy, there were no lurking policemen. After paying for the prescription, they exited the drugstore without any issues.

Attie stopped the RV halfway out of the parking lot. "John, let's go straight to Arkansas."

Shaking his head, he said, "I've trusted people all my life. Tim promised he wouldn't call my son until tomorrow. I believe him. Now," he said, playfully tapping her chin. "We're going to the races."

Chapter 9

Five miles from the pharmacy, they discovered the racetrack in the rolling hills on the city's northeast side. Upon arriving at the large parking lot overlooking the facility, Attie parked the RV. John poured himself a glass of water and took one of his heart pills.

"Races start at one. Maybe we should get a bite to eat at the track restaurant while we wait."

He looked up from the sink at the racetrack's spring greenery. Sparkling with a fresh, new paint job, white stables lined the track that stretched for acres across gently rolling, treeless prairie.

"Good idea," he said.

Grinning, she snapped her fingers. "I have another great idea."

As she rummaged through a closet, he watched with interest. Finding what she was looking for, she returned with a cowboy hat and dark glasses.

"I remembered not throwing away all my husband's clothes."

An almost imperceptible grin rearranged the craggy lines of his typically stoic face as he took the hat. Attie laughed, watching him admire himself in the small mirror. Still grinning, he adjusted and readjusted the hat, tilting it jauntily from one side to the other. Adding dark glasses, he tossed back his head, appreciating the pose.

"Now all I need is a big cigar and cowboy boots."

He turned, surprised, when Attie asked, "What size do you wear?"

Twenty minutes later, they followed the winding path down the hill to the track's entrance. John mimicked a wealthy Texas rancher with a cowboy hat, hand-tooled boots, and a leather vest. Attie looked sleek and lively, appearing much younger than her years in boots, blue jeans, and a flower-print western shirt worn under a mahogany-colored leather vest.

A bright red bandanna kept her silver-gray hair secured away from her face, revealing and accentuating her big dark eyes, high Indian cheekbones, and flawless bronze complexion. She moved along like an energized racewalker, smiling and swinging her arms in wide, synchronized arcs. John trailed behind anxiously, his shoulders tense. Finally, he took her hand and stopped, silently pleading with her through his faded gray eyes.

"Attie, I feel like a fool."

Smirking and nudging him with her elbow, she said, "Don't be so self-conscious. You look wonderful. Besides, I've always wanted to go out with a good-looking cowboy."

His grin grew more expansive, and he wrapped his arm around her waist. "Maybe you should call me Lonesome John, King of the Geriatric Cowboys."

Ignoring his glib remark, she gently nudged his ribs with her elbow. Her light-hearted attitude boosted his confidence and eased his nervousness. He followed briskly down the hill, energized by her vitality, which cracked like lightning amid distant prairie rain.

When they reached the track's entrance, they bought tickets and pushed through the turnstile. Due to their early arrival, the giant complex was nearly deserted. John's boots echoed against the tile as they walked down the empty hallway to the escalator.

The azure sky spilled through the banks of overhead windows, blending with primary colors to create a warm, inviting atmosphere. Bright Oklahoma sunshine flooded the transparent walls, fostering a sense of openness, integration of man and nature, and an instant lightness of being. Holding Attie's hand, he watched the escalator's sleek chrome sides reflect light in sinuous waves.

"I was raised on a cattle ranch and had horses all my life. Now I feel guilty because I never taught my son how to ride."

"Stop this guilt talk. I'll bet he learned dozens of things from you."

He grinned. "Probably all my bad habits."

"If he's anything like you, he's a wonderful man."

When he kissed Attie's forehead, John's face flushed the same color as the bandanna in her hair. Looking away self-consciously, he felt her warm smile and dark-eyed gaze.

"Thanks. He has lots of wonderful traits and hasn't exactly turned out badly. I guess I did teach him a few good things."

As they stepped off the escalator onto the nearly deserted second floor, they saw a uniformed attendant standing next to a bronze statue of a cowboy on a bucking bronco. He was tapping his finger in boredom against the cold metal. Attie playfully slapped John's skinny rear before waving at the man.

"Excuse me. Can you point us toward the track restaurant?"

Removing his hat, the large man scratched his thinning hair. "You bet. Right around the corner, ma'am."

Thanking him, they followed the wide hallway filled with bronze and Western art, reaching the restaurant.

"Do we need reservations?" John asked the white-smocked man standing behind a lectern.

"No sir," he said, words reverberating with deep bass tones. "We got plenty of tables. Eat, watch the races, and stay as long as you like."

"Sounds great."

When John slipped him ten dollars, Attie turned away to keep from laughing.

"Thank you," the man said, beaming.

Motioning a waiter, he said, "Give these good people any table they want."

A middle-aged black man dressed in a white shirt, dark pants, and a bowtie emerged from behind the bar.

"My name is Roy. Where would you fine folks like to sit?"

"Please choose for us, Roy. This is my first visit to the track."

Easing lazily into his role as a Texas rancher, John slipped Roy ten dollars, ignoring Attie's silly grin and wildly rolling eyes.

"Yes sir," Roy said, taking the money.

He escorted them to a table atop the three-tiered restaurant overlooking the track.

Attie couldn't help exclaiming, "This is simply gorgeous!"

Three stories of glass towered above the track. As far as the eye could see, spring colors vibrantly painted the scene while the soft rustle of prairie grass flowed in wind-blown waves across the distant hills.

"Best table in the house," Roy boasted, helping Attie with her chair. "Would you like something to drink?"

Attie said, "Coffee, please."

Roy watched as John gazed thoughtfully out the window, tapping the table with a long, bony finger.

"Bourbon and branch," he finally said, adding an extra swagger to his already contrived southwestern accent.

"Do you prefer a particular brand, or will our house bourbon be okay?"

"I'm partial to Wild Turkey."

Attie smirked. As Roy left to fetch their drinks, her dark eyes sparkled. Lowering her chin, she pushed aside the vase of wildflowers that separated them and gazed across the white-clothed table at him.

"Bourbon and branch?"

Crossing his arms, he leaned back in his chair. "You said I looked like a cowboy. I'm getting into the role."

Attie laughed loudly.

They browsed the menu while waiting for Roy to return with their drinks. Attie picked a simple dinner salad, and John ordered steak and a baked potato. Later, she shook her head when he pushed the mostly uneaten food aside. The restaurant began to fill with fans who were eating, drinking, and talking loudly.

Attie said, "Maybe we should get a form and decide which horses we want to bet on."

John motioned her to keep her seat. "I'll get it, beautiful lady," he said, tipping his hat.

Blushing like a schoolgirl, she glanced around the room to see if anyone had noticed. He winked as he walked away, but she missed it behind his dark glasses. Ten minutes later, he returned with a racing form and nearly a dozen tip sheets. Another ten minutes passed before he looked up from the crumpled racing form, appearing perplexed.

"What's a Daily Double?"

"You pick the winning horses in the first two races. Santa Fe Roy and Red Velvet are the best bets. What do you think?"

After folding the racing form, he placed it on the table beside him and raised his hand for another drink.

"Think I'll wait and look at the horses."

Dropping her pencil, Attie rested her chin on her fists and stared at him. Her studious gaze made him nervous.

"What, may I ask, are you looking at, my dear?"

"I know you said you were raised on a cattle ranch."

"So?"

"Cows aren't horses. I wonder how you plan to tell a good horse from a bad one just by looking."

Tipping the hat over his left eye, he explained in a swaggering prairie drawl. "Little lady, I've been chased by Texas's fastest and meanest horses. My instinct for rapid horseflesh is finely honed."

Attie laughed out loud, and the noisy restaurant quieted briefly as the diners at the nearby tables turned to look.

"You must be kidding!"

He wasn't joking, dragging her to the paddock to see the horses fifteen minutes before the first race began. Behind a whitewashed fence, they admired the magnificent animals. Using the racing form to shield his eyes as the horses paraded by, he nodded and scratched his chin like a knowledgeable buyer at a livestock auction. When the last horse disappeared into the tunnel leading to the track, he grinned smugly.

"When do we place our bet?"

"Now, cowboy. Who are you picking to win?"

"Thunderbird."

Suddenly absorbed, he started, without waiting for her, toward a betting window. Attie shrugged her shoulders and followed.

Calling after him, she said, "Thunderbird? That nag will probably finish last."

He stopped and turned around, wagging his finger at her. "We'll see about that, little lady. Panama Tex is starting to feel mighty lucky."

Chapter 10

Attie gave John a look. "Panama Tex? What happened to Geriatric John?"

"Left him at the turnstile," he said, walking away through the throng of people viewing the horses.

Hurrying to keep up with his long-legged stride, Attie said, "Who is Panama Tex picking in the second race? If you bet the Daily Double, you won't have time to see the horses."

He stopped abruptly. "Hmm! Better look at the racing form."

Attie stepped away from the crowded hallway and rested her elbows on a tall garbage container in a quiet corner. She handed him the form as he detached himself from the flow of people. After studying it for ten seconds, he lowered it to his side and returned to the betting window.

"Well, Tex?" she said, hurrying after him.

Without stopping, he said, "Prairie Sunset."

Attie shouted after him, "Prairie Sunset? You must be crazy. He's a thirty-to-one long shot. The nag has never won a race."

John didn't answer, and he didn't stop until he reached the betting window and pulled out his wallet.

"Ten dollars on Thunderbird to win in the first race and a Daily Double bet on Thunderbird and Prairie Sunset."

"Twelve dollars," the teller said.

John stared at the woman, confused. "Beg your pardon?"

The woman glanced around nervously. John and Attie were alone in the line, so she smiled and explained. "I need ten dollars on Thunderbird to win and a two-dollar Daily Double on Thunderbird and Prairie Sunset. That's a total of twelve dollars."

He shook his head. "Not quite, young lady. I want to bet a hundred dollars on the Daily Double."

Taking the bill, the teller's eyes widened as she handed him a ticket marked with the Thunderbird and Prairie Sunset combination. Attie smiled and shrugged at the clerk as they turned to leave.

Returning to their table overlooking the track, they waited for the first race to start. Breaking cleanly from the gate, Thunderbird immediately took the lead, maintaining a one-length advantage at the first turn. Gradually, he pulled away from the other nine horses on the backstretch.

John sat straight in his chair and exhorted, "Come on, Thunderbird."

"He'll never hold that pace," Attie said.

John's gaze never wavered from the track. His voice grew louder. "Come on, Thunderbird!"

Thunderbird led the other horses into the third turn by three lengths as they approached the final bend and charged down the home stretch. Slamming his fist against the table, he jumped, shouting above the din in the crowded restaurant.

"Come on, Thunderbird!"

Thunderbird crossed the finish line, winning by six lengths. John rushed around the table and hugged Attie. He lifted her off the floor and did a twirling jig to express his excitement, then returned to his chair as many frowning race watchers crumpled their losing tickets and tossed them aside. A tipsy young man with mustard stains on his expensive suit tapped John's shoulder as he passed on his way back from the bathroom.

"Who are you picking in the next race?"

"Take my advice. Go with Prairie Sunset to win."

71

Wrinkling his nose, the man returned to his seat. "Beginner's luck," they heard him tell his friends at the table.

They returned to the betting window to place their bets on the second race and to collect their winnings from the first.

"Ten dollars on Prairie Sunset to win," Attie advised the clerk. "Mother always told me to bet on a winner."

"Prairie Sunset is a winner?"

Patting John's cheek, she said, "Panama Tex."

John placed his bet and followed Attie back to the table. Prairie Sunset bucked like an unruly colt as the horses paraded in front of the stands. The stewards had to load him into the chute, kicking and biting. Attie made a face at the starting bell. Prairie Sunset stumbled and nearly fell as he shot out of the gate, dropping four lengths behind the other horses as they sprinted toward the first turn.

"Come on," John said beneath his breath.

All nine horses showed their tails to Prairie Sunset as they rounded the first turn.

John growled, voice growing progressively louder, "Come on, baby. You can do it."

The lead horse faltered near the end of the backstretch, allowing ten horses to close in during the third turn. Coming from far behind, Prairie Sunset overtook the quickly tiring rabbit and moved toward the middle of the pack.

Squeezing the racing form into a wrinkled wad, he yelled, "Come on, Prairie Sunset!"

Sensing an upset, spectators in the restaurant tensed. Halfway through the last turn, the favorite moved from third to first. Prairie Sunset followed, advancing from ninth to fifth. As they entered the final stretch, the favored horse went wide while Sunset's jockey kept him close to the rail. Suddenly, two stretched-out racers blocked his path. John jumped to his feet, pounding the table and screaming. This time, Attie joined him.

Yelling in unison, they exhorted, "Come on, Prairie Sunset!"

Like any script from a hundred cheesy racing movies, the two galloping nags parted, fading like bleached stones in the hot Oklahoma sun. Prairie Sunset glided smoothly through the gap. Looking triumphant as he sprinted toward the finish line, the favored horse had already established a five-length lead.

John screamed, "Come on, baby! You can catch that nag."

Prairie Sunset charged like a runaway train, quickly narrowing the gap between himself and the front-runner as they sprinted the final hundred yards, stride for stride. Then, like a race-bred champion, Prairie Sunset extended his long neck near the finish line, winning by a nose.

John screamed at the top of his lungs, "All right!"

He grabbed Attie around the waist and did another twirling two-step between the rows of tables. Everyone else in the restaurant frowned and tossed their tickets aside. A surprised cashier counted out nearly five thousand dollars in hundred-dollar bills. As they turned to leave the window, John noticed the same tipsy young man behind him in line.

"Don't worry," he said, patting the man's shoulder. "It was just beginner's luck."

Later, John found the restroom nearly deserted in anticipation of the day's last race. On his way out the door, he noticed someone sitting on the floor, obviously distraught, with a face buried in his hands. Starting to leave, he had second thoughts and returned to speak with the young man.

Blood trickled down his balled hand, and the short sleeve of his red-checkered shirt was torn. Concerned, John dampened a paper towel under the faucet and knelt beside him, wiping away the blood. He examined the young man's puffy face and brushed an unruly shock of orange-red hair from his eyes, discovering they were just as red.

"What's the matter? Need some help?"

Numerous large freckles adorned the young man's pale complexion, making him appear more like a boy than a man. When he didn't respond immediately, John stood up and began walking away. The young man replied before John reached the door.

"I'm okay. Thanks for asking."

Unable to mask the tears in his eyes, he tried to smile. Thinking he was drunk, John walked back into the restroom, kneeled, and held out his hand.

"Let me buy you a cup of coffee. You look like you could use one."

The young man continued staring at the geometric shapes of the black-and-white floor tiles.

In a coherent voice, he said, "Too bad that's not all I need."

"You in some sort of trouble?"

He forced a smile and said, "I'm fine. Sorry to make a spectacle of myself."

Sitting beside him on the floor, John placed a reassuring hand on his shoulder.

"What's your name?"

"Jack."

"I know it's none of my business, Jack, but if you tell me what's wrong, maybe I can help."

Jack's voice was barely a whisper when he answered, "Just lost five hundred dollars."

John glanced around the restroom, checking for thieves, then back at Jack for marks of a scuffle. Looking again at the cut on his hand, he said, "Someone rob you?"

Wiping his hand on his shirt, Jack shook his head. "No, I punched the wall."

John rolled his faded eyes, remembering having done the same thing himself. Touching the white-tiled wall, his frown became a smile.

Jack's lips also curled into a sullen grin when the old man spoke. "Least walls don't punch back."

"My only consolation," Jack said, again dejected.

"Five hundred dollars isn't that much money. This time next week, it won't feel so bad."

Jack closed his eyes, ran his fingers through thick red hair, and slowly shook his head. "It was a whole week's wages."

John commiserated, again patting his shoulder. "Sounds tough, but you'll make do. It's a valuable lesson for you."

"You sound like my father."

"A wise man," John said. "Life is hard. Get up, dust yourself off, and go home."

John helped him to his feet and guided him by the elbow to the washbasin. After turning on the water, he handed him a paper towel from the dispenser on the wall.

"Wash your face," he directed.

When Jack took the towel, John nodded and started for the door. Before he could exit, Jack mumbled something, and John asked him to repeat what he had said. He did, his voice low and filled with ire.

"You still don't understand, do you?"

"Something you need to tell me?"

Glaring at John as if he were the cause of all his problems, the young man turned slowly away from the mirror.

"My wife is eight months pregnant. That money was my car payment, house payment, and Sally's visit to the doctor. I can't face her," he said, covering his face to hide his tears.

Without hesitation, John said, "Be a man and tell her. We all make mistakes. She'll forgive you."

He opened the door and walked away. Halfway back to the restaurant, he stopped and turned around, returning to the bathroom. Jack was still standing in front of the washbasin.

John opened his wallet, handed the young man a thousand dollars, and said, "I'm giving you this, but you have to promise me you won't spend a dime of it at the track."

Staring in disbelief, Jack shouted, "Don't want your charity."

"I didn't have that money when I got here. I don't need it now and never will."

"What'll I tell Sally?"

"Tell her it's a Panama Tex and Prairie Sunset gift."

Letting the door close slowly behind him, he reentered the restaurant. Attie said, "Where have you been? You missed the last race."

He smiled and said, "No, I didn't. Not this time, anyway."

❧

As they slowly walked back up the winding pathway to the RV, arm-in-arm, Attie, and John overlooked the crowd leaving the racing facility. John recounted the incident with the young man in the bathroom during their walk.

"You gave him a thousand dollars?"

"He needed it more than we do."

"Aren't you afraid he'll just squander it at the track tomorrow?"

"It's something I'd never have done for my son. As I left the restroom, I thought about how I raised Dan. I said to myself, what the heck? Maybe I can do a little atoning."

Piloting the RV, Attie exited the parking lot, skillfully weaving through the traffic leaving the track. When they reached the Interstate 40 exit for Fort Smith, Arkansas, she turned onto it. Wispy gray now streaked the sky, and fingers of red and orange began to caress the western horizon. John leaned back in his chair, closed his eyes, and meditated.

Hours later, they stopped at an RV park just off the highway. When Attie retired to her bedroom, he turned off the lights. Undressing, he braced for another uncomfortable night on the couch. As he lay in the darkness, deep in thought, stiff springs dug into his lean back. The bedroom door opened, interrupting his reflection. It was Attie.

"That old couch is mighty lumpy," she said. "I'm replacing it when I get home. Why don't you share my bed tonight?"

Chapter 11

Cynthia sat in bed, watching her pajama-clad husband pace the floor. The deep lines etched on his face emphasized the red glow of his neck. His face became increasingly red as he listened to the one-sided conversation on their house phone. After the caller finished their lengthy discourse, he waved his arm wildly around his head as if he were about to strike the table with his fist.

"Dammit, Blakeman, why didn't you call me earlier? I could have driven to Oklahoma City and caught the old man myself."

Cynthia leaned forward in bed, straining to hear the reply to her husband's angry question. When he glared in her direction, her heart skipped a beat.

Finally, he slammed down the receiver. Before he did, he said, "Thanks for nothing, Blakeman!"

Red-rimmed eyes cast a demented pall over his otherwise handsome features. As Cynthia waited, a muscle in her cheek twitched. She fixated on the dilated blood vessels in her husband's arms and his own involuntary muscle twitch. Many times, she had seen him angry, though never to the point of violence. The look in his eyes pressed her against the headboard. She waited, albeit subconsciously, for the angry condemnation that never arrived. Instead, he continued to rant about his father.

"That son-of-a-bitch Tim Watson talked to Dad today and didn't bother calling me. Believe his nerve?"

he said, glaring wildly around the room while looking at nothing.

Relieved his ire was momentarily directed at someone other than herself, she said, "Dan! Tim is your best friend."

"With best friends like him, I don't need enemies."

Holding the sheet demurely in front of her, she released her grip, allowing the linen to slip through her fingers, hoping the resulting flash of bare skin would change her husband's mood from anger to passion. He turned away, slamming his fist against the wall. She got out of bed and put on her robe. Sitting at the dressing table, she stared vacantly at her reflection in the mirror.

"Can you tell me where Tim saw your father, or are you too angry to discuss it?" Cynthia finally said, interrupting his mumbling soliloquy.

Dan didn't answer right away. Pouring a glass of water from the pitcher on the nightstand, he drank slowly, the cool liquid calming him. When he sat on the edge of the bed, he continued to brood, though at least he had stopped his incessant pacing.

"Oklahoma City," he said. "Dad called him from a pay phone for a prescription for his heart."

Cynthia's hand covered her mouth. After stepping toward him, she paused, holding back, her lower lip trembling. Dan's eyes showed his anguish, and she approached him, gently stroking his shoulder with her fingers.

"Oh, Dan, I'm so sorry."

For a moment, it seemed his anger had dissolved. It hadn't. Igniting again, he wrenched away from her grasp and bounded to the bedroom door.

"Where are you going?"

"To make a few calls."

"Can't it wait until tomorrow?"

Cynthia's words faded into silence as Dan left the room without responding, slamming the door behind him with a dull thud. Still awake when he returned and slid into bed beside her, she closed her eyes, though she couldn't fall asleep.

"Who did you call?"

"I still have some influence in this state," he said.

"That's not what I asked," she said sternly. "Now, explain to me what you just did."

Her outburst briefly calmed him, and he sank onto the bed.

"Blakeman talked with the television people in Oklahoma City after Tim called Tulsa police. They updated the story on the local newscast and reported he might be in Oklahoma City. Several people confirmed seeing him."

"Are the reports valid?"

"Three separate sightings pin-pointed him at one location—the horse track."

Cynthia stared at her husband. "That's not all, is it?"

Dan's nod confirmed her guess. "One person firmly identified Dad as the man who gave him a large sum of money. The man had second thoughts and tried to find him after the races to give it back."

"And?"

"He spotted them in the crowd leaving the track. They left the parking lot in a large recreational vehicle. The RV had Arkansas license tags."

"They?"

"Dad and a woman. They were holding hands."

Cynthia remained silent, digesting the information. Leaning forward and wrapping her arms around her knees, she rocked slowly back and forth, hoping Dan would never learn she already knew about his father's female companion.

She said softly, "Maybe you should just let him go. Maybe he's doing what he wants."

"He's completely off his rocker. No telling what he may do."

"You don't know that."

"Cyn, he gave away a thousand dollars to a stranger. Where'd he get that kind of money? He could be robbing banks for all we know."

"That's ridiculous. You know him better than that."

"Maybe not. I do know I'm not letting him get away with this."

Dan's smoldering anger startled her, and she said, "He hasn't done anything wrong."

"How do you know?" he asked, voice rising.

In a near whisper, she said, "Because your father isn't capable of hurting anyone or doing anything dishonest. You should be ashamed of yourself for even thinking such a thing."

"Well, I'm not ashamed," he said, turning away from her ashen glare.

"You still didn't tell me what you were doing in your office this late."

"State Police are setting up roadblocks all along major thoroughfares leading into Arkansas. By tomorrow, we should have him."

"I don't like your tone. He's your father, for heaven's sake. Not a criminal."

Turning away, he stared sullenly at the opposite wall. "He had no right running away in the middle of the night."

"He's not a convict."

Dan turned off the lamp beside the bed without responding to Cynthia's comment. She stayed seated in the dark, rocking and pondering, long after his heavy breathing indicated that he had fallen asleep.

༄ ❧ ༄

Unlike the curtains in the RV's living area, those in Attie's bedroom blocked out nearly all the light. The morning after the races, something gently nudged John's shoulder. He turned away on the soft bed, attempting to ignore it. Despite his sleepy protest, he finally opened his eyes when the annoying presence persisted. As he adjusted to the dim light, he looked up into Attie's smiling face.

"Sleeping all day, Romeo?"

Rubbing his eyes, he glanced around the dark room, momentarily confused.

"Attie!"

"Forget about last night already, old man?"

His face softened into a smile, remembering instantly that he hadn't. "I'm old, but not that old."

"Amen to that," she said, kissing his forehead. "Better drag yourself out of bed and get dressed, or I'll have to eat breakfast without you."

Attie handed John a cup of coffee and left him alone to get dressed. With his senses feeling pleasantly acute, he sipped the hot coffee and smiled as he got out of bed. After breakfast and a hand-in-hand morning stroll, they continued along the interstate toward Arkansas. When they reached Henryetta, they stopped to fill the RV's large gasoline tanks.

The truck stop spanned several acres of gas pumps and parked semis. One big truck featured a smiling camel painted on the trailer that read Humpin' to Please. Many drivers wandered inside the café and souvenir shop while others rested in their air-conditioned trucks. Idling engines hummed in unison as the acrid odor of burning diesel fuel permeated the damp Oklahoma air. John waited outside, watching the attendant pump gas while Attie went inside for a fountain drink.

Though he appeared young, the attendant was likely almost forty. Still, he had the slump-shouldered posture of someone much older. Dressed in faded overalls over a dirty white T-shirt, his floppy welder's cap rested casually on his head. As he pumped gas, he chewed a wad of tobacco that protruded from his cheek like a chipmunk with its mouth full of nuts. Dark tobacco juice dribbled down his chin. Periodically, he wiped away the juice with the back of his hand and raked his fingers through his greasy hair. When he spat on the cement, some juice landed on his scuffed boot. His dirty name tag identified him as Gus.

"You folks on your way back to Arkansas?"

John grinned. "You bet, Gus. How did you know?"

"Saw your tag," he said, stating the obvious.

Glancing at the back of the RV, John nodded and said, "Oh, of course."

"You going to get stopped when you reach the state line," the man drawled.

"For what?"

"State police got a roadblock. Stopping every RV with Arkansas tags."

"Why?" John asked, trying not to appear overly apprehensive.

"Some old coot ran away from home. Police think he's in an RV, like yours, on his way to Arkansas. They got all the main roads blocked."

John glanced around nervously, not knowing what to do. "We're expected in Arkansas," he lied. "I hope this doesn't detain us too long."

"Heck no," the man said with a grin. "The person they're looking for is lots older than you. They'll know it ain't you right away."

Smiling at the flattering remark, he gently tapped the man's shoulder.

"Thanks, Gus. The second nicest compliment I've had all day."

Hurrying inside, he paid for the gas and Attie's soda. To his relief, the stocky woman behind the register accepted his money without looking up. None of the truckers even glanced his way. After receiving his change, he grabbed Attie's shoulder and rushed her outside, where Gus was still busy washing the RV's windshield. Tossing him a half-dollar, he said, "It's all right, Gus. I'm going to wash it later anyway." Gus waved, watching thoughtfully as they opened the door to the RV and climbed in.

"You take care of yourself now," he said.

Attie had already started the engine before John buckled his seatbelt. He pulled out a road map from the storage flap in the passenger-side door, unfolded it in his lap, and studied it.

She said, "What are you doing? I know perfectly well where I'm going. I've driven this road a thousand times."

"We just changed our plans."

Chapter 12

Attie and John left the interstate, which led to Hot Springs via Fort Smith. Near the edges of Henryetta, they veered south onto the Indian Nations Turnpike toward McAlester. Halfway there, the RV's heat gauge hit the boiling mark.

Attie pulled off the road onto the broad shoulder of the scenic turnpike. She looked disgusted at the gauge as a cloud of thick gray steam billowed from under the hood. John reached across the console, pulled the hood latch, and exited the vehicle to check on the issue. Attie followed. watching with folded arms as he fiddled with a loose hose.

"Maybe we should call a tow truck," she said.

"How are we going to do that?"

Glancing around, Attie wondered the same thing. In the distance, the highway faded into the rolling foothills of the Ouachita Mountains. Overhead, a redwing hawk soared high above the blackened pine stumps leveled by a forest fire the previous summer. Like a watercolor splash against a turquoise sky, the large predator appeared frozen on canvas.

A spring breeze rustled the tall grass off the shoulder of the road, harmonizing with the angry steam hissing from the radiator. Since leaving the interstate at Henryetta, they hadn't seen another car. In frustration, John finally brushed his thin gray hair away from his wrinkled forehead.

"No phone booths around. Maybe I better try fixing it myself." He lowered his head for a closer look and said, "Can you bring me the toolbox from the RV?"

Attie returned with a small metal box filled with various wrenches and screwdrivers. After fumbling through the tools, he picked up a wooden-handled screwdriver, reached beneath the RV's hood, and touched the steaming hot radiator cap. With a startled yelp, he jerked his hand back.

"Dammit, that hurt!" he said, sucking his blistered thumb.

"You don't know what you're doing. Wait until someone stops and helps."

Frowning, he placed the screwdriver on top of the radiator and soon returned with a pitcher of water and a towel from the RV.

"Start the motor," he said, sounding almost angry. "Think I see the problem."

"Sure?"

"Attie, I'm not a mechanic, but I can fix this contraption if you'll start the engine for me."

Attie narrowed her dark eyes at his fractious tone. Indignantly, she kicked a rock into the ditch before heading back to the RV to start the engine. After pouring half the water from the pitcher onto the steaming radiator, John pried off the cap with the screwdriver, using a wet towel as a pot holder. When the cap popped loose, he poured the remaining water into the steaming hole and rushed back into the RV for another pitcher.

With the radiator filled and the cap securely in place, John quickly checked the wires and hoses before wiping his face with the damp towel. Slamming the hood, he looked over at Attie. Frowning, she stood directly behind him, her arms tightly folded.

"May not know what I'm doing," he said. "But I think the old bucket will at least get us to Arkansas now." Attie's direful expression didn't change. Seeing her staring at him, he suddenly became sensitive to her injured feelings, took her hand, and kissed it.

"Sorry. I can be an old bear sometimes."

When her frown softened into a smile, she said, "I'm not a pouter."

A twinkle glossed his faded eyes. Staring intently down his hawkish nose, he put his arm around her waist, grinned, and said, "I am."

They gazed silently at the pine-covered hills for several wistful seconds while holding hands. Appearing ageless and cloaked in vivid green, the low-lying promontories of the Ouachita foothills stood in stark contrast to the clear blue Oklahoma sky. A gentle breeze ruffled Attie's silver-streaked hair, which she adjusted with her palm. After squeezing John's hand, she led him back to the RV.

"Radiator cap's worn out," he explained when they were again on their way. "Anti-freeze evaporated through the loose fitting."

"Can we make it to McAlester?"

"No problem. The water will boil off again after a couple of days. When we get to town, we'll buy anti-freeze and a new radiator cap."

Attie remained silent for several miles, and John did the same, gazing out the large windshield at the rolling hills and swaying pine trees that appeared to grow taller with each passing mile. Finally, she broke the silence.

"You said back there you're not a mechanic. It made me realize I know very little about you. What did you do before you retired?"

Chuckling, he said, "Guess."

"All right. I'll play your silly game." Drumming the steering wheel with her fingers as she thought, she finally said, "We've ascertained you're not a cowboy."

"No, I'm certainly not a cowboy," he said, still chuckling.

"But you are handy with tools," she said suggestively.

John raised his bushy eyebrows. "That I am, young lady."

"Tell me. I don't want to guess anymore."

"Doctor."

Turning her gaze away from the road, she glanced at him. "A medical doctor? I should have known."

"And what might have led you to that conclusion?"

"You have steady hands."

"Not so steady when you're around."

Attie took her hand off the wheel and reached across the console to pat his bony knee.

"You always know just the right thing to say, old man?"

Grasping Attie's hand, John held on tightly as she continued down the four-lane divided highway. They traversed the remaining distance to McAlester, listening to Mozart on a radio station that featured classical music. He pointed to a service station when they reached the outskirts of town.

"Pull in. I'll buy some anti-freeze and a new radiator cap."

Attie continued without stopping. "If you don't mind, I'd rather find a garage and have a real mechanic take a look. No slight against your ability as a mechanic, mind you."

Attie's disbelief in his mechanical ability miffed John more than he cared to admit.

"Suit yourself."

John held his tongue until Attie looked at him, then winked and grinned to show he wasn't upset. Fifteen minutes later, she found a garage and wheeled the RV into its graveled lot. After consulting with the mechanic, they waited beneath a giant elm tree growing alongside the metal prefab building.

Weathered letters identified the place as Big Al's Garage. Big Al was buried deep beneath the open hood, examining the RV's engine. Mechanical debris, ranging from wheel casings to wrecked vehicles, cluttered the surrounding yard. John leaned back against a rusting engine block and shook his head. Attie glanced at her watch.

"You think this is a waste of time, right?"

Allowing the barest glimmer of a knowing smile to betray his feelings, he said, "Mechanics always find something wrong. It's their job."

"Seems like a few doctors I've known."

Dutifully chastised, he winced.

"Touché, my dear."

After squeezing his hand, she said, "John, I'm worried."

"Don't worry. I'm sure it's nothing serious."

"I'm talking about the roadblock, not the RV. Why are they doing this to you? It's almost like you're an escaped criminal instead of a respected, retired doctor."

"My son," he said softly.

"But why go to such lengths?"

"I've known him all his life. I still don't understand him. He seems to feel the need to control me. For the life of me, I don't understand why."

"Maybe because he felt controlled and constrained by you all his life," she said.

John blinked and thoughtfully studied Attie's face.

"He had more freedom as a child than most grown-ups. I went my way. He went his."

"I'm not a psychiatrist. Maybe he's lashing out at you for that very reason. Maybe, subconsciously, he's trying to be your father."

John let Attie's words sink in and gradually dissolve within the framework of his understanding. Big Al's appearance interrupted his thoughts, and her theory continued to trouble him.

Big Al was short, his belly bulging from his greasy blue jeans. Spitting on the ground, he wiped his face with the sleeve of his dirty western shirt. Like Gus, the service station attendant in Henryetta, tobacco dribbled down his cheek. Oil had already darkened the graying stubble. After removing his worn-out cap, he raked his calloused hands through his thin hair, oddly brown from repeated applications of cheap men's hair dye. John glanced at Attie and winked, amused by his apparent vanity.

"The water pump and the thermostat are out," he said.

It was Attie's turn to wink. Looking pointedly at John, she nodded.

John shrugged.

"Can you fix it?"

"Course I can fix it," Big Al said gruffly. "This here's a garage, ain't it?"

"I mean, can you fix it today?"

"Shore. I'll start on it now, and you can get it a little later."

"How much later?" asked Attie.

Big Al glanced at the broken crystal of his oily watch and said, "Bout two hours ought to do it."

"Fine," she said. "Can we use your phone to call a cab?"

"Ain't no need for that," Al said. "McAlester ain't that big. I'll give you a ride."

By now, it was well past noon. The sunshine had started to fade. Their engine troubles had carried them past lunch without a break.

"I'm hungry," John declared, glancing at Attie.

"So am I," she said. "Is there a good place to eat here, Mr. Al?"

Big Al grinned, further emphasizing tobacco-puffed cheeks. "Where you folks from, anyway? This here's the biggest Italian colony west of the Mississippi. Ever known an Italian that couldn't cook?" he asked rhetorically.

Attie and John shook their heads. Five minutes later, they found themselves in the front seat of Big Al's wrecker, a six-wheeled behemoth with a massive winch on the back. He drove them into a nearby neighborhood to a restaurant that resembled many white-framed houses, except for the gravel parking lot surrounding it and the neon sign that read Mike's.

"Best steaks and pasta in town," Big Al assured them. "And tell Mike you want a glass of Choc."

Attie cleared her throat and said, "Choc?"

Big Al spat tobacco out the window and wiped his mouth. "Choc beer is homemade and used to be illegal."

"Oh," Attie said.

John asked, "Why do they call it Choc beer?"

"Short for Choctaw," he explained. "Indians once made it." John nodded knowingly as he stepped out of the truck to give Attie a hand. "Just stick around, and I'll be back to pick you up when I finish with the water pump and thermostat."

Attie waved as Big Al drove away. John sensed what was coming but tried to avoid the reprimand by walking carefully toward the restaurant's front door. Grabbing his elbow, she turned him around, her usual smile replaced by a stern expression. He winked and walked away before she could accost him with the inevitable I told you so.

Flippantly, he said, "When it comes to a doctor's prognosis on broken cars, take my advice and get a second opinion."

Chapter 13

A blue and white police cruiser screeched to a neck-popping halt in front of Vince Blakeman's condo complex. The detective tapped the dashboard before exiting, thanking the uniformed driver for the ride.

"Sure you won't join us for a beer at Ten Pin Annie's?" the driver asked.

"Like to, Joe, but I got paperwork coming out my butt. Maybe I'll make it next time."

Joe smiled as if he expected as much, "Yeah, sure. You bowling this year?"

Glancing at his watch as if the thirty-dollar timepiece somehow held the answer to his question, he said, "You know I usually bowl."

"All right. See you tomorrow."

Spinning the tires, Joe, the patrolman, drove down the elm-lined boulevard while Vince strolled along the sidewalk, passing the neatly manicured lawns. With the weather still cool, the complex managers had yet to fill the swimming pool, which appeared like a dull gray hole in the ground. Four elderly men with spindly legs, warmly dressed in sweaters and soft hats, were playing tennis on one of the green-surfaced courts. When he waved at them, they merely grumbled and continued their game.

Communal flower beds burst with red and yellow blooms, none of which he recognized. Picking up the evening paper from his front steps, he spotted his attractive neighbor on her knees, planting a tomato vine. Brief cut-off blue jeans hugged her shapely rear end. Vince whistled softly under his breath. Although they had been neighbors for almost a year, the shy detective had never introduced himself or even spoken to her. Realizing how close they were, he sucked in his belly and straightened to his full five-foot-nine height. His lips quivered when he opened his mouth, but no words emerged.

From the name on his neighbor's mailbox, he knew she was Marla MacDonald. He recognized her as a nurse from her usual work uniform. Although they had never spoken, she'd smiled at him once. He still remembered that smile.

Marla's yellow bikini top showcased her shapely shoulders and golden tan, marred only by a crisscross band of ivory. Tanning booth this time of year, he deduced. He slipped into his condo after giving her long legs one last appreciative glance.

"Some day," he said to himself.

Dropping the newspaper into his faded recliner, he went to the kitchen for a beer. When he returned to the small den, he noticed the light on his answering machine blinking red. Two people had called, or perhaps the same person twice. Wiping the dribble of beer from his chin, he rewound the recorder, interrupting a tinny computer voice mid-sentence.

"This is Cynthia Warren," the second message began. "It's about five on Monday. I need to talk with you. I'll be at Michael's Bar for the next hour or so. Please meet me if you can."

Vince replayed the message and checked the time on his watch. Chugging the beer, he grabbed his jacket and started out the door. At least he'd get another glimpse of beautiful Marla, he thought. Maybe even another smile. He was wrong on both counts. Her front door was ajar, and her gardening spade was abandoned in the dirt.

"One of these days," he said.

Ducking around the corner to the covered parking lot, he pulled out his car keys and gave Jezebel, his twelve-year-old Ford, an affectionate pat. Even with 132,000 miles on the clock, she was still a crème puff, boasting dark blue leather seats and all the options. Starting the engine, he headed downtown to see what Cynthia Warren had on her mind.

In one of downtown Tulsa's newer hotels, the gold letters on dark oak paneling at Michael's immediately signaled that the place was upscale. Unlike Little Annie's Ten Pin Lounge, Michael's was the preferred gathering spot for many city attorneys and oil executives.

Stepping into the paneled hallway, the cheerful buzz of relaxed conversation welcomed him at the front door. When the hostess arrived, he noticed she was more attractive than any waitress at Little Annie's, and her low-cut outfit overshadowed the jeans and sweatshirts they wore at Little Annie's.

She asked, "Table or stool at the bar?"

"Meeting someone," he said, glancing around the room as his eyes adjusted.

"And their name is?"

"Cynthia Warren."

"This way."

Vince followed the hostess past an ornate brass and oak bar to an even dimmer corner at the back of the smoke-filled room. She yanked a velvet-covered chair from the table and waited until he sat down.

"Mrs. Warren will be right back. Would you like something to drink?"

"Light draw, please."

Her dark eyes signaled distress. "We only have imported beer in bottles. Heineken, Moosehead, and St. Pauli Girl . . ."

"Moosehead," he said, not letting her finish.

Pivoting on her heels, she vanished into the smoky nightclub. Michael's was tiered like a Roman amphitheater around the circular bar. Packed to near-capacity with after-work patrons, the club buzzed with music and small talk.

A woman across the room giggled uncontrollably, making him wonder what she was drinking. Finally, a waitress in a red velvet uniform, even skimpier than the hostess's, interrupted his idle thoughts. The young lady's blouse revealed much cleavage, even while standing straight. The good detective nearly choked when she reached across the table to set the distinctive green bottle and frosty mug before him.

"Three-fifty," she said as he unglued his eyes.

Vince handed her four crumpled bills from his wallet and suggested that she keep the change. She must have pegged him as a cheapskate because she wrinkled her nose when accepting the money. Still, he thought, it was worth four bucks, and her evident disdain was a small price to pay for the privilege of watching her shapely legs in dark stockings disappear. After whistling softly to himself, he immediately regretted it.

"Ahem!" a voice behind him said.

It was Cynthia Warren, smiling like a Cheshire cat. Vince jumped up and pulled out a chair for her, grateful she couldn't see how red his face had turned.

Instead, she pointed. "This isn't very private. Let's grab that booth."

Several strategically placed potted plants partially concealed the booth in the club's dim recesses. Wearing a stylishly short mauve dress, Cynthia presented a delightful view of her shapely legs as she slid across the velvet-covered booth. She caught him watching, her big blue eyes sparkling with electricity as she acknowledged his silent compliment with a knowing smile. Loosening his paisley tie with a nervous forefinger, he slid beside her.

"How are you, Vince?"

"Fine, Mrs. Warren."

"Cynthia," she corrected. "I need to talk about Dan."

Before she could explain further, their pretty waitress returned and said, "Your usual, Mrs. Warren?"

"Yes, thank you, Kelli."

As Kelli nodded and returned to the bar, Vince reached for his wallet, wondering if he'd brought enough money.

"Don't worry," she said, responding to his distress. "Dan keeps a running tab here. We'll let him pay."

Relieved, he downed a shot of cold beer straight from the bottle, pouring the rest into the frosted glass when he noticed her raised eyebrows. The heavy imported beer foamed over the rim, soaking the cocktail napkin. She grinned again as she helped him clean up the spill with her napkin. As she did, he caught an elusive whiff of expensive perfume, and warmth flushed his face and neck.

"Sorry I'm such a klutz," he said.

Averting her amused gaze, she said, "Dan has acted strangely since his father disappeared. It's getting worse."

"Worse?"

"Scooter Bates."

Vince nodded, already knowing the story she was about to tell. "The interview he gave the newspaper was pretty tough."

"Made Dan seem like an unfeeling ogre," Cynthia said. "The man's been on television and every radio talk show. Dan is outraged."

"Bates made some strong statements. Sentiment around town's running toward letting the old man go free."

"Dan will never let that happen."

"Your husband has powerful friends," he said, stating what everyone at the precinct knew.

Kelli returned with Cynthia's champagne cocktail before she could respond to his comment. Though Vince tried not to stare, he couldn't help but gawk at the statuesque waitress as she bent over the table with the drink. This time, Cynthia feigned ignorance. Instead, she scooted closer around the circular booth until her bare knees brushed against the detective's trousers.

"Are there any new developments in the case? Anything on the horizon that might return us to normality?"

By now, Vince had a buzz from the strong Canuck beer and couldn't help feeling nervous about discussing the case in a darkened hideaway.

Leaning closer, he said, "Your father-in-law was spotted at a gas station in Henryetta. State Police have checkpoints along all the major roads entering Arkansas. They're showing Mr. Warren's photograph to the locals. That's how they learned he stopped at the gas station."

When she grasped his wrist, he had to steel himself to keep from recoiling. "Did they get the license number?"

"They didn't."

Dissatisfied with his answer, Cynthia raked her nails across Vince's wrist and turned away. The action did little to conceal the tears welling in her eyes. He offered her his handkerchief this time, patiently waiting as she dabbed her tears and softly blew her nose.

"Sorry," she said, regaining her composure.

Vince pushed Cynthia's champagne cocktail closer to her and waited while she took a sip. She didn't say anything until she had finished it, the sweet drink visibly calming her.

"Do you understand how I feel?"

Vince could only nod.

Cynthia leaned in close enough for Vince to feel her warm breath against his neck. Kelli rescued him by checking on their drinks. When Cynthia straightened in her chair, he held up two fingers. Understanding his gesture, Kelli returned to the bar without asking.

"I'm amazed by your husband's connections. I've never seen a simple disappearance get this much attention."

"Dan networks more than CNN," she said, smiling at her joke.

It didn't seem like much of a joke to Vince. "With all the attention, we could likely find your father-in-law before the end of the week."

"Think so?"

"Don't know how he can continue to elude us, though it's obvious he doesn't want to be found."

Cynthia lowered her head as Vince pushed the crumpled handkerchief that was still lying on the table in front of her toward her hand. In response, she smiled, revealing no tears.

"I know you think we should just let him go. I feel the same way. What can we do?"

Kelli returned with their drinks just before he had to answer her question. When he poured the Moosehead this time, he hit the frosted glass perfectly without spilling a drop.

Chapter 14

Relaxed by three champagne cocktails consumed rapidly, Cynthia leaned against the velvet booth and slowly deflated. Vince waited, wondering if he should offer advice or order another drink from Kelli when she returned to check on them. He finally decided to do both.

"You all right, Mrs. Warren?"

"Cynthia. Sorry, I'm making such a spectacle of myself."

Breaking away from her stare, he said, "No way."

Closing her eyes, she tilted her head against the cushy chair. Her face looked ghostly white in the dimly lit bar.

"I don't have many friends except Trish and Emily. Sometimes, it seems I go days without talking to anyone else. Before Grandpa disappeared, I seriously considered asking Dan for a divorce."

Disturbed again by her stare, he turned away, glancing at a rumpled cocktail napkin on the floor.

"Mrs. Warren . . ."

"I decided to stick it out," she said, ignoring his discomfort. I'm sorry. I just needed someone to talk to, and you understood the other day. I hope I haven't confused professional courtesy with genuine concern."

Cynthia was drunk. Having helped her reach that state, Vince thought it unwise to tell her. He finally managed a response, realizing how insensitive it sounded before the words left his mouth.

"Can't you talk to your mother or sister about this?"

"My parents have both passed away already, and I was an only child." The light in the bar changed slightly. Burnished azure radiated from her eyes. "I'm making you uncomfortable, aren't I?"

Vince could only blink and nod. Cynthia propped her chin in her hands and leaned across the table toward him. When she spoke, her words came out slurred.

"Mom died when I was twelve. I lost touch with my friends from high school years ago. I'm not close to any of the ladies I do charity work with or the girls at the tennis club."

He slurred his words when he replied to her sorrowful admission, causing her to smile and clutch his hand.

"Your husband sounds like a real jerk."

"I've given all I have. All he returns is cold passivity. With his father missing, it's even worse."

"Was he always this way?"

"Oh no. He was the most thoughtful and caring person until his father disappeared."

"He has a problem. It's definitively him and not you."

"Where does it leave me? I have to do something, or Dan will ruin the rest of his father's life and ours."

Cynthia's whispered confession blended into the dark woodwork as Vince enjoyed his Moosehead. This stuff tastes great. Suddenly realizing there were beers other than Budweiser, he lifted it to his lips, savoring its rich flavor. He finally managed a tipsy grin. Once more, Cynthia rested her chin in her hands, elbows on the table, leaning close to him. He thought she was admiring the shadows of his quickly growing beard or the amusing dimples in his cheeks.

"Let me call your husband down to the station tomorrow. Tell him I have some important info. The police shrink bowls on my team, and he owes me a favor or two. I'll have him give your husband the once-over. Maybe set him straight."

Cynthia sipped the remnants of her drink, a growing smile returning a glow to her cheeks. "I knew you were the right person to talk to about this."

Vince finished the Moosehead, drinking straight from the bottle.

"You know," he said. "This stuff's pretty good."

᠑ᢣᢦᢖ

Later, he led Cynthia into the parking garage, steering her toward the car with a shaky elbow. Too many champagne cocktails had left her in a state of giggling inebriation. He wasn't much better off. Still, he probably had more experience handling the situation. When they reached her silver Mercedes, he left it and drove her home. Ten blurry blocks from downtown, he decided to stop for coffee first.

Slumped against the door of the Ford, Cynthia sang a bawdy sea ditty that would have made him blush if he hadn't also been drunk. Finding a Big Boy, he parked the car. When he opened the passenger door, she tumbled out into his arms, still giggling like a teenager on her first good drunk. Once inside, it took two pots of hot coffee, toast, scrambled eggs, and a short stack of pancakes drizzled with blueberry syrup before she regained her Nordic coolness.

Then she said, "I feel like a fool."

"So do I."

Vince felt his face dimpling into a smile and reddening from the neck up. Scarlet replaced the ashen pallor of Cynthia's neck and face, and she managed to grin.

"What will your wife think of all this?"

"Not married," he said.

"Divorced?"

"I never had the pleasure."

"Sorry I'm so nosy. I feel close to you now that we are conspiring against my husband. What's your girlfriend's name?"

Eric Wilder

"Marla," he blurted.

She smiled and said, "I think the coffee has sobered me enough to make it home now. Take me back to my car?"

Seeing the logic in Cynthia's request, Vince paid their tab and escorted her from the restaurant. Back in the parking garage, he opened the door of his car for her, noticing as her skirt rode ten inches up on her thighs. She knowingly glanced up just at the right moment to catch him looking but only smiled and winked.

"Dan and I are having a cocktail party at our house on Saturday at seven. I'd like you to attend. And Vince, be sure to bring Marla."

Before he could beg off, she slid behind the wheel of her car and drove away into the night, leaving him alone in the dark parking garage.

John and Attie walked hand-in-hand up a flower-lined sidewalk to Mike's Restaurant. A dark-haired little man in a short apron met them at the door.

"Come on in here," he said, his words ringing with a strongly accented Okie accent. "Lunch for two?"

The man's smile seemed perfect, except for a quarter-inch gap between his two front teeth, one white and one gold. A dark, bushy mustache capped his large mouth.

"Don't mind if we do," John said.

"I'm Mike," the man said, grabbing two menus from a stand.

Mike led them across the hardwood floor to a table near the window at the back of the open restaurant. Once they were seated, he handed each of them a menu. Amateur photographs of various celebrities adorned an entire wall: movie stars, politicians, and other luminaries. The noise from a distant lawn mower echoed through the open window, blending with the fragrant scent of early spring and freshly cut grass. John arranged his chair with his

102

back to the window. Still standing by their table, Mike brought them back to reality with a start.

"You folks from around here?"

"Just passing through," John said, adjusting the reading glasses he'd borrowed from Attie as he scanned the menu.

"What's your special today?"

"Steak and pasta. Just like every day."

"Then that's what I'll have," John said, smiling and returning the menu.

"Dinner salad for me," Attie said. "Steak sounds a bit heavy this early in the day."

"Not the way Norma cooks it, it ain't. It'll melt in your mouth. I guarantee."

"I'll take your word for it," Attie said. "But I'll pass and save the calories."

"Suit yourself, ma'am. Bet you can't resist a bite of the gentleman's here."

"You're probably right, Mike."

"What would you folks like to drink?"

Attie said, "Coffee, please, with cream."

"I'll try your choc beer," John said.

Mike let the pencil and pad drop to his side. "Are you sure about that? Some people don't like the taste. Maybe you'd rather have a domestic beer or glass of wine."

"I had my heart set on a choc. Big Al told me to ask for it."

"Big Al?"

"Big Al's Garage," Attie said, clarifying John's statement. We're from out of town, and our vehicle broke down. He's fixing it."

"Don't worry about the choc. Just bring me a Coors," John said.

Mike nodded and disappeared into the kitchen, returning in five minutes with Attie's coffee and a frosted Mason jar brimming with a foamy head of golden beer.

"I brought you a choc to try. It's on me. You'll like it if you're a fan of full-bodied beer."

"Thanks," John said. "Appreciate it." He sipped the sparkling beverage and smiled. "It's delicious. This could grow on you."

Due to the hour, there were no other customers. Mike and his wife Norma made up the entire restaurant staff. When the meals were ready, they both appeared at the table. After serving the food, they seemed hesitant to leave. Norma was two inches taller than her husband. Fine reddish hair fell around her shoulders in a relaxed style that framed her face. Amber freckles dotted her otherwise pale complexion, and her brightly colored peasant dress with balloon sleeves highlighted her strong arms. Her pixie nose seemed out of place, and she had a larger frame and a vast country smile.

"Mike says you folks are from out of town," she said, imitating Mike's regional accent.

"Arkansas," Attie said.

"Whereabouts in Arkansas?"

"Eureka Springs. I'm Attie, and this is John."

"Proud to meet you folks," Norma said, pumping Attie's hand and then John's. "I'm Norma."

Mike flashed his patented gold-toothed grin. "My name's on the sign outside, though Norma runs the place."

Norma wrapped her big arm around Mike's shoulder and squeezed. "Don't matter. I still love the little guy."

Mike ignored the bone-crushing hug and stared at John as if he recognized him, though he couldn't quite remember from where.

"You know, you look familiar. Just can't place you."

John cleared his throat and bent his head toward the plate of steak and pasta. "Common features."

Before Mike figured it out, Big Al burst through the front door. Tipping his feedlot cap to John and

Attie, he rushed past their table, oblivious to the open button at the bottom of his shirt that exposed his hairy belly. His dark eyes flashed a serious message to Mike and Norma, prompting them to follow him into the kitchen.

Attie finished her salad, rocking nervously in her chair as John continued to work on his pasta and steak. He noticed her agitation. Placing his fork on the plate, he joined her in watching the animated conversation inside the kitchen door.

"Looks like we have a problem," he said.

"Maybe we should make a break for it."

John stretched his shoulders until his vertebrae popped. "We're on foot and wouldn't get far."

"Then what will we do?"

"Hope for the best."

John picked up his fork and continued eating. Attie tapped her toe and rocked.

"How can you be so complacent?" she finally asked. "Big Al must have reported us to the police."

"Nothing we can do about it now."

"I know, but it's so frustrating."

"It'll be all right. They can only take me back to Tulsa. They can't eat us."

Attie didn't seem convinced, so he took her hand, gently patted it, and consoled her while trying to prevent the redness around her eyes from turning into tears. After five minutes, the discussion in the kitchen stopped. Mike, Norma, and Big Al peeked out from behind the door at them.

John focused on the mower's grating noise near the window. When the blade struck a rock, it flew from beneath the mower, slamming into the side of the building. John turned to look. When he pivoted back in his chair, he found Mike, Norma, and Big Al in front of their table. Their country smiles were gone, and he held his breath when Big Al spoke.

"Folks," he said. "We know who you are."

Chapter 15

Waiting for the proverbial other shoe to drop, John and Attie sat frozen in their chairs. Big Al, Norma, and Mike stared down at them, almost as if they were viewing criminals through jail cell bars. Finally, Big Al removed his cap and wearily shook his big head.

"Don't know how they tracked you here, but this-here town's swarming with State Police. I heard it on the scanner on the way over here. They have roadblocks on all the main roads. But," he said, drawing out the word. "If we hurry, we can lead you through the neighborhoods and into the mountains."

John looked first at Attie and then into Big Al's sad cow eyes. "You'd do that for us?"

"If you hurry."

"But why?" Attie asked.

Norma said, "Dearie, ain't you heard?"

Attie shook her head. "Heard what?"

"You two are the biggest celebrities to come down the pike since Bonnie and Clyde. Ever since that talk show on Tulsa television, the whole state's been buzzing about you. Our radio station gives an update every hour on your reported whereabouts. We know all about the money you gave to the man in Oklahoma City and the paralyzed fellow in Red Rock."

Again, John looked at Attie. Mike explained, "People are calling in and talking. No one wants to see you sent back to Tulsa and put away in an old folk's home. People 'round here don't cotton to that sort of thing."

"Scooter," John said.

Attie grinned. "Good ol' Scooter Bates."

Shuffling nervously in his chair, he grabbed his wallet and looked up with a grin. "Norma, the lunch was lovely. Best steak I've ever eaten. And Mike, I'm going to miss your choc beer."

"Put your money away," Mike said. "It ain't no good 'round here."

"We would like one thing, though," Norma said, rushing away into the kitchen and returning with an instant camera. "I'd like to get your picture for our wall collection."

John and Attie indulged in their picture-taking frenzy for the next half hour. Mike and Norma stood behind them while Big Al shot a half-roll of film. Mike captured more images of Big Al with the two celebrities. One roll of film later, they found themselves back in the front seat of Big Al's wrecker, heading through town to pick up their RV from his shop. Dark thunderclouds, rolling in from the southwest, obscured the sun. When they arrived at the town center, Big Al pointed to a black-and-white police car turning a corner just ahead.

"Third trooper car we've seen since leaving Mike's." Glancing at his worn watch, he switched on the radio and said, "Let's see what the talk show's saying."

A local disk jockey's twangy voice instantly flooded the cab. "A McAlester man reported seeing the RV of run-away geriatric John Warren and his unidentified female companion. Local police called for immediate back-up to assist in the . . ."

"Son-of-a-buck," Big Al said. "Good thing your RV's out of sight. I parked it inside my shop."

Big Al switched off the radio and turned on the high-pitched squeal of a police scanner. They learned that roadblocks were set up on all routes in and out of town. Additionally, State Police actively asked locals to pinpoint their exact location.

"Maybe you shouldn't get involved in this," Attie said, touching the big man's wrist.

Big Al's ruddy neck flushed red. "Already am. Don't you worry about me, little lady. Going to get you two out of here, though it looks like we'll have to wait till after dark."

Big Al rounded a corner and immediately slammed on the brakes. Blocking their path was a black-and-white cruiser. Three troopers in Smokey hats leaned into the open windows of a row of backed-up cars, checking drivers' licenses.

"Oh-my-God!" Attie said.

"Back up, Big Al," John said. "Go the other way."

Big Al shook his head. "There's a truck blocking me in."

John opened the front door and grabbed Attie's arm. "Slow down and let us out. Meet you around the corner."

As John stepped off the running board, he helped Attie to the curb. Lowering her head, she covered her face with her hand and hurried toward the sidewalk in the opposite direction. After giving Big Al a quick wave over his shoulder, John followed her. Their ruse worked. The truck was high enough to conceal their exit from the troopers' view.

By now, late afternoon shadows and dark clouds had completely cloaked the once-pale sky. Sprinkles of rain began to fall as John hurried after Attie. He was out of breath when he caught up to her near the end of a narrow alley that separated two old brick buildings. Grabbing her arm, he wheeled her around. Her dark eyes widened as he clutched his heart, his face suddenly ashen.

"John! Are you all right?"

"I'm fine. Just need a second to catch my breath."

She looked back up the alleyway. Silent lightning framed the eastern mountains. Grabbing his elbow, she said, "Let's stop this madness and get you to a doctor."

"No," he said, leaning against the brick wall. "I'm okay."

Fishing in his pocket for the bottle of tiny pills, he swallowed two and then slumped against faded bricks. His cheeks reddened. Attie clutched his arm. Her tears, trickling down his neck, returned him to his senses.

"I'm all right," he said, touching her shoulder and consoling her until she stopped crying.

"What are we going to do?"

"Find Big Al before he leaves us," he said, leading her toward the beckoning opening at the far end of the alley.

When John and Attie emerged at the corner of the deserted side street, they found Big Al and his wrecker patiently waiting. Spotting them in his rearview mirror, he exited the cab to help them into the truck.

"What happened? I thought they must have caught you."

Nearby, thunder boomed, punctuating John's terse answer. "No lawman alive is slick enough to take Panama Tex."

Big Al's drooping eyelids opened an extra confused millimeter as he cranked the engine, offering no comment on the vague response. When they arrived at the prefab repair shop, they found Mike and Norma waiting outside in their car. Worry cast dark shadows across Norma's pale face as she waited for them to leave the truck. Mike followed, carrying a large box.

Thunder heralded a heavy downpour as they opened Big Al's office door. In the dusky clutter, two fugitives and three would-be protectors waited, watching the rain stream down the single dirty windowpane and beat a hollow timpani on the building's tin roof. John and Attie slumped on a threadbare old couch while Norma helped Big Al start a pot of coffee. Mike opened an ice chest he'd brought, fishing out a Mason jar of choc beer.

"Couldn't let you get away without some of my special recipe," he said. "Got a week's supply for you in this here foam chest."

John grinned and unscrewed the lid, sipping the golden liquid. "Mike, you're a lifesaver. It's just what I needed."

Though Mike beamed, Attie frowned. "I'm frightened. Why are you two so happy?"

Licking foam from the lip of the jar, John said, "We may be fugitives, but we're not guilty of anything. If they catch us and take me back to Tulsa, I'll leave again. My son doesn't own me."

"Tell him that," Attie said.

John placed the jar on the cluttered coffee table, his knees brushing against Attie's hand. Suddenly, pent-up emotion surged between them like a current through an electrical conduit, and she began to cry. Embarrassed, Mike turned away and peeked through the tattered curtains. Finally, the rich aroma of freshly brewed coffee started to fill the damp air as Big Al poured from the pot.

"Coffee's ready," he said, walking out into the garage's open bay, leaving them to their lonely reflections.

"You folks in a heap of trouble," Mike said. "Police have roadblocks on every road out of town."

"We know," John said.

"You'll have to stay till they get tired of waiting and leave," Norma said.

John began nervously pacing the floor. After screwing the top back on the Mason jar, he returned it to the Styrofoam chest.

When he Attie on the lumpy old couch, he said, "Might take a week."

She squeezed his hand. "Or longer."

Mike's bushy mustache twitched. "You folks can stay with us."

"Absolutely," Norma said.

"We appreciate your hospitality," John said. "The problem is, with all this publicity, someone is bound to recognize us."

Attie leaned forward on the couch. "We could hide in the trunk of Mike's car. Let him take us beyond the outskirts of town. We can hitchhike to Arkansas."

John shook his head. "I can't let them risk it. Besides, how far would we get trying to cross the mountains on foot in the middle of the night?"

"We got a car you could borrow," Mike said.

"Everything we own is in the RV," Attie said.

John resumed pacing in circles around the room. A well-worn path on the rug suggested that pacing was also one of Big Al's problem-solving strategies, as he was doing the same in the concrete bay of his shop. Mike, Norma, and Attie had fallen asleep on the couch. John settled in behind the cluttered government-issue desk belonging to Big Al. Amid the storm's cacophony and Mike's loud snorts, he finished the pot of coffee by himself.

Two hours later, Big Al returned from the shop to find Mike, Norma, and Attie on the couch and John asleep at the desk. The storm had finally passed, leaving only a moonlit darkness in its wake. As he started a new pot of coffee, the two couples began to stir, waking up one by one. As he watched them blink the sleep from their eyes, he scratched his scruffy day-old beard.

After refilling everyone's coffee cup and ensuring they were all alert, he said, "Folks, I believe I got a plan."

Chapter 16

Big Al waited until everyone was awake and had finished at least one cup of his strong shop coffee. Mike woke up out-of-sorts, glaring at Big Al as he brushed past him for a second cup.

He asked, "Fixing to load 'em up in a hot air balloon and fly 'em out of town?"

"Nope," Big Al said. "But it wouldn't be a bad idea. If we had a balloon, that is."

"Tell us your plan," John said, ignoring Mike's sarcasm.

"After dark, we'll hook the RV up to my truck, and I'll tow it up into the hills."

Mike smiled cynically and winked at Norma. "That won't work because authorities have a description of the vehicle and its tag number."

Big Al agreed. "That they do."

"Then how . . ."

Raising his palm to quiet Mike, he folded his hand, leaving a single upraised finger, which he crooked, motioning for them to follow him into the bay. Attie gasped when he switched on the overhead lights.

"My God, what have you done to Ol' Nellie?"

Big Al didn't have to answer. Gone was its well-preserved white paint job, replaced by bright fluorescent yellow. Lightning streaks emblazoned both sides of the RV and several dark blue peace symbols. One slogan said Free Mandela and another said Save the Whales.

Mike's gold tooth glinted in the light as he gazed at the RV, his mouth agape. Norma's ruddy complexion flushed bright red. Attie's hands covered her mouth and nose. John simply leaned against the corrugated metal wall, grinning like a fox.

"Always wanted to do one up like that," Big Al said.

"But why? Surely . . ."

John didn't let Attie finish. Instead, he answered for him. "Perfect. It's so obvious that the police will never suspect it. How did you think of it?"

Big Al beamed. "Even a blind hog finds an occasional acorn. Dawned on me that the only way to hide something as big as your RV is not to hide it at all; make it so visible that it becomes invisible. Even put on a California tag from a wrecked car out in the lot. Make it seem even more normal."

"You're a genius," John said, slapping his meaty shoulder.

"Can't take all the credit," Big Al said. He pointed to a snapshot on the wall—a Volkswagen bus, painted garish yellow, bearing precisely the same slogans as those now found on Attie's RV. "It was my daughter's. She dropped out of college in the sixties and went to live in a California commune with a surfing bum turned hippie."

"Your daughter lives in a commune?" Attie asked.

Big Al smiled. "Not anymore. She practices law in Los Angeles and has three kids. She married the surfing bum, though. Now he's a Dean of one of them fancy west-coast colleges."

"That's a wonderful story and a great idea. What now?" John asked.

"It might be risky, but Mike and Norma will have to take you two out of town in the trunk of their car. I'll hook Ol' Nellie to the back of my truck, and we'll all meet at Four Mile Flats."

Attie crossed the bay and gingerly touched the side of the RV. Yanking it back, she grinned when she saw yellow paint on the tip of her finger.

"Ain't quite dry yet," Big Al said.

Attie looked at Mike and Norma. "Sure you want to do this for us?"

Returned to his former state of cheerfulness by Big Al's strong coffee, Mike said, "As John says, they can't eat us. When do we leave?"

Big Al glanced at his watch. "Now's good a time as any. We'll stay in contact by CB."

Attie hugged Mike and Norma, and Big Al blushed when she kissed him square on the mouth.

At precisely a quarter to twelve, the two couples left the garage. Anticipating the extra time needed to reach the rendezvous, they had given Big Al a fifteen-minute head start. Muddy pools of rainwater and deep darkness were all that remained after the passing storm. Mike's old Cadillac trunk provided ample room for Attie and John, although the air grew stale. They could also hear every word of the other couple's conversation and Mike's occasional flatulence eruptions.

"You two okay back there?"

Attie giggled, and John said, "Fine, Mike. It's just a bit stuffy."

"What'd you say?"

"We're fine," John said again, almost shouting.

"They're fine," Norma said.

"Yell if you need anything," Mike said.

"Fat chance," John said with a grin.

Attie elbowed him, realizing Norma and Mike couldn't hear his rude comment. She grabbed his hand when Mike slammed on the brakes, throwing them into the firewall.

"Oh hell," Mike said.

John clutched Attie's hand. "You all right?"

"I'm okay."

114

Norma called, "You two all right back there?"

"None the worse for wear," John said.

"Hold it down back there," Mike said. "There's a roadblock up ahead."

In a moment, the car halted. Glass ground against metal, screeching as Mike lowered the window. John held his breath and Attie's hand, her pent-up anxiety launching her into another giggling fit. Clutching her shoulder, he clamped his hand over her mouth. He needn't have bothered. Neither the policeman nor Mike and Norma could hear a thing above the engine's clatter.

After showing them a snapshot through the window, the policeman asked, "You folks seen this man?"

"Not me, officer. You, Honey?"

"Nope," Norma said. "What's the problem?"

"Nothing to worry about," he said, slapping the car door. "You folks can move along now."

Mike didn't move along. Instead, he said, "Is he an escaped murderer?"

"Mike," John said, still holding Attie's mouth. "Get the hell out of here."

"No, sir, he's just a missing person."

"Seems like quite a fracas for just a missing person. You boys have three cruisers alone on this street. Do you have any big leads?"

"Mike!" John exhorted beneath his breath.

By this time, his hand had become ineffective. Despite Attie's attempt to hold her breath, a full quaking fit wracked her body. John stiffened, closed his eyes, and crossed his fingers.

The policeman said, "We know he's going to Arkansas and in town. We've got every man on the force working overtime to see that he doesn't make it out of here."

When nervous Norma elbowed Mike's ribs, they heard a whoosh of expelled air. "We'll keep a look out for them," she said. "Let's go, Mike."

115

When the policeman slapped the door again, Mike accelerated away a little too fast. "Mike, you idiot," Norma said. "Trying to get us caught?"

"Sorry, Honey. I couldn't resist."

No sooner than they were past the roadblock, Attie's laughter subsided. Hugging John and thinking they were safe, she said, "We made it."

They hadn't.

"We got problems, folks," Norma said.

John asked, his voice a near shout, "What's wrong?"

"Cops had Big Al pulled over at the roadblock. He was standing outside the RV, talking with three of them. They didn't look any too happy."

⁕

Five minutes later, Mike stopped the car again. The heavy Cadillac door swung open, and gravel crunched underfoot as he walked around to the back. Even Attie's usual humor had faded as the key turned, echoing hollowly in the lock. When the large trunk popped open, fresh air and a chill darkness greeted them. Having reached the eastern outskirts of town, the blacktop had ended abruptly, replaced by a narrow dirt road that stretched into the tree-covered mountain range separating eastern Oklahoma from western Arkansas. Norma joined them as Mike helped them out of the trunk.

"What now?" Attie asked.

"We wait," John said. "And hope for the best."

When Attie hugged Mike and Norma, the big red-headed woman began to cry.

"I was so frightened," Attie said.

"I about wet my pants," Norma said.

"Not me," Mike said. "I knew they weren't going to search the car."

Norma elbowed her little husband and said, "You didn't know anything. For a minute, I thought you would open the trunk for them."

Again, Attie began to titter. John grabbed Mike's hand and gave it a hearty shake. His gesture was somehow not enough, and he embraced Mike and Norma like children.

"You two are the best friends a lost soul could ask for. You were both wonderful at the roadblock. I don't want you to take any more chances. Go back to McAlester. Attie and I will wait for Big Al alone. If he doesn't make it, we'll hitchhike to Arkansas."

"Hell no," Mike said. "I'll drive you there myself before I let that happen."

Norma and Attie were now both in tears. A chorus of crickets and a gentle breeze whistling through pines interrupted the sniffles and anxious chatter of the two couples waiting in the dark. Finally, a distant moan disturbed the silence. John heard it first, and then Attie. It was the throaty drone of a diesel engine.

Attie asked, "Is that Big Al's truck?"

"Sounds like it," Mike said, glancing at his watch. "It's been a long time. Hope he ain't got the police with him."

"He wouldn't do that," Attie said.

"He might have broken down under their questioning. Better get back in the trunk," Mike said.

John shook his head. "No, Mike. If it's the police, it's over, and I'll go back to Tulsa with them. You can tell them you found us walking beside the road."

"No, John," Attie said, tugging at his hand.

Shaking his head, he leaned against the fender and folded his arms. "Folks," he said. "Whatever happens from here on out, it's in the hands of fate."

Chapter 17

Vince grabbed a towel from the rack and girded it around his waist as he stepped from the shower. With the back of his hand, he wiped a circular swath from the steam-fogged mirror, raking critical fingers through thinning hair as he stared at his hazy image. He moaned in disgust. After wriggling the loose skin around his neck one last time, he drained his warm beer waiting on the dressing counter.

He'd begun worrying about Cynthia's party shortly after leaving her in the downtown parking garage. Now, he could kick himself for blurting out that Marla was his steady girlfriend. Sleepless hours had convinced him Cynthia's inebriation would preclude her from remembering the invitation. Her call to him at the station the following morning informed him otherwise.

"Vince, you haven't forgotten about Saturday, have you?"

"Saturday?"

"The party is at eight. And Vince, I want to thank you."

"Thank me?"

"For arranging Dan's talk with the police psychologist."

"Oh yeah. Hope it does some good."

"It's already helped me. And Vince, don't forget to bring Marla. I'm dying to meet her."

She'd hung up the phone before Vince could contrive an excuse to skip the party or explain why he wouldn't bring Marla. Hell, he'd thought, refilling his cup with strong precinct coffee. I'll ask her. Why not?

Why not? Vince could think of no valid reason, except the very idea frightened him worse than cornering a serial killer in a dark alley. Still dripping from the shower, he tossed the empty beer can into the trash and trudged into his small kitchen for something to eat.

After breakfast, Vince picked through his clothes closet, searching for an appropriate outfit to wear. Something to impress Marla when asking her to go to the party. Even though it was Saturday, jeans seemed too casual for a first meeting. He settled on blue dress pants and his last starched white shirt. Somehow, the selection seemed benignly incongruous with white socks and sneakers.

"Hell," he mumbled. "All she can do is say no."

The thought terrified him.

At eleven, he could think of no further reason to delay confronting her, so he edged toward the door and peeked out the window. There she was, wearing a skimpy purple tank top and abbreviated khaki shorts, stooping in the flower bed, tending her irises. Her outfit framed darkly tanned shoulders and long winsome legs and tied a knot in his throat as he edged outside.

Standing frozen on the doorstep, his hands trembled, and his heart beat reveille against the old rib cage. Oblivious to the creaking door, Marla continued spading dirt around the flowers as he walked up behind her. Blinking, he drew a deep breath and tapped her shoulder. His action resulted in an unexpected reaction.

Eyes wide, Marla wheeled around, shaken from her concentration by Vince's cautious touch. Like a released spring, she jerked up from her squatting position, catching him full in the crotch with the

119

gardening spade. The ensuing blow doubled him over. Losing his balance, he tripped and tumbled forward. With a dull thud and explosion of soil and blossoms, he landed in her bed of orange and burgundy irises.

Lying motionless on the trampled flowers, Vince choked on their licorice aroma, wincing as Marla screamed and ran inside, slamming the heavy condo door behind her. Shaken, he eased out of the flower bed. After brushing the dirt from his white shirt, he knocked on her door. When she opened it, he missed the glint of fear in her big brown eyes, seeing only the barrel of a .38 police special staring back at him. Immediately, he raised his hands above his head.

"Please don't shoot me," he said. "I'm your next-door neighbor."

Vince waited until Marla lowered the pistol before dropping his hands. Her handsome face flushed, and an errant dark hair was caught between her quivering lips.

"You scared me half to death."

"Sorry. I was just trying to get your attention."

"You ruined my irises," she said. The worried timbre of her voice darkened with anger as her flush of fright subsided."

"It wasn't my intention."

Glaring at him, she spouted, "You ruined my flowers and my whole weekend. Thank you very much."

With that, lovely Marla slammed the door unceremoniously in his face.

"I'm really very sorry," he said, voice raised so she could hear him through the door.

When Marla didn't answer or return, Vince began to feel like the queasy loser in a pie-eating contest. Backing away, he beat a hasty retreat to his condo, hurrying to the refrigerator for another beer to calm his shattered nerves. He found the cupboard bare, his last beer consumed before the confrontation.

Fishing desperately through a lower cabinet, Vince managed to find the bottle of Jack Daniel's leftover from New Year's Eve. Tipping back his head, he poured bourbon directly into his mouth, a position he held until the strong brown liquid dribbled down his neck.

Cynthia was worried. Dan hadn't spoken to her since his meeting with the police psychologist. That night, he'd eaten alone in his study. When he finally came to bed, icy silence pervaded the room, and he ignored her when she crawled in beside him. Rolling over, he turned out the lights without giving her as much as a peck on the cheek. The tightness she felt when she touched his face caused her to instantly withdraw her hand.

Dan left for work without eating breakfast and didn't return until six. Cynthia greeted him at the door, already dressed for the party.

"Where have you been? Our party starts in two hours."

Dan went to his study without answering, not emerging until a quarter of seven. A less-than-subtle click of the bathroom door lock resounded like a brass clapper in Cynthia's brain. Turning helplessly away from the indifferent door, she went to the kitchen to help Billie with the refreshments. When she returned to the bedroom, she found herself locked out, literally and figuratively.

Knocking lightly at first and then more forcefully, she finally gave up and returned to the living room to await their guests alone. They began arriving by seven-thirty, mostly Dan's business associates and influential clients. By eight, well-dressed party-goers crowded their large living room. Dan made his appearance at eight-fifteen. Until then, the bedroom door remained locked.

Cynthia, distraught, tripped on a stool and almost fell after drinking her third glass of champagne. Still, the warming effect of growing anger and too much alcohol replaced her worried flush. They'd hired a string quartet for the party, and dulcet melodies melded with conversation dissonance and champagne glasses clink.

A senior partner's wife clutched her arm, backing her into a corner to spread the latest society gossip. After five minutes of inane conversation, Cynthia realized she hadn't heard the woman's words. Begging off, she retreated through the crowded living room to help Billie clean a spill.

Too upset to fret over a fresh cigarette burn on the couch, she asked, "Seen Dan?"

Billie pointed at the French door. "On the patio, getting some air."

"I could use some myself," Cynthia said.

Handing Billie the glass-filled tray, she started through the packed room. Robert Baker, a senior law partner in Dan's firm and former U.S. Senator, spotted her, waving to get her attention. Dan's mentor, Baker, was also one of Cynthia's closest confidantes. Still, she had other things on her mind. Pretending not to notice, she masked her departure behind an enormous rubber tree plant.

Finding the empty kitchen, she exited the moon-bright yard through the back door. The night air was clear and cool, and she clutched her arms around the low-cut party dress. Slipping on slick grass as she rounded the house, she broke a heel. This time, an opportune tree branch kept her from falling.

Holding her breath, she assessed the rip in her blouse, trying unsuccessfully to regain her composure. When she opened her eyes and unclenched her fists, she removed her shoes and continued around the house. There, light from a flickering cigarette formed shadows on the porch. Suddenly, someone grabbed her from behind, and she screamed, but not before one looping arm went around her waist and a hand over her mouth.

"Cynthia, what the hell are you doing out here? I thought you were a prowler."

Dan's voice instantly soothed her frazzled nerves and wildly racing heart. "And I thought you were a rapist."

Releasing her, he blew smoke into the air and turned away. "I'm going back to the party."

She grabbed his arm and said, "Not until you talk to me."

"What do you want to talk about? That the police shrink thinks I'm off my rocker? I haven't smoked in months. Now, this little episode has me started again."

"You're angry about the meeting with the police shrink."

"Damn right, I am. Who gave you the right to pull a silly stunt like that?"

Caressing his arm, she let her hand drop slowly to his side. Her touch failed to dissipate his glare, and she turned away into the darkness.

"I'm worried about you," she said.

"Worried?"

"Yes, worried. You're acting so irrationally lately. I don't even recognize you anymore since your father disappeared."

Light from the streetlamp blurred the dark lines of his face. Stepping backward, he tossed the cigarette, stamping it out with his shoe.

"So that's what this is all about. Just butt out and let me handle it."

"You are handling it," she said, again touching his arm.

Wrenching away, he backed even deeper into the shrubbery. "You think I don't know about your secret meetings with Columbo? You must think I'm a complete moron."

It was Cynthia's turn to step backward. "Dan, I . . ."

"Don't Dan me," he said, almost shouting. "I know what game you're playing."

"I'm not playing games."

"The hell you're not. Don't you want to find him?"

"Maybe he doesn't want to come home just yet. Is that so terrible?"

She clasped her arms tightly around her chest after he backhanded the bushes with such force that she flinched.

"Yes! Yes, it's terrible!"

She watched, tears in her eyes, as his words ended, though his mouth remained open. She caught her breath and wiped her nose.

"Why is this so important to you? Can't you just let go?"

Backing away, he folded his arms, his jaw clenched into a tight mass of angry muscle.

"This is an important party, Cyn. Important for my career. Now you've upset me, so I don't know if I can go back in there."

Putting her arms around him, she began rocking him like a baby. Oblivious to her gentle pressure, his neck and shoulders only stiffened, and she could feel his tortured apathy.

"Don't be self-destructive. Let's sneak back in the house and lock ourselves in the bedroom," she said. "The guests won't miss us for thirty minutes. I'll make it better. I promise."

He only shook his head, darkness still reflecting from his eyes. "Don't you think the guests would notice their hosts missing for half an hour? Come on, Cyn. Change clothes. You look like you've been in a catfight."

Pulling away from her, he disappeared around the house. Feeling the fool, she leaned against the wall, tilting her head until it touched brick. Remaining there for five long minutes, she waited for tears to dry and emotions to equilibrate. When they finally did, she returned to the kitchen, slowly opening the door.

"Miz Warren! Are you all right?"

Billie stood in the doorway, holding a fresh tray of champagne.

"I was looking for Dan in the yard and stumbled over the shrubbery. I'm going to my room to clean up and change clothes."

She grabbed a glass of champagne and exited with no further explanation. Halfway down the hall, she drained the glass and turned around, suddenly determined to face Dan and force him to explain his actions. She spotted him across the room talking with Robert Baker. Dan saw her at the exact moment.

Angrily rolling his eyes, he started through the crowded room toward her. "My wife tripped in the garden," he explained to a guest in his path.

When he reached her, the party suddenly went ghostly quiet, with all eyes on the young couple. The incessant ringing of the front doorbell interrupted their studied voyeurism. As one, they turned to see who was demanding entrance to the party at this late hour. Billie squirmed through the mass of people, reaching the door.

"Hold your horses," she said. "I'm coming."

As Billie threw open the door, she and the guests emitted a communal gasp. It was Detective Vince Blakeman, dressed in navy blue polyester pants and his best plaid sports coat. Tumbling face-first onto the floor, he shattered the half-empty bottle of Jack Daniel's clutched beneath his arm. As everyone watched, their mouths agape, he sprawled in a heap, bourbon seeping onto an expensive rug.

Chapter 18

Cynthia pulled away from Dan and pushed through the crowded room. The shock of seeing Vince lying drunk in her foyer was more than her already shattered confidence could take. Mixed feelings darkened her face as she stared down at the floor. Behind her, Dan whispered apologies to curious guests, crowding closer for a better look.

When she knelt and pressed her finger against his neck, a loud snort informed her, without the need to feel his pulse, that he was merely inebriated and not injured. Robert Baker touched her shoulder, and their glances conveyed everything they needed to know. Nudging her aside, he slipped his shoulder beneath Vince's arm and hoisted him off the floor, dragging him to the kitchen and into a chair. For privacy, Billie shut the door behind them.

"Miz Warren, if you don't mind me saying so, you look like hell. Why don't you go get yourself cleaned up? I'll take care of this gentleman."

"Do as she says, Cyndi," Baker said, leading her to the side door. "Get cleaned up. I'll help Billie."

"There's something I have to do first."

Wrenching free of his grasp, she opened the kitchen door. Baker called after her, and she stopped in the doorway.

"I can't leave Dan in there alone, looking like a fool."

She grinned when Baker said, "You can't stop an avalanche."

Sticking her head into the living room, she raised her arms, momentarily muting the noise.

"Folks, I'm fine. I thought I heard a prowler in the backyard. I tripped on a bush and made a mess of my dress." A worried titter circulated the party when she laughed at her little joke. "The prowler was just our neighbor, having some fun of his own. Billie and Robert are cleaning him up before his wife finds out. Please excuse me and enjoy the party while I clean up a bit myself."

Laughter dissolved into relieved applause. On her way out the door, she caught a glimpse of Dan, smiling confidently, again in control of the situation following her slightly stilted explanation. When she returned twenty minutes later wearing a different dress, she found the decibel level even higher than before, as Billie had wisely dispensed extra bottles of champagne.

After spotting her, Robert Baker sidestepped his wife and their circle of friends. Easing through the guests, he grasped her hand and squeezed.

"What's this all about?"

Standing on her tiptoes, she gave him a brotherly peck on the lips. "Next time we have two free hours and a nice bottle of chardonnay, I'll explain."

With a wink, she pulled away from his insistent grasp, joining Dan and a throng of admiring guests.

Due to the extra champagne, the party ended later than expected. When it finally did, Cynthia pushed Billie out the door, telling her not to return until much later. After heading straight to the bathroom, she brushed her teeth and washed her face. She pulled on one of Dan's t-shirts and skipped her lacy negligee. She found Dan waiting in bed. Contrary to her fears, he didn't appear angry. When she crawled in beside him, he even managed a half-hearted smile.

"Cyn, I'm sorry."

Surprised by the unexpected apology, she pulled him closer, cradling him in her arms.

"Don't be sorry. I'm the one who should be sorry."

"No. I have a confession."

Suddenly fearful he was about to tell her something devastating, she pulled away, instantly imagining the admission of an affair or maybe worse.

"What do you mean a confession?"

Nodding, he said, "I know you'll think I'm a monster when I tell you."

"Tell me what you've done," she said.

He paused before answering as if trying to recall the exact nuance that would express the magnitude of his malfeasance.

"Remember when I told you I had Dad give me his power of attorney?"

"Yes, to protect his assets and administer his affairs. At least until he accepted your mom's death."

"There's more to it than that."

"Like what?"

In a whisper, he said, "I got more than Dad's power of attorney. I had him ruled incompetent and made him my ward. I'm Dad's legal guardian."

Cynthia shook her head, trying to understand the full significance of his admission. "What does that mean?"

"It means I manipulated his situation to gain control of his affairs."

"But that's not so terrible. He couldn't take care of himself."

"That's the point. He could then, and he obviously can now."

"I don't see the problem. Just go back to court and have them dismiss you. Return your Dad's rights."

"Not so simple."

"You're a lawyer. What could be simpler?"

His sullen expression explained before his words had a chance. "I not only sold Dad's house, I also liquidated all his assets."

It was her turn to pause. After letting the ramifications of his story sink in, she said, "Then return the money."

Dan's eyes lowered to the satin sheets, and he slowly shook his head. "We don't have it anymore. I paid off the house with part of the money. The rest went into a business venture with some of the partners at the firm. There's no cash left."

Staring at him, stunned, she said, "Can't you sell your interest in the business venture?"

"Maybe for ten cents on the dollar. Real estate belly-flopped this past year, you know."

"I can't believe you spent all his money."

Anger, so apparent in his eyes since his father's disappearance, flashed anew. Turning away from her, he glared at the wall.

"I expected a full return on the investment. Besides, Dad has shown no signs of coming out of his malaise until now. And I did intend to care for him as long as he lived."

"He's not that old, Dan. He might live ten, maybe twenty more years."

"He's an old man," Dan said. "He doesn't need the money anymore."

"He's your father, not a steer on his way to the slaughterhouse."

He faced her again, and his anger bled away, this time replaced by guilt-laced pain.

"What'll I do? What can I do? Everyone will think I stole Dad's money. They're already talking behind my back at the office."

"You're being paranoid. No one thinks anything except you want to see your father returned home, safe and sound."

Like an errant gust of wind, the demented glint, present since his father's disappearance, returned to his eyes. Springing out of bed, he began pacing the bedroom floor, mumbling.

"I've got to do something. I can't afford to let this continue."

Upset and anxious, Cynthia said, "Just call off the dogs. Let your father come home of his own accord. When he does, you can tell him the truth."

Vince awoke in a strange bed, his head throbbing and ears ringing like a recess bell. Two little giggling girls were staring at him.

"You're the policeman looking for Grandpa."

He massaged his throbbing temple and closed his eyes, not immediately recognizing the twins.

"I'm Vince. Who are you?"

"Trish. This is Emily and Sparky."

When she handed the squirming animal to him, he held on tight, grimacing as the black cocker puppy licked wet swaths across his mouth and nose. One of the little girls grabbed the playful puppy and put him on the floor. He ran out of the room, toenails rasping against wood.

"What's your last name, Trish?"

"Warren."

He failed to suppress a low moan at hearing the name. He massaged his aching temples and said, "I was afraid of that. Where are your mommy and daddy?"

"Still sleeping. Billie fixed breakfast and cleaned up the house from the party."

"Billie?"

"She helps Mommy," Emily said.

Before he could ask another question, the two little girls said, "See you later, Vince."

They hurried out the door after the black cocker. Vince slowly peeled the sheet away from his neck and peeked down at his chest. Realizing he still had on all of his clothes, except for his coat and shoes, he felt an ounce, though only an ounce, of relief.

It suddenly occurred to him that a significant gap occupied much of his memory of the prior day. It wasn't all missing. Seared into his brain, surreal and painful, the humiliating encounter with Marla remained. He began to remember trying to kill the bottle of Jack Daniel's and vaguely recalled driving alone to the party.

Finding himself fully dressed in one of their bedrooms chilled his neck like a shot of ice water. He wondered what he had done and what price he would ultimately pay for his actions. Easing out of bed and limping into the bathroom, he searched the cabinets for a much-needed aspirin. Returning to the bedroom to search for his shoes and sports jacket, he came face-to-face with Billie. She was propped against the open doorway, staring at him as if he were a serial killer. Under her arm, she held a silver serving tray.

"Had yourself quite a time last night, didn't you?"

He ignored her reproachful remark and dropped to his knees to search beneath the bed for his shoes.

"Wish I could remember it if I did. How did I end up here?"

"Me and Mr. Baker drug you in here and threw you in bed."

"Is Mr. Warren angry?"

Billie snickered. "Oh, he forgot all about you as soon as we carted you out of the room. Mrs. Warren just told everyone you were a drunken neighbor."

"He doesn't know I'm here?"

"No, and if I was you, I'd pack my butt on out before he gets up and you refresh his memory about your grand entrance to the party last night."

Again, he moaned and rubbed his head. "You wouldn't happen to know where I can find my shoes and coat?"

"Maybe," she said. "What's it worth to you?"

"Look, I'm in no mood for games. Sorry for whatever I did last night, but I could lose my job if I don't get out of here."

Beginning to feel sorry for him and perceiving correctly she'd ribbed him enough, she poured coffee from a carafe on the nightstand, handing him the cup.

"You just relax. After last night, those two won't be up for at least another hour. Your shoes and coat are in the closet," she said.

The coffee tasted like manna from heaven. Billie waited patiently until he'd finished it and then poured him another cup. She watched as he retrieved his sports coat and shoes from the closet. When he finished dressing, he returned the empty cup and hurried from the bedroom, carefully looking both ways before entering the hall.

Billie followed him. At the front door, he crooked his finger, still having some difficulty functioning correctly.

"Billie, right?"

With a grin, the big woman nodded.

"Thanks, Billie," he said. "I owe you."

On his way home, Vince passed a florist, going half a block down the road before slapping the dashboard and turning around in the vacant street. He returned to the nearly empty shop, where a surprised clerk sold him two dozen roses. With blurry eyes and a trembling hand, he scrawled two message cards. With what was left of yesterday's lunch threatening to come up, he could only acknowledge the florist's thanks with a weak grunt as he hurried for the door.

Upon arriving at his apartment, Vince rushed into the bedroom and fell onto the bed. He stayed under the covers for the rest of the weekend, his thoughts flickering between painful reality and troubled dreams.

Chapter 19

Hazy moonlight, filtering through wispy cloud cover, lightened the eastern Oklahoma sky. Leaning against the fender of Mike's Cadillac, John and Attie held hands, listening to the low diesel drone of Big Al's wrecker coming up the hill. Norma waited nearby, arm around her short husband's shoulder. Even in dim light, no one could miss her tears that mingled with many freckles, creating unique patterns on her face. Staring at the pavement with a frustrated frown, Mike curled strands of dark hair between anxious fingers.

Far down the hill, truck lights appeared through the trees, laboring up the steep pavement with the yellow RV behind it. When Big Al reached them, hydraulic brakes screeched as he eased two vehicles behind Mike's Cadillac. Holding their collective breath, they watched as he exited the wrecker and joined them beside the white Cadillac. Seeing he was alone, Mike's frown changed to a grin, and he rushed over to shake his hand.

"Al, we thought they had you back there."

"Thought so, too," Big Al said. "Head trooper turned out to be my nephew." Chuckling, he scratched his stubbly chin. "Said the RV must be my daughter's—his cousin's—since he remembered seeing one like it years ago."

Norma said, "He believed your story?"

133

"Believe it, hell! He spouted it out to the other police before I got a word out of my mouth."

"Then what took you so long," Mike asked, glancing at his watch. "We've been worried sick."

"Drank coffee with the boys and swapped a few lies. Didn't want to appear too anxious, you know." He chuckled again.

Attie smiled. "What's so funny?"

"The boys were leaning against the RV. Hope the paint's dry. If not, their wives will be surprised when they see yellow paint streaked all over those nice khaki uniforms."

Norma began to giggle, and Attie joined in, with the five conspirators howling with moon-mad laughter. When Attie put her arms around the big mechanic's neck, even the Oklahoma darkness failed to hide his blush."

"Thanks, Big Al," she said.

"My pleasure, Attie."

When she let go of him, she hugged Mike and Norma, her laughter turning into tears. "Don't know how we can ever thank you," she said, finally pulling away.

"We will miss you two," Norma said.

"We'll visit again when this whole mess is settled," John said. "It's not the end of the world."

A pregnant silence followed his pronouncement. Finally, Big Al slapped his shoulder and pointed up the hill.

"This here road goes up over the mountains, eventually into Arkansas. Ain't got no name, so all I can tell you is to keep heading east till you hit Arkansas blacktop. It might be kind of dangerous, so be careful. Sorry to send you this way, but it's probably the only road to Arkansas without a roadblock."

"Thanks, Big Al," John said. "We better go before a stray patrol car decides to take a moonlight drive to the Arkansas border."

"Wouldn't worry about it on a night like this," Big Al said. "Be sure to send us a postcard when you settle down."

"We'll do more than that," John said.

"Wish I could do more," Big Al said. "A man's got rights. Don't matter how old he is. God bless you, you hear?"

The big man fell silent, turned away, and returned to his truck. After one last hug and handshake, Mike and Norma followed him. John and Attie watched the wrecker and Mike's Caddie turn around on the narrow road, their taillights disappearing beyond a distant bend. Attie patted the RV's hood, opened its door, and went inside. After a last glance at the cloudy sky, John followed her.

Attie pulled away from the curb with her tires slipping in the mud. Mud splattered up from the road, soon covering the windshield and headlights and diminishing visibility. Attie pumped the washer button until it ran dry as the winding dirt road replaced the moderately steep Oklahoma blacktop. After ten miles, the slippery byway showed no signs of flattening out.

Lost in thought, Attie finally said, "I'll miss them."

"So will I, and if you don't keep your eyes on the road, we may see them again sooner than we'd like."

Attie tapped the brakes at John's concerned tone, involuntarily sending the RV's nose into a lateral slide toward the right-hand ditch.

"Steady, now. Straighten her up, but don't stop," he warned. "You'll stick us for sure."

Riveting Attie's attention and forcing her to plant both hands firmly on the wheel, she regained control as the big RV shimmied first to the right and then to the left.

"Looks bad, John."

His attention was concentrated on the narrow strip of muddy road illuminated by a dull headlight

Eric Wilder

glow. Reaching across the console, he touched her shoulder.

"Easy, Attie," he said softly. "You're doing just fine."

For the second time that night, rain began to fall slowly and in ever-increasing waves. Mud, thrown by the front wheels, impeded the windshield wipers clacking against the window frame, further obstructing their vision. Attie remained silent as she feathered the throttle and gingerly twirled the wheel to stay centered on the road. The RV began to fishtail.

"Almost there," he said. "It's only a hundred feet or so to the crest."

Too engrossed with the muddy road to respond to his subliminal exhortations, she didn't answer. Unable to do anything else, he kept up a constant, encouraging banter. As they neared what appeared to be the crest of the hill, both held their breath. Unfortunately, it wasn't the crest they'd reached. After flattening briefly, the road continued increasingly steeper into rainy gloom.

By now, John's mouth was dry, his throat lumpy. "False alarm," he said.

Attie maintained even pressure on the throttle and a delicate touch on the wheel. Ten frantic minutes passed before the road flattened enough to stop the RV. Switching off the engine, she let go of the wheel and closed her eyes. When she glanced up at John, she found him smiling back at her.

"Mario Andretti's got nothing on you."

Attie leaned across the console and hugged him.

"We made it," she said.

As the RV slowly slid backward, its metallic groan interrupted their moment of elation. "Not yet," John said. "Start the engine. Hurry!"

Spinning its wheels in the mud for one heart-stopping moment, the vehicle regained traction and moved slowly up the narrow road.

Unable to mask his concern, he said, "Still haven't reached the top. Have to keep going."

Attie needed no prompting. Though she tried centering the RV on the road, she could barely see beyond its stubby hood through thick and cloying fog.

"We're losing traction and still going uphill," she said, voice cracking.

"Keep going as far as you can. I'll walk the rest of the way and get help."

John's suggestion seemed, at best, futile. Still, there was little else to do but continue up the slick grade. They did just that, slowly, slipping and sliding. Before long, even that became impossible. Despite Attie's efforts, the RV sputtered to a halt and started sliding slowly back down the mountain road.

Desperately, she gunned the engine, spinning the wheels to stop their backward momentum. It didn't help, and they continued losing traction. When the rear end spun sideways, John slammed his foot against the floorboard as they lurched into the ditch with a sickening thud.

Canted at an odd angle, the RV rocked once and stopped dead in the ditch. Unlatching his shoulder harness, he stumbled to the door, grabbing his jacket. He realized he'd made a mistake when he stepped outside the RV. It was dangling and canted at an odd angle, and even in foggy darkness, he sensed the big vehicle was near the edge of the narrow mountain road, its left rear wheel two feet lower than its right. Cautiously, he stepped from the ramp, probing for solid ground. Finding none, he stepped down anyway. A stupid mistake, he instantly learned.

Mud in the ditch immediately sucked up his foot. When he yanked upward to free himself, he lost his balance and grip on the door, sliding into sticky muck and not stopping until he'd rolled ten feet down the hill. He found himself hopelessly mired in glue-like mud. Lightning flashed and thunder sounded nearby.

A steady rain began to fall. Attie heard his surprised cry and rushed to the door of the RV.

"John. Where are you?"

"Down here."

"You okay?"

"Stuck against a rock. It's too slick to crawl back uphill."

"I'm coming."

"No," he shouted. "Then we'll both be stuck. Get a rope from the tool chest. Tie it to the steering wheel and throw me the other end."

Attie hurried to the back of the RV and began searching through the tools, finding the utility tow rope. Following his instructions, she returned to the open door.

"Where are you? I can't see you."

Even through the murky fog, dim light from the RV's open door silhouetted Attie's rain-soaked image.

"Directly below you, about ten feet. Give the rope a good toss and stand back."

She threw the rope, landing it just two feet from his grasp. Despite his efforts, he couldn't climb the slick incline far enough to reach the dangling lifeline.

Out of breath and exhausted, he called hoarsely, "Any slack on the other end?"

"Just a little. Stay there. Be right back."

Even in his pressing predicament, he had to smile. "I'm going nowhere," he said to himself.

Propped against a big rock, he waited for her to re-tie the rope to the steering wheel. A flash of yellow lighted the foggy western sky, followed by a nearby clap of thunder and an even heavier downpour. Attie shouted from the door.

"Here it comes."

Wet rope dropped from the RV, striking him in the face. Thinking she'd missed, she pulled it back toward her. John made a diving grab and held on to the slippery line.

"Attie, I have it. Let me get a grip."

Barely able to hear his voice above wind and pounding rain, she reeled in the wet rope. She tossed it again, connecting with John and waiting until his shout and tug signaled he'd tied it around his waist.

Bracing against the door frame, she pulled. John reached the door ten grueling minutes later. Attie grabbed his shoulders, yanking him into the RV. She collapsed on top of him as he flopped in a muddy pile on the floor.

When her labored gasps subsided, she said, "What now?"

"Wait until morning so we can see what we're doing. And hope the police aren't fool enough to search this road on a night like this."

For moments, they lay there, coated with thick brown mud. Then Attie began to chuckle, and despite their tense situation, they both rolled in laughter on the floor.

Chapter 20

Bright sunlight streamed through the RV's unshaded window, waking John early the next day. Groggy and still exhausted, he found himself lying on the floor with Attie sprawled unceremoniously on him. Dried mud caked both of them. Something pecking at the window caught his attention. He rubbed his crusty eyes and craned his neck to look at the window. It was tilted at an absurd angle, and it took him a moment to remember why.

"Hello," someone from outside the RV said. "Is anyone in there?"

Recalling the muddy accident the night before, John briefly closed his eyes. Attie was still asleep, but someone, likely the Oklahoma State Police, had found them. Gently pushing her off his chest, he carefully extricated himself from the wall. He slipped on the slanted floor when he tried to stand, crashing into a cabinet with a bang.

"John . . ."

"It's all right. I just slipped a little."

Following a moment of confusion, she rubbed her mud-crusted eyes and glanced around the RV. Again, a man's voice called outside the window.

"Are you all right in there?"

Glancing first at Attie, John said, "We're fine. Had an accident last night and slid into the ditch."

"Need some help?"

"We can't get out the door," John said, remembering their predicament.

"Hang on. I'll climb up on the roof and give you a hand."

They waited as the unknown person went to the ladder in the back, listening intently as he crawled across the roof, making his way to the side door facing the drop-off.

"This could be the end of the road, Attie."

"Not on your life, old man. If it's the police, I'll return to Tulsa with you."

"And bust me out of the old folk's home?"

"With chisel and crowbar, if I have to."

"Hey in there," the man called. "Give me your hand, and I'll lift you out."

Resounding with the same country twang as Mike, Norma, and Big Al, the voice on the roof had a strangely friendly and reassuring tone. John and Attie glanced up and spotted a big, hairy arm reaching into the window. Thankfully, it was draped in red flannel instead of khaki. John helped Attie to her feet and guided her to the door, where the unidentified man hoisted her up to the roof as effortlessly as lifting a baby from its crib. When John cautiously stepped out the door, he noticed the man's curly red hair and ruddy face.

"Grab hold," the smiling man said, extending a muscular arm.

He lifted him out the window, up to the radically canted roof with one easy motion. Dressed in blue jeans and a bright flannel shirt, their rescuer looked like an overgrown Huck Finn. Instead of Huck, it was Hulk.

"Name's Hulk," he said, extending his meaty hand in John's direction.

"You don't know how glad we are to see you, Mr. Hulk," John said. He winked at Attie, still precariously clutching the roof's chrome luggage rack. "I'm John Warren, and this is Attie Johnson."

"Pleased to make your acquaintance," the man said. "Ain't Mr. Hulk, though, it's just Hulk."

141

"We thought you were the Oklahoma State Police," Attie said.

"No way," Hulk said. "You're five miles into Arkansas."

After climbing down from the RV roof and brushing off as best they could, John and Attie could only stare. Mud-streaked Big Al's yellow paint job and the RV's two left wheels were firmly planted in the ditch. Gone was rain and fluffy cumulus clouds, replaced by sunlight and a clear blue Arkansas sky. They could see fifty miles in every direction from their vantage at the top of a gently rounded mountain. Below the RV, a cliff of solid chert plunged several hundred feet down to a wooded valley far below.

Behind them, on the hood of a blue Ford pickup, sat an attractive young woman about the age of the man who'd rescued them. A large camper occupied the truck bed. From the travel decals on its tan corrugated surface, the couple appeared to be on permanent vacation. A large bass boat on a trailer, attached to the rear of the camper, reinforced this observation.

"That's my wife, Lillie Mae," Hulk said, pointing.

John and Attie smiled and waved. "Thanks for helping us out of the RV, Hulk. Now, if you could get us off the ledge."

John expected no positive response to his flippant statement. Hulk glanced at the big RV as if weighing that possibility.

He finally said, "I can do it."

"You have a tow truck hidden in the trees somewhere?" John asked, disbelieving.

"No, but I got a tow rope. I'll jerk you out of that hole."

Without waiting for John to scoff at his offer, he headed to his pickup for the rope. On hands and knees, he attached the line to the towing connection on the RV's frame. Spitting on his oversized palms, he disengaged the boat trailer from the back of his camper and attached the other end to his truck.

"One of you will have to get back in and drive it out of the ditch," Hulk said.

John immediately started for the ladder at the back of the RV. Attie stopped him and grabbed his arm.

"No, you don't. I brought us this far. If anyone drives Ol' Betsy off that ledge, it will be me."

John grinned and raised both hands into the air. "I wouldn't have it any other way."

Hulk helped Attie back into the RV. "Put it in drive and rest your foot on the gas. Don't spin the wheels. When I jerk it, you feel it starting to inch out of the ditch. Give it a little. Just don't let the back wheels break loose," he said, wagging his finger at her.

Hulk climbed down and hurried to the wheel of his camper. John waved his arm and said, "What can I do?"

"Stay out of the way," he said.

John did just that, moving to the far side of the road. Lillie Mae, Hulk's diminutive wife, joined him. She was small as Hulk was large, her face fresh, and her blond hair sharply contrasted with Hulk's red mane. Brushing curly-blond hair out of her big blue eyes, she smiled at John and grabbed his elbow, directing him further off the road.

"Hulk gets a going, that camper's going to be all over the place," she said with an accent far sharper than her husband's. "Better steer way clear."

"You don't think the RV will turn over, do you?" John asked, suddenly very concerned.

Lillie Mae shook her head. "Ain't no better driver in Arkansas than Hulk. He can't get her out of there, no one can."

"That's good to know, I guess," he said.

As they watched, Attie cranked the RV's engine and Hulk did the same with the camper, backing until he had about ten feet of slack in the rope. Moving forward slowly, he tested the tautness, barely letting the camper's rear tires break loose as the engine strained against the RV's weight.

Every time the camper moved forward, Attie applied gas. As she did, its rear wheels slipped on loose rock, and the RV began creeping sideways. It crept toward the drop-off and not the road. John held his breath, seriously contemplating running up to Hulk's truck and aborting the attempt. Again, Lillie Mae grabbed his arm.

"Give him a chance."

Something in her sweet, country voice made him do just that. Backing away from the road, he folded his arms and watched. Again, Hulk backed toward the RV. This time, instead of creeping forward, he gunned the engine. Like a giant rubber band, the slack in the rope popped and disappeared, yanking the RV and lifting its front wheels physically off the ground. This time, Hulk reversed the engine, moving only two feet before jamming the gears into forward, again popping slack from the rope.

Back, forward, back, forward; the maneuver became almost a single fluid motion. Getting a feel for what Hulk was trying to do, Attie furiously worked the gas pedal, gunning the engine when Hulk jerked forward, letting off when he went back. The RV jumped and bumped and began to come loose from the embankment. In one last fluid effort, Hulk launched the truck into a series of reverse and forward motions so fast it seemed the camper was going in both directions simultaneously.

With a crunch of crushing rock and lurching protest of six tons of combined steel, the RV seemed to bend in the middle. Its rear tires popped off the rock a distance of at least three feet, and the massive vehicle pulled free of its fetters, spinning wildly on the gravel, tossing stone and mud for a frenzied moment before coming to a halt on the flat roadbed. Attie switched off the RV's engine and exited the door with a mile-wide grin. John looked at Lillie Mae in amazement.

"I wouldn't have believed it."

Meeting Hulk halfway out of his camper, Attie shook his hand. He gave her a smiling thumbs-up and continued past her to detach the rope from the RV. After performing the same task on the camper, he grabbed Attie's arm and escorted her to the spot where John and Lillie Mae waited by the side of the road.

Shaking his hand, John said, "I wouldn't have believed it possible if I hadn't seen it with my own eyes."

"Seen it done once. I wasn't sure it would work with that big bus, though."

"Hulk, you're a genius," John said.

"Ain't nobody ever called me that before," Hulk said with a satisfied grin. "Where you folks headed?"

John glanced back down the steep winding road they'd so recently traversed and said, "Hot Springs."

"Well, you ain't going to make it today."

Visibly disturbed, Attie asked, "What's wrong?"

"You got a hole in your gas tank, and it's leaking fast."

Attie's hand went instantly to her mouth, her questioning gaze to John.

"What will we do?"

Hulk answered the question before John confused as Attie, had a chance to comment.

"We're camped right down the road a bit. You got enough gas to make it. When we get there, you folks can relax, and I'll fix the tank for you."

"You can do that?" John said, still confused.

"You bet he can," Lillie Mae said. "Hulk's got welding equipment and tools back at camp. Fix you up in no time. You can camp the night with us and head for Hot Springs when you feel like it."

"We're most grateful," Attie said.

"Then let's get it on," Hulk said, raising his thumb skyward again. "If we finish soon enough, we can get

Eric Wilder

in some river fishing before sundown. You game,
Pops?"

"Lead the way," John said.

They followed the young couple over the crest to
a spot near the top of the weathered mountain range.
Complete with switchbacks, u-turns, and blind
chutes, the flattened roadbed, still muddy from the
recent rain, traversed an ancient hogback ridge. In
places, sheer drop-offs occupied both sides of the
narrow road. They felt like nineteenth-century ridge
runners thrown back in time to a simpler existence.

Old oaks, pine trees, and bare rock cuts
punctuated the short trip. After ten miles of slow
going, Hulk's blinker signaled he intended to turn
right. For a moment, John and Attie studied the thick
foliage, wondering where and how he planned to turn
off the road. After a perfunctory blink of his brake
lights, he disappeared into the trees.

When Attie reached where his camper had
vanished, she found an even narrower road. Scraping
muddy yellow paint on both sides of the RV, she
negotiated the turn and immediately started downhill
on a fairly steep grade. Only gravel, kicked up by
Hulk's truck and the absence of an intersecting road,
told them they were on the right path. The narrow trail
was like a tunnel through the thick cover of trees,
becoming even narrower as they descended the steep
road.

"Hope Hulk knows where he's going," John said.
"No place to turn around, and we sure can't back out
of here."

After five minutes, they saw that Hulk knew
where he was going. A clearing suddenly appeared
through the trees, and the RV's nose leveled. Hulk and
Lillie Mae's camper was already parked. With massive
waving arms, he directed Attie to a flat parking place
beside his truck. When they got out of the RV and
looked around, they realized they had somehow

stumbled on a little Shangri-La hidden deep in the mountainous backwoods of western Arkansas.

Chapter 21

Shangri-La indeed! Behind them, a sheer limestone cliff jutted straight into the stratosphere, a distance of at least two hundred feet. Making a gentle crescent, a solid rock wall curved around, enclosing a clearing on two sides. Steady sun had replaced the rain, and the day had grown warm and humid. Hollowed back into the mountain, the resultant cave-like indention in the cliff emanated a sudden abundance of refrigerated air, forming a naturally air-conditioned amphitheater.

A short distance down the hill from the camp, a meandering river flowed slowly by. Eons ago, the river had carved a path through a steep-walled valley. Now, in shifting shades of azure and emerald, the still water contrasted beautifully with the greens and earthy tones of the surrounding trees and rock ledges. Together, they glimmered in the refracted light on the valley floor. Wading in the shallow water, a blue heron seemed oblivious to them.

"Gorgeous, absolutely gorgeous," Attie exclaimed.

"It is that," Hulk said as he crawled beneath the RV with a pan to catch the gas still dripping from the tank. "That'll hold it till we can patch the tear."

John asked, "How in the world did you ever find this place?"

At the same time, Hulk and Lillie Mae exchanged glances. A rush of red crept up his neck, making the numerous freckles on his face less noticeable. Lillie

Mae smiled, stood on her tiptoes, and kissed her rosy-cheeked husband.

"Hulk was looking for a place off the main road to do a little parking," she said.

"Lillie Mae, you didn't have to tell them that," Hulk said, even more flustered.

She laughed and said, "It's true, though."

Hulk wrapped his large arm around Lillie Mae's neck and pretended to thump her head. She elbowed him in the stomach and wrenched free. Attie and John watched, concerned, as the young couple dashed down the hill toward the river. When Hulk caught up with Lillie Mae beneath a giant pine, they embraced passionately, like eager newlyweds. After observing them momentarily, John squeezed Attie's hand and kissed her.

Attie said, "Feeling a little frisky, old man?"

"Must be the mountain air," he said, pulling her toward him.

Imitating Lillie Mae, Attie playfully cuffed him on the cheek, then turned and dashed for the RV. With aging legs and a youthful heart, he chased after her, breathing heavily when she let him catch up at the RV's door.

After showering and changing into fresh clothes, John and Attie spent the rest of the morning exploring their newly discovered mountain hideaway's rocky crevices and wooded areas. Hulk rummaged around camp, setting up lawn chairs, tables, and a portable generator. Finally, he backed his boat down the gentle slope and launched it into the river. At noon, Lillie Mae called them from the tranquil clearing below.

"I got some sandwiches ready. Let's eat."

They made their way back down the trail hand in hand. When they reached the clearing, they discovered a portable picnic table. Lillie Mae had already covered it with cold cuts, white bread, salad dressing, and a large bowl of potato chips. Hulk

149

signaled for them to help themselves. Sitting on boulders overlooking the river, they did just that.

Between bites, John said, "How long have you been married?"

"Five years," Lillie Mae said. "Right out of high school."

Attie asked, "Live around here now?"

"Just up the road, near Conway. Hulk's got a welding shop there."

"Come here every chance we get," he said, smiling at Lillie Mae. "It's kind of our special spot."

"It is a special place and so peaceful," Attie said.

Hulk and Lillie Mae beamed at the compliment. Throughout the light lunch, they held hands as they ate. Hulk dwarfed Lillie Mae but catered to her every wish like a devoted servant. It was obvious, almost embarrassingly so, that they were deeply in love. Between bites, they would kiss like smitten teenagers, or Lillie Mae would pinch Hulk in an awkward spot, causing his big face to turn bright red. Attie and John pretended not to notice.

"We never caught your last name," John said, interrupting their mutual groping.

"Dancer," Lillie Mae said proudly.

"How did you come by your nickname? John asked.

"From the cartoon."

"The Incredible Hulk," Lillie Mae said.

Attie grinned. "You're certainly not green."

"But he's big and beefy," Lillie Mae said, trying, but failing, to extend her tiny hands around his huge biceps.

"Any children?" asked John.

Hulk's blush and Lillie Mae's impish grin faded as one. Lillie Mae's pretty features contorted into a grimace. Without saying a word, she pushed away from the table and hurried to the camper, slamming the door behind her with a resounding thud. John could only sit with his mouth open, aware of Attie's fingernails digging into the back of his hand. Noticing the pallid blankness of Hulk's expression, Attie reached across the table and touched the young man's wrist.

"We're sorry. Why don't you go see about her?"

Hulk nodded and got up from the table. As he vanished into the camper, John looked over at Attie.

"Did I stick my foot in my mouth?"

"Yes, though I'll bet you're not the first."

He gazed at the camper, slowly unwinding his lanky limbs from beneath the table. "Shall I knock on the door and apologize?"

Attie held up her hand in a halting motion. "Let's just pretend nothing happened. If and when they want to tell us about it, they will."

They went about their business, with Attie straightening the RV and John washing the mud off its new yellow paint job using a bucket of water from the river. Hulk and Lillie Mae left the camper feeling much lighter an hour later. Lillie Mae smiled at John as she brushed past him on her way into the RV to assist Attie. Hulk strolled up with a friendly grin on his Huck Finn face, admiring the older man's effort with the bucket and sponge.

"Looks a sight better than it did this morning when I pulled you out of the ditch," he said, his lilting Arkansas twang reverberating off canyon walls. "Are you and Attie hippies?"

John didn't understand the implications of Hulk's question. Then, recalling the sixties graffiti on the RV, he recognized that he was entirely serious.

"There were no hippies in the forties." Seeing Hulk's confusion, he added, "A long story goes along with the paint job. I'll tell you when we both have a few hours to spare."

Thankfully, changing the subject, Hulk said, "Know anything about engines?"

Remembering his failed prognosis of the RV's overheating problem, he grinned and said, "Not much, but I'm game to look. What's the problem?"

"My truck has a funny noise under the hood."

"Let's check it out," John said, motioning Hulk to follow him. "Maybe we can get a handle on it before dark."

John spent the rest of the afternoon assisting Hulk with various tasks around the campsite. They disassembled, cleaned, and rebuilt the truck's carburetor and chopped a stack of firewood. Lillie Mae and Attie relaxed in lawn chairs, chatting like schoolgirls.

The two couples watched the sun relinquish its command of the heavens to a big yellow moon and thousands of glittering stars, a river loon's mournful cry punctuating the darkness. Attie and Lillie Mae prepared a spicy hot pot of chili and beans. Back-dropped by a chorus of frogs and crickets, they savored the chili with cornbread and some of John's large stash of choc beer. In addition to frogs and crickets, they heard an occasional hoot of an owl, a wolf's howl, or a bobcat's snarl tracking its luckless prey. No traffic noise or any human sound disturbed the tranquility.

Comforting darkness, piquant chili, and the pacifying effect of strong beer combined to loosen their tongues. Coaxed by Attie, Lillie Mae, and especially Hulk, John told several amusing vignettes from his youth.

Hulk finally asked, "John, were you in the war?"

After hesitating, he said, "Yes, I was."

"Then tell us a war story," Hulk goaded.

Poignant memories flooded John's mind, and he smiled sadly, unconsciously grinding his toe against an empty cardboard carton.

Hulk prompted, "Were you in the Battle of the Bulge?"

Waves of nostalgia crested John's bow, and he said, "Wasn't supposed to be, but I was."

"Please," Lillie Mae said. "Tell us."

He did, beginning slowly and then warming to the tale. "The Bulge was Hitler's last attempt to turn back the advancing Allies. For a month and a half, the battle lasted, and it was called the 'Bulge' because Germans failed to break through the line, only succeeding in bending it. I was a radio man in the signal corp. One night, an old colonel appeared at the communications tent, needing to relay a message to Patton. Since we were out of direct radio communication with the main force, he decided to deliver it in person and conscripted me to drive the jeep for him.

"The night turned bitterly cold. Snow had fallen for days, piled high on both sides of the road. Continuing night and day, the battle line had spread out many miles, constantly moving like an angry sidewinder. We realized we had somehow crossed the line when the sun rose the following morning.

"Germans, besides many other things, were excellent soldiers. We found ourselves caught, along with an advancing column of American infantrymen, in a crossfire ambush. Fresh from the States, our boys were young, mostly teenagers. Barely trained, none had ever seen a German, much less been under fire.

"Finding yourself caught in a firefight is like walking a railroad track at night. Hearing the loud blast of a whistle behind you, you turn and stare into the lights of the monstrosity twenty feet away and bearing down on you—the remains of your best friend already chewed up beneath its wheels.

"When the attack began, the noise was frightening and extreme—beyond imagination for the uninitiated—with gunfire and violent explosions, steel, dirt, and stone whistled randomly around our heads. Our boys tossed their rifles and ran for cover. German marksmen began dropping them in their tracks. Blood was running in the ditches, staining the snow crimson, when we reached the center of the column. Unarmed, the old colonel jumped from the jeep and ran directly into the path of the retreating GIs."

"Thrusting rifle after rifle back into the hands of those child soldiers, he admonished them to hold their ground. Around us, the battlefield was alive with explosions, hot lead and wounded soldiers screaming for help. A mortar round exploded near the jeep, spraying me with dirt and shrapnel. When I wiped my face, the blood on my hand wasn't my own.

"Any one of a hundred Hun marksmen could have dropped the colonel. None did. Maybe they were awed by his bravery and coolness under fire. With confused soldiers dying all around him, he coursed the length of that bloody road, exhorting them to turn and fight. One by one, their youth dissolved in a mire of smoke and torn flesh, and they became men in the hot cauldron of battle. Turning around, they fought, hanging on until reinforcements arrived."

John grew silent, and Attie squeezed his hand, feeling the intensity of his pain. Finally, he chuckled, and his laugh drew into a hoarse laugh.

"Know what's funny?" His rapt audience shook their head without answering. "I remember the Colonel as old, but he was probably no more than forty. Forty years younger than I am now, and I still think of him as an old man. I can't remember his name, and I don't suppose you'll ever read about him in any history book, but he was a true American hero."

Suddenly aware of frogs, crickets, and distant owls, John realized no one had spoken for an interminable period. Lillie Mae put her arms around his shoulder like a mother comforting a child when she saw he'd finished the story. Hulk remained silent, torn by his own conflicting emotions.

Having nothing more to say, the young couple said goodnight, leaving John and Attie alone beneath a yellow moon and sparkling stars. He hugged Attie, drawing for a moment on her strength before speaking.

"In all these years, I've never told that story to another soul."

Attie patted his shoulder and said, "Some of us hold painful memories inside till the day we die. It's good you let one of yours go."

Chapter 22

Awakened from an early morning Technicolor dream, John rolled over in bed. Groggily aware of an incessant tap tapping outside the RV's bedroom window, he opened his eyes enough to see his watch dial. When he cracked the curtain, Hulk's smiling face, his freckled nose pressed against the window pane, stared back at him. It was still dark outside.

Recalling their planned fishing trip, John got out of bed and put on his pants and shoes, still buttoning his shirt as he stepped out the door. Hulk greeted him with a friendly smile and a steaming mug of coffee. With a glum expression, he accepted both.

"When you said fishing, I didn't realize you meant in the middle of the night," he said, sipping the hot coffee.

"Need to be on the river before first light. Don't want to spook the fish," Hulk explained.

Too early for conversation, John nodded. After helping Hulk with the gear, he followed him down the winding path to the river. The first morning light filtering into the valley shone through the fog wafting from the river's tranquil surface, turning its algae-covered cobbles a dull gray. Attracted by insects that had fallen into the shallow water, schools of minnows created ripples against the boat's bow. Hulk lifted the ice chest, rods, reels, and fishing tackle into the boat. After stepping over the gunwale, he offered John a hand.

The electric trolling motor powered the craft silently away from the bank, propelling it toward the center of the river. In the hazy distance, a beaver's burrow dammed the water flow. This, along with the slow current resulting from a bend in the river, had formed a wide, lake-like environment.

When the sun crested over sheer rock ledges, John gazed up in awe of their physical setting at the imposing walls enclosing them. Draped in the full bloom of early spring greenery, limestone cliffs jutted high into a cloudless sky. Their camp seemed to be the only evidence of human presence in the lush valley. A large bass breaking the water's surface brought him back to reality, as did the younger man's grinning face.

Hulk said, "It's really something, ain't it?"

"Yes, it's like we're the only humans to have ever visited."

"That we're not. They're arrowheads all along the river and corncobs in the cliff hollows. Indians lived here hundreds of years before Columbus left Spain."

"What about now?"

"This is National Forest land. Except for squirrels and other critters, no one lives here permanently."

Switching off the trolling motor, he let the bass boat drift lazily toward a brush pile near the opposite edge of the river lake. Grabbing two rods, he handed one to John.

"I caught a six-pounder right over by that brush pile last week."

John lifted the rod once or twice to get a feel for the well-balanced tool.

"Feels great," he said. "I haven't fished in years."

"Don't like fishing?"

"I love to fish. I just never seemed to have the time."

Hulk grinned and flipped his silver lure into the water near the brush pile.

"There's always time to fish."

John hefted the rod again. Flipping his lure into the water beside the brush pile, he slowly reeled it back toward him. The polished smoothness of the mechanical reel sent soothing sensations up his arm, directly to his brain. Within minutes, his neck and facial muscles began to relax, as if he were taking a warm bath.

Leaning back in the comfortable seat, he stretched his long legs, propping them idly against the footrest. Pacified by the mindless mechanical motion of casting the lure into the water and reeling it back, he nearly lost his grip on the rod when a large fish snatched the bait. Grabbing it with both hands, he held on as the fish swam beneath a submerged bush.

"Oh gosh!" he said. "That caught me by surprise."

Before he could coordinate his brain and hand, the big fish vanished beneath the brush pile, hopelessly tangling the lure around the submerged tree branch. Without saying a word, Hulk grabbed the nylon line and swiftly cut it with his pocketknife.

"Sorry Hulk."

"Don't worry about it. I've lost so many lures in that brush that I could start my own tackle shop if I fished them all out."

Reaching into his well-stocked tackle box, he pulled out another brightly shining lure and attached it to the nylon line at the end of John's rod. On his next cast, John felt another bite. This time, he twisted his wrist and skillfully set the hook, reeling in the fish like a pro.

"All right!" Hulk said, grinning broadly as he netted the fish and raised it into the boat. "It's a beauty."

"My, my, my," John said as the glistening silver fins of a largemouth bass reflected light from the early morning sun.

Removing his camera from his flannel shirt, Hulk motioned him to hold up the fish. He snapped a photo.

Pumped up like the winner of the Boston Marathon, John said, "What now?"

Returning the camera to his shirt pocket, Hulk searched his tackle box until he found a hand scale. Hooking it through the fish's mouth, he held it up, weighing it carefully.

"Three pounds, two ounces," he said.

While holding the big fish with both hands, he carefully lowered it back into cool river water and held it until it swam away.

"Catch it again another day. I got a trotline up the river. We'll check it after lunch. Probably catch a mess of catfish for dinner tonight. Maybe just my opinion, but they're better eating than most fish."

"Hey, you won't get any arguments from me."

"Lillie Mae can cook them any way you like, fried, baked, barbecued, you name it. She's the best."

Relaxed, John placed his rod back in the boat, put his hands behind his head, and reclined against the headrest, satisfied to watch Hulk fish for a while.

"Why is it I forgot how relaxing this is?"

"Have to ask somebody besides me about that," Hulk said, getting a bite.

Failing to set the hook, he grimaced, watching the fish disappear beneath clear water. John grinned and said, "Let me show you a trick."

Appearing confused, Hulk said, "Trick?"

Adjusting the young man's large hand with his own, he said, "Hold your rod like this. It'll give you an angle. When a fish takes the lure, your reflexes will respond with an automatic wrist twist to set the hook for you."

Even though he held the rod as instructed, his expression mirrored skepticism.

"Trust me," John said. "Kind of like the western grip in tennis."

Hulk blinked without replying. Another bass nibbled the silver lure as it trailed back toward the boat. He twisted his wrist just as John had said,

159

automatically setting the hook. With a mile-wide grin, he reeled the big fish to the side of the boat.

"Unbelievable," he said as John took his picture.

"A little trick my father taught me," John said. "A variation for use with a cane pole," he added with a smile.

He instantly noticed Hulk's cheerful demeanor darken. Although he flipped the lure back into the water, his big shoulders seemed to slump.

"Something I said?" he asked, leaning forward and touching the young man's shoulder. "What's the matter?"

"Guess I'm just feeling a little sorry for myself."

"Because of your father?"

"Never had a father. No one to share fishing tricks with. No father at all."

"Hulk . . ."

"No matter. I ain't a kid no more. I can handle it."

John answered in a low voice, almost a whisper. "I said my father taught me that trick. A slight exaggeration, I'm afraid. My uncle raised me. I never had a father either."

Hulk faced John. Nodding, he said, "Least you had an uncle. Catholic nuns raised me in an orphanage."

"Sorry. Seems I have a penchant for sticking my foot in my mouth."

"No problem."

"I have a problem, and I'm almost ashamed to tell you."

He paused as Hulk raised his chin, staring at the older man, waiting for him to finish his statement. When he didn't, he said, "Ashamed?"

"I am ashamed because I always intended to share that little trick with my son someday. After all these years, you're the only person I've ever told."

Hulk remained silent, assessing the apparent regret expressed in the old man's pale gray eyes. Finally, he said, "Ain't nothing to be ashamed of."

Staring back at him, John's sallow expression softened into a smile.

"You'd have made someone a fine son. I never shared that fishing trick with my real son. I doubt now I ever will. Could you humor me a bit? Let an old man pretend, just for the day, you're my son."

Hulk's boyish grin returned. "One thing I learned at the orphanage is how to pretend. Maybe I'll pretend I'm on a fishing trip with my dad."

John patted his cheek affectionately and said, "Maybe I'll be a better father to you than I was to my biological child."

"I'm sure you raised him just fine."

"One likes to think so. Being a parent is mighty hard. Someday, you'll find out yourself."

John's reply failed to produce the desired response. Instead, Hulk's dark frown returned. Reeling in his lure, he placed his rod inside the boat holder, hurriedly cranked the gasoline engine, and pointed the hull toward the far bank. Petrified by his reaction, John gripped the armrests, mouth agape.

With his voice permeating unexplained bitterness, Hulk said, "That is something that ain't never going to happen."

Chapter 23

John remained silent during their trip back across the lake created by beavers. Already high above the valley walls, the sun beat down on his head, and he regretted not having a cap to wear. Hulk tapped his shoulder and handed him a cap as if he could read his thoughts.

"Almost forgot. Arkansas sun will fry your brains if you don't wear one of these."

John glanced at the logo, smiling before plopping it on his head. It said, hottest chicken, coldest beer—Vian, Oklahoma.

Attie and Lillie Mae were awake and moving around the campsite when Hulk plowed the boat into the rocky shore. Both men grabbed a handful of gear and proceeded up the graveled path to join them. The aroma of bacon and eggs wafted down the slight incline. It was breakfast, cooking outdoors on a portable, three-burner propane stove. John realized what an appetite he'd worked up.

The valley, alive with the sounds of birds and squirrels, engulfed his thoughts. After devouring his third homemade biscuit stuffed with strawberry preserves, he realized that, like the valley, all his senses were alive, heightened, just beneath his skin. He could see they felt the same from the smiles on everyone's faces. Later that morning, he helped Hulk drop the RV's gas tank and fill it with water. Once there were no remaining fumes, Hulk welded the tear and set the tank in the sun to dry.

"Good as new tomorrow," he said.

After lunch, Attie and Lillie Mae searched for a highly touted blackberry patch. Hulk and John returned to the river to run the trotline, a passive southern fishing device used to catch bottom-dwelling catfish. After landing three fair-sized fish, they returned to camp. Lillie Mae and Attie's blackberry expedition also proved a success. They were already preparing a pie. More hungry than afraid, a ground squirrel hustled up to Hulk, snatching a blackberry directly from his palm.

"Take a load off, John. I'm going to fillet these catfish for dinner tonight."

"I don't mind helping."

"Won't take me long, and I'm taking a nap in my new hammock when I finish."

John nodded, glancing at the sizeable net hammock between two pine trees. "You girls need any help?" he asked, turning his attention to Attie and Lillie Mae.

"Nothing you'd know how to do, old man," Attie said teasingly.

"Try me sometime. I might surprise you," he said, pinching her elbow.

Swatting his hand away, she returned to stirring milk and flour. Seeing he was being ignored, he went to the RV to wash up. When he finished, he sprawled on the couch and fell asleep, not waking until five, the pleasant aroma of frying catfish permeating the RV.

He found Hulk laboring beneath the vehicle, reinstalling the gas tank. Attie and Lillie Mae were busy at the propane stove, frying catfish and hushpuppies in a big stainless-steel boiler. He sauntered over and poked one of the pies with his finger.

"Keep your hands off," Attie said sternly.

"Not even one little piece before dinner?"

"You can wait."

"Don't know," he said, grabbing her shoulders and nibbling her neck. "I'm mighty hungry."

Playfully poking his ribs, she said, "After dinner, we'll be so full we won't be able to eat for a week."

"Then we'll have to work it off before we sleep."

"Maybe," Attie said. "If you don't pass out before the sun goes down."

"Let's just make a little bet on who passes out first," he said mischievously.

Smiling at John's implication, Attie pushed him away to finish cutting potatoes into long, slender strands. Wandering to the ledge overlooking the lake, he stretched out in a canvas lounge chair. He rested his head in his hands, observing peaceful stillness until Lillie Mae's shrill call alerted his dinner was ready.

"Let's eat!"

They ate. After his second helping of catfish, hushpuppies, green tomatoes, and fried potatoes, he realized he wouldn't have room for blackberry pie if he didn't slow down. After dinner, they cleared the dishes and leftovers and brewed strong coffee on the stove. Relaxing in lawn chairs overlooking the lake, they watched a crimson sun drop behind the valley walls as frogs and crickets tuned up for their nightly concert.

Just before darkness enveloped them, John retrieved the coffee pot from the burner. He'd saved a bit of room for a small slice of blackberry pie. Hulk lit a lantern and hung it in a nearby tree. When he returned, they engaged in idle chatter, letting the satisfying meal digest further.

As they gazed across the valley, faintly illuminated by flickering lantern light, John and Attie held hands. Hulk stretched out on the canvas chaise while Lillie Mae sprawled lazily on top of him. Just like before, the young couple kissed and nuzzled like love-struck teenagers.

"Quite a meal," John finally allowed, breaking the silence.

"Everything tastes better outdoors," Hulk said.

"Maybe. There's also something about eating food you caught and gathered that makes it even more wonderful. It does something for you."

"Makes you sleepy?" Attie said, referring to their earlier exchange.

"Not a bit. We might even stay up all night."

"Hah!" Attie said, laughing and giving his hand an expectant squeeze.

"You two turned in early last night," John said.

Hulk smiled. Lillie Mae giggled and said, "Didn't go to bed. We went skinny-dipping in the waterfall pool."

"Oh?"

"Up the hill," Lillie Mae said, her voice flavored with deep country inflection.

John and Attie turned their heads toward the direction Lillie Mae was looking. Although it was too dark to make out the color of Hulk's neck, John could tell by his expression that it was red.

"We're going again tonight. Want to come with us?"

"Sounds like a grand idea. A swim is just what I need to work off some of this dinner," Attie said.

Too old to blush, John opened his eyes and mouth wide at Attie accepting Lillie Mae's invitation.

"Maybe if I wore a bathing suit," he said.

"Don't be like that," Lillie Mae said. "It's too dark to see anything, and being naked in a mountain pool is like nothing you'll ever experience again."

With an enthusiastic smile, she sprang to her feet, grabbing Hulk's big hand and pulling him up from the chaise. Hurrying to the camper, she said, "Doff your clothes and wrap yourself in a towel. It's all you need, except maybe a pair of sandals or flip-flops."

Smiling, Attie grabbed John's hand and pulled him to the RV. "Surely you're not going to make me go skinny-dipping alone?"

"Don't you think we're too old for this?"

"You may be. I'm not."

"Hulk, come on," Lillie Mae said, sticking her head out the camper door.

Hulk shook his head, shrugged his shoulders, and followed his diminutive wife into the camper. Whistling a nervous tune, John glanced at the starless sky before proceeding to the RV.

Ten minutes later, the adventurous quartet, looking like Roman citizens bedecked in their finest togas, made their way up the hill. Despite appearances, they were American campers, high in the Ouachita Mountains of Arkansas, traversing a steep trail by flickering lantern light. John realized as much when he stubbed his bony toe on a rock.

"Oh, oh, oh!" he said, holding the injured digit while attempting to hop up the trail on one foot.

"Don't be so melodramatic," Attie said, not bothering to turn around.

Holding the lantern and leading up the trail, Hulk said, "Almost there."

Realizing he was getting no sympathy for his stubbed toe, John asked, "How can you tell?"

Hulk stopped along the path, motioning for them to halt.

"Listen."

At first, John only heard the familiar chorus of crickets and frogs. Then, as his senses heightened in the relative darkness, he noticed the sound of falling water.

Lillie Mae nudged Hulk forward. "It's the waterfall, just over the next rise."

Hulk, Attie, and Lillie Mae quickened their pace. So did John, feeling very nervous but eager to lift his sore feet from the trail's sharp rocks. Around the bend, illuminated by lantern light and the soft glow of the half-moon, he caught his first glimpse of the waterfall pool.

Shangri-La indeed! No movie director or scriptwriter could have captured the beauty before them. A perfectly circular pool, thirty feet wide, carved from solid limestone, lay before them. A concave stone wall extending deep into darkness framed the west end of the pool. A steady stream of water cascaded from somewhere high above, creating the fall that gave the pool its name.

Ferns and flowering bromeliads thrived in every cavity formed by time in the ancient monolith. Various lichens grew on the rocks and near the waterfall, displaying chameleon-like colors and rapidly shifting hues, depending on their proximity to or distance from the pool. Water spilled over the pool's east edge, plunging straight down to the river below. From their vantage point, they could see the entire valley, including their camp, which looked tiny in the distance.

Without waiting for the others, Lillie Mae tossed aside her towel and dove into the water, swimming under the surface to the far bank. Attie joined her. Climbing a ledge ten feet above the pool, Hulk dropped his towel and plunged headfirst into the water.

"Don't be a sissy," Attie said, submerged to her neck.

"Is it cold?"

"It feels good."

Cautiously sticking his toe into the pool, he pulled it out. "Too cold."

Lillie Mae crawled out of the pool and climbed along a crevice etched into the limestone wall.

"Don't be a baby," she said.

"It's freezing."

"Not cold once you get used to it," Hulk said as he swam laps.

"Maybe not for a polar bear."

Eric Wilder

Slipping his toe into the water again, he removed it immediately.

"Can't just ease in," Attie said. "Dive in. It's really not cold as you think."

"If it's half as cold as I think, it's too cold," he replied.

Grinning, Lillie Mae said, "Too embarrassed to let us see your bare butt?"

Goaded by her insinuation, he followed Hulk's steep path to the ledge overlooking the pool.

"I've done lots of things during my many years. Skinny-dipping isn't one of them." Letting the towel drop to his ankles, he said, "Guess it's time I made the plunge."

168

Chapter 24

John yelped when he touched the water. Not from the cold but elation at having taken a naked plunge into the unknown. He swam beneath the water's surface with powerful strokes, finally touching a solid undulating stone ten feet below. When he emerged, he yelped again, this time from pure exhilaration.

Swimming to meet him, Attie wrapped her arms around his neck, nearly drowning him in the wake of their kiss. Laughing as he choked, he started treading water, trying not to sink them both. Attie pulled away and swam effortlessly to the shallows, and he followed.

With both feet planted firmly on the pool's limestone bottom, he hugged her, acutely aware of the sensations her bare body evoked against his own. His entire being relaxed, leaving him quite lightheaded. Goosebumps on her taut skin sparked a stimulating awareness he had never felt before. It was a feeling, he speculated, akin to walking barefoot across cool, tactile mounds of silver coins.

Now, it seemed John had never felt as close to another living being. When Attie playfully pushed him away to continue her exploration of the pool, he experienced a momentary sense of loss. Somewhere, beyond awareness, on the other side of reality, he drew the analogy of a newborn suddenly expelled from its womb. Like an infant, utter exhilaration overwhelmed him, flooding his senses. Emitting another ear-splitting war-whoop, he plunged backward into the water.

As he backstroked across the pool, time lost its meaning. Hours or minutes may have passed as he explored the rugged limestone encasing the pool. After bathing beneath the cascading water, he leaned against the stone adorned with epiphytes. Night-blooming orchids clung to the rough limestone walls, filling the warm air with their intoxicating perfume. On a ledge above them, night birds sang a late-night melody.

As John watched, Attie walked around the pool to the waterfall, realizing he had never seen her completely naked. He swam beneath the falls and waited for her to join him. When she did, they embraced beneath the cascading water, feeling enraptured, enamored, and enthralled all at once. Closing his eyes tightly, he lost himself in chilled, hedonistic bliss.

Eddies, ripples, and whirlpools formed in the water, accompanied by currents of varying temperatures, some nearly hot. John soon lost track of the others, as well as time. Cold water pouring into his crooked nose brought him to his senses, and he suddenly realized he was alone. Looking around, he couldn't find Attie, Hulk, or Lillie Mae.

"Hey! Where did everybody go?"

"Up here," Hulk called.

As he climbed out of the pool, a cool breeze chilled the backs of his legs and reminded him of his initial apprehension about the water's likely temperature.

"John," Attie called. "Up here. It's wonderful."

When John pulled himself over the limestone wall, he discovered what Attie was talking about— Attie, Hulk, and Lillie Mae were sitting in a perfectly circular miniature of the pool below. Streams of vapor rising from the steamy surface gave it the look of a health club hot tub. Testing the water with his toe, he realized it was hydrothermal, heated by hot mineral water from the very core of the eroded mountain range.

"Come in," Attie said. "What are you waiting for?"

Easing slowly, he waded through steam and hot water to join the smiling trio on a submerged ledge. The night air was damp and heavy, filled with pungent mineral salts. He took a deep breath and grinned ecstatically as he sank into the hot water up to his neck.

"Wonderful," he said, closing his eyes and savoring the moment. "I had no idea there were hot springs in this part of Arkansas."

"Neither does anyone else," Hulk said. "Lillie Mae and me found it accidentally."

Around the pool, stunted trees grew, their bark adorned with brightly colored epiphytic growths. Moss draped over the limbs, giving them the appearance of gray old men, and varicolored algae flourished both above and below the water. Lichens, orchids, and other air plants thrived in the moisture of the hydrothermal basin. The scent of night-blooming orchids mingled with tangy mineral salts as hot water percolated from the subterranean spring—everything combined to heighten John's aural, tactile, and olfactory senses.

"How hot is the water?"

"About a hundred degrees," Lillie Mae said. "Hulk measured it once."

"Perfect," he said.

"More than perfect," Attie said. "It's paradise."

Glancing upward, he asked, "What causes the dancing lights?"

"Some sort of mirage, I guess," Hulk said. "Sometimes it's even brighter than tonight."

Above them, violet, purple, and orange lights danced like excited electrons on a portable computer's plasma screen, illuminating the pool with an eerie glow. Since taking the plunge, John had forgotten his nudity and inherent modesty. When Lillie Mae emerged from the water, he was reminded. His flushed neck would have turned crimson if the warm water hadn't already caused that specific reaction.

Sitting at the edge of the pool, she seemed unbothered by her nudity as she dangled her tiny feet in the water. Although no more than five feet tall, her body was lithe, well-shaped, and perfectly proportioned. John observed through the eyes of a former practicing doctor. He also noticed something else: a cesarean scar on her abdomen. Attie caught him watching and nudged his ribs, returning him to reality. When Hulk dragged his muscular frame out of the water, John grinned and returned the nudge.

As time lost its direction, they remained in the warm, spring-fed pool. Finally, unaware of the hour, they noticed they were rapidly becoming shriveled prunes and decided to leave its comforting embrace. They retrieved their towels and sandals and returned down the winding path to their camp. Accustomed to the dim overhead lights, they continued along the hilly path without using the lantern. Upon reaching the clearing, a rattling thud from a garbage can behind Hulk's camper startled them. He raised his hand and strolled behind the truck to investigate who, or what, was there.

"Got you."

A loud screech echoed after Hulk's retort. He returned, carrying a reluctant cat that was so flea-bitten and skinny it could barely make a sound. Lillie Mae rushed forward, grabbed the cat, and cradled it to her ample bosom. The captured feline had no energy to resist and closed its eyes, surrendering into Lillie Mae's arms, resigned to its fate.

"Poor little thing," Lillie Mae commiserated.

Grabbing her elbow, Attie pulled her toward the RV and said, "I have milk in the kitchen. It must be starving."

Lillie Mae followed and said, "Hulk, go get that left-over catfish. Poor little thing."

Turning toward their camper, Hulk complied. John followed Attie and Lillie Mae, still clutching the hapless cat, into the RV. Attie poured a bowl of milk and placed it on the floor. John watched as Lillie Mae gently set the cat before the bowl. Hunger overcoming its fright, the ginger-brown cat touched the milk delicately with its nose and began lapping it up furiously.

Hulk returned with flaky chunks of leftover catfish. When the stray cat finished lapping the milk, it devoured the fish. Then, momentarily satisfied, it lay on the RV floor, licking its paws and trying to groom the matted fur on its coat.

"We're keeping him," Lillie Mae said.

"Oh, no, we can't."

Tears formed in her big eyes. Kneeling beside the now-purring feline, she lifted it to her bosom and repeated, "We're keeping him."

Rocking the cat like an infant, her face became red and puffy. Through anguished tears, she wailed, "Skittles, Skittles, Skittles."

Hulk's freckled face turned red. To Attie and John's trepidation, he also began to cry.

"He ain't Skittles. He ain't Skittles."

Attie pointed John toward the refrigerator and said, "Get something to calm them."

John returned with an icy Mason jar of Mike's choc beer. Not bothering with a glass, he handed the jar to Attie. Hulk and Lillie Mae were hugging each other, tears streaking their faces. Attie put the jar under their noses until they both drank.

As John helped Attie hasten them to the couch, Lillie Mae kept saying, "Skittles, Skittles, Skittles."

"It's all right," Attie said, trying to soothe the young couple and find out what their crying was all about.

From the scar on Lillie Mae's abdomen and the peculiar way she and Hulk reacted when children were mentioned, John already suspected the reason.

When they finally settled against the couch, and their crying turned into a gentle stream of tears, he asked the question that had been on his mind.

"I know it's painful. Can you tell Attie and me about Skittles?"

His question sent the couple into another fit of tears and earned him a sharp reprimand from Attie. Unfazed by her disapproval, he took the Mason jar, brought it to their lips, and gently poured more cold beer down each of their throats. The cold chocolate served its calming purpose.

"Skittles was our baby's cat," Lillie Mae said.

Her words brought a sorrowful grimace to Hulk's face as if she had plunged a knife into his chest and was twisting the blade.

"Tommy died in his sleep."

Her words ended with a high-pitched wail. Once more, John touched choc to her lips, administering the only anesthetic he had. In a moment, she hiccupped and blinked twice, her tears momentarily settling down.

"Died in his sleep, and we weren't there to help," she said.

"No, Lillie Mae, no," Hulk blubbered, her admission of their baby's death too painful for him to bear.

After handing Attie the remaining beer, John returned to the refrigerator for another jar. Sitting next to the weeping giant, he held the beer under his red nose until he swallowed some. Once Hulk started to drink, he lapped up all the beer in the jar like a thirsty hound.

Lillie Mae cried softly as Hulk continued the explanation she had started. "A stray kitten wandered into my shop when our Tommy was born. We named him Skittles. He loved that baby as much as we did. When Tommy died, Skittles ran away and never returned," he said, his face bright red.

Hulk cried some more and then hugged Lillie Mae again. When Attie's dark eyes reddened, John gave her a sip of the cold choc.

He said, "When did this happen?"

"Just a year ago, but it seems like forever," Lillie Mae stammered. "Don't know how I've gone on living this long."

"Sudden Infant Death Syndrome," John said.

Neither Hulk nor Lillie Mae answered though both nodded.

"SIDS," he said, looking at Attie. "Nothing anyone could have done."

Taking Lillie Mae's hand, Attie softly said, "Tommy's passing wasn't your fault. Nothing you could have done would have prevented it."

"We miss him so much," Lillie Mae said.

Attie probed further. "Have you thought about trying again?"

Shaking her head sorrowfully, Lillie Mae said, "Couldn't bear to lose another baby."

"What happened was beyond your control," Attie said. "You have to put it behind you."

"It's normal to feel great loss, accompanied by feelings of remorse and guilt," John said. "But it wasn't your fault, and there's no reason to believe it will happen again."

"How do you know?" Lillie Mae lashed out. "How could you possibly know how we feel?"

"Because I also lost a son," Attie said softly. Their attention was suddenly riveted. Hulk, Lillie Mae, and John listened as she continued her story. "His name was Roland, like his father's. My husband Roland ran his car off the road in an ice storm. Though he wasn't critically injured, our son Rollie died in the crash."

John clutched her hand, feeling her pain.

"It's okay," he said.

Seeing she wasn't finished, he handed her the jar of Choc, and she drained it before resuming the story.

"Roland and I were heartbroken. He blamed himself because he hadn't made Rollie buckle his seatbelt. Consumed with guilt, he took his own life a year later, to the day."

Hulk, John, and Lillie Mae sat mesmerized by Attie's story. By now, her face was puffed and pasty. Barely able to suppress her emotion, she said, "Roland and I were married ten years before we had little Rollie. I was fifty-two when he died—too old to replace his memories with another child. The void he left was filled with years of pain and unanswered anguish."

"Attie," Lillie Mae said. "We're so sorry."

Attie put her arms around Lillie Mae and Hulk's shoulders and said, "I was denied the joy of another child. You're not. You can keep Tommy's memory forever, but you must let him go. Forgive yourselves for whatever you think you may have done wrong. You may never get another chance. If you can't do it yourself, please do it for me."

Later, in bedroom darkness, Attie nestled in John's arms. "In ten years, I've never told that story to another living soul," she said.

Remembering the bathroom picture of the dark-haired man with his arm around his son, John hugged her and said, "Attie, I think tonight you freed one of your own painful memories."

Chapter 25

Detective Vince Blakeman's hands and clothes still reeked of refrigerated death, even though he had left the morgue more than an hour ago. Reaching home, he hurried along the condo sidewalk without bothering to wave at the old men playing tennis. Skipping the refrigerator, he used both hands to turn on the faucets in the bathroom shower, then stripped off his clothes and stepped beneath the water, not waiting for it to get hot.

Vince stood under the hot water spray until it turned lukewarm and cold. Feeling better, he wrapped a blue terry cloth towel around his waist and headed to the kitchen for a beer. Like a balm for the soul, the first Moosehead steadied his trembling hands. The second relaxed him. The third nearly made him forget the mutilated teenage body in the morgue. The persistent ring of the house phone interrupted his grim thoughts. It was Cynthia Warren.

"Vince, the roses are lovely. They weren't necessary."

Remembering his impulse purchase at the florist, he asked, "Is your husband upset?"

"He wouldn't have noticed if I'd put them under his nose."

"I meant the scene I made at your party."

Cynthia giggled behind her cupped hand on the receiver. "Considering his intelligence and advanced education, Dan is lucky if he manages to put on matching socks in the morning. He didn't even realize it was you, not our neighbor."

"I'm very sorry for my actions."

"Vince, I'm not mad. No harm done. If anything, it broke the tension and livened up the party."

"I know, but I'm . . ."

"The flowers are lovely. Now, no more of that."

"Thanks, Mrs. Warren."

"Cynthia."

"Thanks, Cynthia. Afraid I was having a bad night."

"So was I. Mine didn't end with the party."

"Sorry to hear that."

"I need to talk. Can I come over?"

"You mean to my place?"

"Is it all right?"

"I suppose so, but . . ."

"Great. Give me directions, and I'll be there in an hour."

Vince was waiting and answered the front door on the first ring of the door chime.

"Come in," he said, motioning toward the living room. "I have an opened bottle of wine. Like a glass?"

"That would be lovely."

Grabbing two clean tumblers from the kitchen cabinet, he filled them and joined Cynthia in the living room. Ignoring the tumbler decorated with red sailboats and blue jumping porpoises, she sipped the wine, savoring it an extra moment on her tongue.

"Delightful," she said. "I didn't know you were such a connoisseur."

"Someone gave it to me. Now what's the problem?"

"I want to apologize. Dan pulled some strings to remove you from his father's case."

"No matter."

"I hope it hasn't hurt your career."

Mention of his career caused him to grin. "Don't worry about it."

"After the party, Dan was distraught but talkative. I cajoled him into explaining why he's so intent on returning his father to Oklahoma."

"Oh?"

"He had Granddad ruled incompetent. The rest of the story is very embarrassing to me."

"There's not much I haven't heard."

"Dan liquidated his father's assets. Now he's afraid if he doesn't do something to show Granddad is incompetent, everyone will think he's an unfeeling ogre."

Vince began slowly massaging his temples. "I've seen this before. Sometimes, their children are old people's worst enemies."

"Dan can't see that. He's just worried about his reputation."

"And if the police return him to Tulsa against his will, well then . . ."

"It'll look as if he were incompetent or senile when he ran away from home in the middle of the snowstorm," she said, finishing his sentence.

"I wish there was something I could do. It's likely the old man somehow made it to Arkansas. Your husband won't benefit from his statewide influence bartering over there. Mr. Warren may never come home."

Cynthia's raven hair rippled in the dim light as she slowly shook her head. "How do you know that?"

"We don't, for sure. No one's spotted him in Oklahoma for days. Still, we've traced the RV to a woman named Attie Johnson, who lives in Eureka Springs, Arkansas. It seems likely that's where they're headed. Even if we know where he is, it won't be easy to make him come home if he doesn't want to."

Cynthia slugged her wine and poured another glass without asking.

"Dan's seen the report. He's talked with the District Attorney, trying to get Ms. Johnson charged with kidnapping and extortion. If he's successful, the

179

police will have her house staked out. She'll be arrested and imprisoned when they show up in Eureka Springs. They'll take Granddad into custody and return him to Oklahoma. I don't know what to do."

"I'm sorry. I have no authority in Arkansas. Your husband works for the biggest law firm in Tulsa. Isn't there someone you know who can pull a few strings for you?"

Cynthia's frown suddenly turned into a smile, and he blushed when she hugged him like a giant Teddy bear.

Chapter 26

After their late night with Hulk, Lillie Mae and the cat, John, and Attie slept late the following day. When they awoke, they found Hulk and Lillie Mae already up and about, the stray cat nestled in her arms. Much more so than the previous night, their demeanors were cheerful. Hulk bounded about the campsite, cleaning this and repairing that. Lillie Mae had breakfast ready, and the satisfying aroma of bacon and eggs greeted them when they exited the RV.

"Morning," Lillie Mae said. "Sleep well?"

"Like a top," John said. "And you?"

"Hulk and me didn't get a wink of sleep," she said with her patented impish grin.

"Oh?" Attie said.

"Had some catching up to do," she said, winking. "And we're keeping the cat. We named him Charlie."

John and Attie exchanged hopeful glances. "Does this mean Attie and I could be godparents someday?"

Hulk's face turned red, and Lillie Mae grinned.

After breakfast, they packed the RV and prepared to depart. Hulk filled their repaired tank with gas from a five-gallon container. After packing, Attie glanced at her watch, seeing it was nearly eleven. Hulk and Lillie Mae waited by the camping table to say goodbye.

"We're going to miss you two," Attie said.

"And we'll miss you," Lillie Mae said, dropping the cat.

Tears welled in her eyes as she threw her arms around Attie's neck and hugged her. When mutual tears finally ceased, amid many hugs and handshakes, Attie and John turned to the RV.

"We're keeping Charlie," Hulk said.

Lillie Mae added, "Hulk and I talked it over. We took what happened last night as a sign. With a little luck, Charlie will soon have someone to grow up with."

"That's wonderful," Attie said, hugging them again before saying final goodbyes at the RV's door.

After turning the big vehicle around, they drove slowly away, back up the lonely narrow path. John was chuckling to himself.

"What's so funny, old man?"

Crossing his arms and legs, he turned his knees toward the door.

"Nothing," he said.

"You tell me now, or I'm going to throw you out of this RV."

"It's just that Charlie, Hulk, and Lillie Mae's new cat is a calico."

"So?"

"So, all calicos are female."

"Why didn't you say something?"

"I didn't want to spoil things for them, and they'll find out soon enough, anyway."

"You're hopeless," Attie said, shaking her head.

Halfway to Hot Springs, they stopped at a roadside stand for sandwiches and cold drinks. Again, on their way, Attie slowly and cautiously negotiated switchbacks and U-turns on the narrow road. A decrease in pine trees and an increase in souvenir shops and filling stations signaled their proximity to the old resort community. After one last sweeping turn, John finally found himself in Hot Springs, Arkansas.

Attie asked, "Shall we get a hotel room, take a real bath, and sleep in an honest-to-goodness bed for a change?"

"Fine idea," he said. "Let's drive through town first. It's been years since I visited this old place."

"It hasn't changed much."

"No, it hasn't," he said, chuckling.

Attie navigated the narrow street slowly, flanked on both sides by shops, hotels, and limestone cliffs. She continued past Bathhouse Row. Caught amid horse racing season, tourists thronged the dreary old town, and cars lined both sides of the street. When they reached Hot Springs National Park, near the town center, John asked her to find a place to park and stop.

Hot Springs had all the characteristics of a worn-out resort town. Dull stone buildings with cracked mortar and dirty windows loomed over the rolling streets like tired gargoyles. Young couples with runny-nosed children and elderly folks—very elderly folks—converged around monuments and cheesy souvenir shops. Taking Attie's hand, John led her to a sparkling spring bursting from a fissure in a gray limestone cliff. He cupped his hand beneath the gushing water and brought it to his lips, smiling at its taste.

"We made it, Attie. It still tastes the same."

"Told you I'd get you here," she said.

"That you did. I never had a doubt."

An old man wearing alpine shorts, a hat, and lederhosen appeared from the sidewalk. Upon seeing John drinking from his palms, he smiled and handed him an empty cup. Gratefully, John thrust it beneath the stream of water, drank some more, and passed the half-empty cup to Attie. After quenching her thirst, she returned it to the gray-haired old man. Time's weight had withered his body, and he appeared almost like a little boy in his colorful alpine outfit.

When Attie thanked him again, he began speaking in French that neither she nor John could understand. Smiling and nodding, John shook the man's hand until he realized they didn't comprehend him. Finally, with a sad smile, he waved and limped away.

Attie said, "Wonder what he's looking for?"

"Maybe the Fountain of Youth."

"Is that why you had me bring you here?"

"I thought I knew. Now, I'm not so sure."

They watched as a hawk swooped down, nearly to the ground, then floated slowly upward, vanishing into a fluffy cloud. Turning away from the spring, John clasped his hands behind his back and surveyed the flower-filled courtyard. After five long, reflective minutes, he closed his eyes. When he opened them again, he was smiling.

"You know, Attie, we live in a garden of mirages and illusions. For years, I've dreamed of this place. I see it in every detail, exactly like when I last visited. Somehow, it's not the same as what it had become in my imagination."

She patted his hand knowingly. "Let's find a hotel."

"No. It just dawned on me. Last night, we found the real Magic Fountain in the mountains of western Arkansas. Hot Springs is nothing but a sad illusion. Now that I've found what I was looking for, I want to keep going until we reach home."

Chapter 27

John's expression was so focused as he left the fountain that Attie didn't question his choice to head straight to Eureka Springs. Neither spoke until they were heading north, ten miles from the old Arkansas spa town.

"It'll be dark before we reach Eureka. Sure you don't want to stop along the way? Get a room for the night?"

"If you're tired, let's stop."

"I was worried about you."

Turning with a smile, he touched her hand across the console. "Not to worry. Can't remember when I've had more energy."

Glancing at the dashboard clock, she said, "We should make it home by nine unless we stop for dinner."

"Let's don't stop. I'm not hungry and anxious to finally see where you live."

"You'll like it. My house is a sprawling old wood frame on an Arkansas mountaintop." Giggling, she said, "Mountains in Arkansas aren't high, especially the Ozark Mountains. But they are massive, rounded, and covered with trees. You can see all the way to the next county from the top of my mountain. Vital hues of green, mixed with floating swaths of flawless gray, caress endless brilliant blue. It's quite spectacular."

"I can see it," he said. Do you have a back porch?"

"Of course I do, and it reminds me quite a lot of you."

"Me? I don't recall ever being compared to a porch."

Laughing, she said, "It's old and has lots of character. My porch stretches around the entire house, and it's a perfect place to watch golden Arkansas sunsets while sitting in an old swing. Rusted chains suspend it from the ceiling and harmonize like dueling harps when you rock."

"Wonderful," John said. "You think we'll be there to see the sunset?"

She put her foot on the gas. "We'll give it a shot, old man."

❦

Laboring up steep Highway 71, Attie managed to pass several slower-moving, sight-seeing vehicles. When they reached the highest point, south of Canada, on the old highway, she pointed into the distance.

"Eureka's just beyond the horizon, not really that far away, as the crow flies."

"Look there, Attie, it's a rainbow on the horizon. Must be where our pot of gold lies."

"I don't see it."

"There, in the distance," he said.

"Road's too steep to look away. I'll take your word for it."

They neared the final stretch of highway before reaching Eureka Springs, where a road sign warned that the next fourteen miles were steep and winding. It certainly was. Spiraling upward, the narrow road flattened briefly, forming a river valley. Having carved its way between two rounded peaks, the river meandered lazily into the distance, creating a beautiful mountain vale.

Attie crossed the river and pointed the RV up the steepest mountain they had yet encountered. As they ascended the incline, the engine coughed and struggled. Overlooking the river below, their view became even more spectacular as they climbed higher.

The winding roadway took a wide loop near the mountain's crest, offering an incredible view of the meandering river far below.

"Pull over, Attie."

Responding to his urgency, she wheeled the RV to a scenic turnout by the side of the road.

"You all right?"

"We're not going to make it to your house before dark. Let's stop here and watch the sunset."

The golden orb had already begun its descent in the western sky. Attie parked and waited until he opened the door. Fresh air, heavy with impending rain, filled the vehicle. As he stepped onto the ground, he smiled and stretched his arms.

"Attie, I feel as if I've finally come home."

"You have," she said, taking his hand. "We both have."

They walked together to the cliff's edge and sat on a large limestone boulder overlooking the valley. Purple martins, departing their daytime roosts in search of insects, swirled high overhead. In the distance, a chorus of tree frogs began their nighttime serenade. A damp breeze whistled through the pines, joining the melody and harmonizing with a chorus of crickets lilting like a thousand violins.

Tightly squeezing Attie's hand, John said, "It's beautiful."

"Yes, it is," she said, gazing at the red radiating sphere burning a luminous swath in the fading sky as it descended toward the valley floor.

"Once," he said. "On a spring night in western Oklahoma, I saw a sunset almost as beautiful. Particles of dust from some volcanic eruption in the Pacific filled the sky. Invisible during the day, dispersed particles became fiery streaks of crimson incandescence at dusk."

"A beautiful sunset is something to remember."

"Attie, you remember the races?"

"Of course I do."

187

"Remember when I told you which horse I was betting on? You said he was the biggest nag on the track and had never won a race."

"And you were too stubborn to listen."

"I bet on his name, Prairie Sunset, because until I met you, that sunset in western Oklahoma was the loveliest vision I'd ever seen."

"You're incurable," she said, nudging his ribs and moving closer. Putting her arm around his waist, she felt a tremble beneath her touch, like a bridge abutment, stressed with age, beginning to tire and collapse.

"John, do you need a heart pill?"

"Already took two," he said, his breathing suddenly coming faster and in short gasps.

"John!" Not answering, he closed his eyes and shrank back against her. "Get up, John. We're just outside town. There's a hospital there."

Neither speaking, nor opening his eyes, he grasped her hand. Squeezing it tightly, his lips began to quiver and he fought to open his eyes.

"Attie," he said in a whisper. "Help me up."

"No!" she said, tears welling in her red-rimmed eyes."

"Help me Attie," he said, his voice low and becoming increasingly hard to hear.

Encircling his waist, she struggled to lift him. Managing somehow to boost him into a sitting posture, she positioned herself behind him, bracing his frail weight between her legs, against her body, embracing him as death's head danced ever-narrowing circles above them.

"This can't be happening. Not now. Not so close to home. Let me help you to a doctor."

Still holding her hand, he said, "Don't cry, Attie. This has been the happiest week of my life. I never met a kinder, sweeter person than you." His voice was barely a whisper when he squeezed her hand. "I love you, Attie. You kept your promise and took me to the

Magic Fountain. Before I go, I want you to make one more promise."

Clutching his hand in a desperate clasp, Attie nodded sadly as tears streamed down her red and puffy face.

"Bury me on an Arkansas hillside close to you, facing west. I'm home now, and I never want to leave again."

Attie rushed up the hill to the RV, using her CB radio to call for help, even though it seemed hopeless. It was probably too late. Then, until the sun dipped below the western horizon and distant thunder announced a gentle rain, she held him tightly to her chest, shedding silent tears as she rocked him in her arms.

Chapter 28

They weren't far from Eureka Springs, and an ambulance arrived, its siren drowning out the night's other sounds. Two EMTs hurried toward John and Attie, one with an oxygen bottle and mask. Both were young and looked concerned. They didn't bother asking what had happened as they tried reviving John.

"Let's get him up the hill. They'll have better luck in the ER."

Placing John on the stretcher, they carried him to the ambulance. Attie joined him in the back.

"Against regulation but no time to argue. Every second counts right now. You okay?"

Attie whimpered. "I think it may already be too late."

"Don't give up yet. He still has a pulse."

Tattoos covered the EMT's meaty arms as he worked on John, giving him an injection and then administering an IV. As they raced toward the hospital in Eureka Springs, siren blaring, Attie closed her eyes. When they finally pulled into the entrance to the emergency room and wheeled John out, Attie followed them through the swinging doors. A nurse grabbed her arm.

"Please wait in the reception area. We'll call you when we have him stabilized."

"But he's dying."

"The doctors will take good care of him. Come with me to the waiting room. I'll call you when it's okay to see him."

Attie followed the nurse up the long hallway to a waiting area. She was the only one there, at least for the moment. An hour passed before a doctor joined her.

"Did you come in with Mr. Warren?"

"Yes, is he . . .?"

"He's alive though hanging on by a thread."

Attie started to speak, but her words caught in her throat. "Can I see him?" she finally said.

The doctor led her down the hall and pointed to a door. "He's in intensive care. I'll show you."

In the hushed ICU, John lay with his eyes sealed shut—a fragile figure encircled by the relentless chorus of beeping machines, rhythmic drips, and the soft hiss of oxygen. Tubes and wires painted a stark portrait of life hanging by a thread. Attie knelt by his side, her tears falling silently onto the sterile sheets as grief mingled with desperate hope.

The doctor, his face etched with regret, squeezed her trembling hand briefly. "I'm sorry," he whispered, his voice carrying the weight of unspoken truths. He then quietly exited, leaving her with her heartache.

Lost in the depths of her sorrow, Attie barely registered the sound of measured footsteps until the ICU door creaked open. In stepped an older nurse whose presence felt both unexpected and otherworldly. Her silver-threaded hair framed a weathered face, and her eyes—wise and enigmatic—held hints of endless compassion and untold stories. The frayed edges of her uniform spoke of countless nights wrestling with fate in this room.

Without explanation, the nurse rested an assuring hand on Attie's shoulder. "He needs your help," she said in a hushed tone. With surprising strength, she assisted Attie to her feet, guiding her closer to John's bed.

"Touch him," the nurse instructed softly. With trembling fingers, Attie let her hand graze over John's angular features— sculpted cheekbones and crooked nose that suggested a lifetime of resilience and imperfection. A subtle warmth spread across his pallid skin, and for a fleeting moment, Attie thought she detected the faintest flutter—perhaps a sign that he might still return to her.

Her gaze lifted, desperate for reassurance, only to find that the enigmatic nurse had drifted toward the darkened corridor. "Wait—" Attie's voice cracked as she called after her. "Is he going to make it?"

The nurse paused at the door, her expression unreadable yet touched with a melancholy mystery. "Don't know," she replied softly, almost as if sharing a secret. Then, in a whisper that hung in the still air, she added, "How deep is your love?" Before Attie could question further, the nurse melted into the shadows, leaving only a lingering sense of wonder and foreboding.

Moments later, another nurse entered as if summoned by the weight of the unanswered question. Attie, trembling with urgency, asked, "Who was that nurse?"

The newcomer offered a gentle smile. "I'm Mr. Warren's nurse," she said quietly.

That simple statement revealed an unspoken truth: no one else had been in the room apart from the young doctor. The inexplicable presence of the other nurse deepened the mystery, leaving Attie to grapple with the fragility of John's life and the incomprehensible allure of the night itself.

When Attie left the ICU, a commotion erupted behind the swinging doors leading to the hospital's main reception area. Someone was arguing with the receptionist. A man pushed through the door without waiting for her to grant him entry into the emergency area. Many more people followed: a cameraman and another person with a microphone, which he shoved into Attie's face.

"Are you Attie Johnson?" Not waiting for her to answer, he asked, "Is John Warren alive or dead?"

Attie remained silent, tears streaming down her cheeks as three uniformed men pushed through the ever-growing crowd of people watching the melee. One of the policemen was someone Attie knew well.

"Attie, I'm sorry. I have to arrest you."

"Arrest me? For what reason?"

"Can't tell you."

"You've known me all your life, James Simpson. You know I'm incapable of committing a crime."

The clean-cut young man wearing the Sheriff's badge could only shake his head.

"Afraid I got no choice."

"What did I do?"

No one responded to Attie's question. Simpson's two deputies cuffed her, forcing her hands behind her back and jamming them into handcuffs. In addition to TV cameras, still photographers started flashing pictures. She turned away and closed her eyes as one of the deputies yanked the cuffs and pushed her through the crowd toward the swinging door.

"Ms. Johnson, did you kidnap Mr. Warren?" a reporter asked, her microphone stuck in Attie's face.

The crowd swelled further as they left the hospital, camera flashes going off, and the noise level was intense. It seemed like everyone within earshot of the news had come to town to see the spectacle.

"Out of the way; we're coming through," Sheriff Simpson said, leading them to a police car parked on the sidewalk.

After cramming Attie into the backseat of the police car, they sped away, tires screeching. With sirens blaring, they left the crowd behind and drove her to the small jail in downtown Eureka Springs. Sheriff Simpson shook his head, turned, and walked off.

"Jimmy, why are you doing this to me?" Attie called after him.

Simpson didn't answer, and the jailers took her to a cell, mercifully releasing her from the cuffs.

"When can I call my attorney?" she asked as a burly jailer with a crew cut shut the door, leaving her alone in the tiny cell.

Her question went unanswered.

Sheriff Simpson returned later that night, sitting with her on the cell's lone bunk.

"Attie, I hope you'll forgive me for all this. Mom's already called and threatened to disown me if I don't release you."

Attie smiled. "You should listen to your mom."

"You're a real celebrity. Every major network and all the cable channels have crews in town."

"What's going to happen to me, Jimmy?"

"Not a damn thing. There are no charges against you."

"Then why did you arrest me?"

"We didn't arrest you so much as we took you into custody."

"But why?"

"You're like the eight ball in a political pool game. My department's caught in the middle."

Sheriff Simpson nodded when Attie asked, "Is John Warren's son behind this?"

"I don't know what really happened, but the law enforcement grapevine says Dan Warren tried to get the Tulsa D.A. to file kidnapping charges against you."

"Oh my!"

"The D.A. supposedly told him no way, and neither he nor anyone else in his department believed you kidnapped Mr. Warren."

"That's a relief," Attie said.

"Warren's son is politically connected, pulling all the strings he has. Higher-ups told me to bring you in. At least make it look like you were being arrested."

"How long will I have to stay here?"

Sheriff Simpson looked at his watch and smiled. "About thirty more minutes. Wayne's waiting outside, and he's mad as hell."

Sheriff Simpson embraced her and left the cell, allowing Wayne Taylor, Attie's family attorney, to enter. Clad in shorts and a t-shirt, he resembled someone who had just come from a company picnic. The lawyer settled on the bunk beside her.

"Attie, I'm sorry you had to go through all this. They don't have anything on you; this whole mess is a sham."

"Jimmy said John's son tried to file kidnapping charges against me."

Wayne smiled. "Hell, Attie, I don't think you've ever had a parking ticket."

"Can you get me out of here?"

"Lady, you're sprung. I must tell you a few things before you go leave."

"Like what?"

"This town's turned into a three-ring media circus. Everyone's talking about you and Mr. Warren. Half the people think you're an angel, the other half the Devil. You got to really watch yourself these next few days."

When he stood from the bunk, the jailer opened the door, letting him exit.

"The sheriff will release you soon," he said.

It was dark when Sheriff Simpson, with an enormous smile, led her down the hallway.

"You're out of here, and someone's waiting to pick you up."

Attie was surprised and relieved to see Norma, Mike, and Big Al waiting for her.

Following a group hug and a few tears, Norma said, "We came as soon as we heard the news."

"Let's get you out of here," Mike said.

When they exited the jail, Attie realized the circus wasn't over. A large crowd had gathered, complete with cameras and reporters. Mike, Norma, and Big Al surrounded her, with Big Al leading the way. It quickly became a shoving match, everyone pushing closer, eager to see, talk to, or touch Attie.

"Everybody step back. Give this lady some air," Big Al said.

A large man became offended, shoving Big Al until he stumbled and fell to one knee. The man was completely bald, with tattoos covering his muscular arms.

"Who are you telling to step back? You may be big, but I'll whip your ass."

Someone else pushed through the crowd. It was Hulk, with Lillie Mae beside him. He grabbed the tattooed man by the neck and lifted him off the ground. The man struggled, trying to break Hulk's grip as his face progressively reddened. Finally, Hulk released him, and he dropped to the ground.

"You want to whip somebody's ass, maybe you ought to try picking on someone your own size."

Hulk glared at the man on the ground as a woman pushed a man in a wheelchair through the crowd. It was Scooter Bates and his girlfriend Sue.

"If anyone else wants to hassle Ms. Attie, they'll have to go through me first. And don't let this wheelchair fool you."

Hulk grinned and reached down to shake Scooter's hand. "You're Scooter Bates. I saw you on TV. I'm Hulk, and this is my wife, Lillie Mae."

"Pleased to meet you. This is Sue," he said, introducing a slightly overweight woman with short brown hair and a big smile.

"I'm the one that pushes him to safety when his mouth overloads his rear end."

Attie hugged them before they began carving a path through the crowd. Hulk and Big Al followed closely behind, keeping anyone from getting too near to Attie. They arrived at the parking lot, where Mike and Norma's Cadillac awaited.

"Where to?" Mike asked.

After introducing everyone, she said, "My house is about ten miles from here."

"I'll drive to the end of the road," Mike said. "Get your vehicles and flash your lights twice when you pull up behind so we'll know you're friendly."

Norma opened the front door, gesturing for Attie to slide into the front seat. She nestled in beside her while Big Al climbed into the backseat.

"We've been so worried," Norma said, hugging Attie.

"You and John have been the number one news story for the last two days," Mike said. "When we saw they arrested you, we headed this way."

"This whole thing just ain't right," Big Al said.

Norma continued hugging Attie until she finally stopped crying. "I don't know what I'd have done if you hadn't shown up."

"We're not the only ones," Mike said. "You and John made many friends, some in the vehicles behind us. Please tell me where to go, and I'll lead the way.

Chapter 29

Scooter's van and Hulk's camper followed Mike's Cadillac out of town, heading toward the winding road to Attie's house. They noticed they weren't alone; television and radio vehicles and many private cars also followed them. Mike pounded on the steering wheel.

"Dammit! Why can't they leave you alone?"

"Pull up in one of those dirt roads that goes up into the hills," Big Al said.

Attie shook her head. "Not a good idea. Most are dead ends."

Someone keyed the CB radio. "This is the Hulkster, over. Can you read me?"

Attie clutched Mike's arm. "It's Hulk. He's in the camper behind us."

Mike grabbed the handset. "I read you, Hulkster. This is Choctaw speaking. Over."

Another screech. "This is Ironsides, over. I'm right behind you, Choctaw, and just in front of you, Hulkster. Over."

"These idiots are right on my back bumper. I'll drop back and hold them up. You two get the hell out of here. We'll hook up later. Over."

"Roger that, Hulkster. Sounds like a plan. Over."

"This is Ironsides, boy. Don't let 'em wreck you. These roads are tighter than Dick's hatband. Over."

Attie grabbed the handset from Mike. "This is Attie. You two be careful."

"Over," Mike said, grabbing the handset from Attie and flooring the gas pedal.

Scooter followed, though his old white van wasn't as fast as Mike's Caddie. They began pulling away from Hulk, who had started swerving from one side of the road to the other.

"I hope they're okay," Attie said, squeezing Norma's hand.

Norma and Big Al gazed out the back window, observing the lengthy parade of vehicles behind them playing bumper cars, unsuccessfully attempting to pass Hulk's camper. Norma gently patted Attie's wrist.

"Don't worry, honey. That boy doesn't need any help. He's good."

Big Al had his elbows propped on the back of the seat, watching the skirmish behind them.

"Good, hell! I've seen NASCAR drivers that couldn't block any better than he's doing."

Mike glanced in the rearview mirror as a deer bounded out of the ditch and into their path. He slammed on the brakes, causing the car to swerve violently. It slid to the edge of the ditch before screeching to a stop. Their heads snapped as Scooter, too close to stop, crashed into the rear bumper.

"Sorry," Scooter's voice said, sounding over the CB. "Everyone okay up there? Over."

Attie grabbed the handset. "Mike did a wonderful job of keeping us out of the ditch. We're okay."

"Not quite," Mike said. "We got a flat tire."

"The broken chat they rock the road with is sharp as knives," Attie said. "Sorry, Mike. I'll buy you a new tire."

"No, you won't. It's not your fault."

Big Al slid out of the back seat. "Pop the trunk."

"No time," Mike said. "The mob will be on us in a minute or so."

"Don't matter. We're stuck here unless we change the tire. Pop the trunk."

Mike popped the trunk and watched Big Al unload the spare tire and tool kit. Scooter had already joined him, doing his best to help. Hulk's camper pulled to a stop behind them, along with the two dozen or so vehicles in pursuit. Within seconds, reporters, cameramen, and paparazzi swarmed the area, snapping photos and demanding insider interviews.

"Just stay in the car, honey," Norma advised. "Don't talk to those bloodsuckers."

Attie took Norma's advice and watched as the insistent crowd began to push and shove. When Scooter's wheelchair tipped over, and he was dumped onto the ground, she could no longer stand it. Shaking off Norma's grasp, she unlocked the door and exited the car. Camera flashes began immediately, accompanied by microphones and spotlights in her face.

After finishing with the tire, Big Al joined her, trying to fend off the throng of curious onlookers. The area was as bright as day, with spotlights aimed at them from the filming crew vans. Someone stood on a ladder directing traffic with an electronic megaphone. Big Al pushed his way through the crowd.

"Get back. Leave this woman alone. She ain't hurt nobody and don't deserve this."

"It's all right. Help me up on the hood. I'll say a few words. See if that does the trick."

Big Al picked her up, depositing her on Mike's Cadillac hood. Then he began shouting.

"All right, listen up! Mrs. Johnson's got something to say. Shut up and listen."

Lillie Mae and Sue piled into the Cadillac on the passenger's side while Hulk, Mike, and Scooter joined Big Al, doing their best to form a human shield between themselves and Attie.

For a moment, the crowd grew quiet.

"I'm Attie Johnson. I'll answer your questions, then please, leave us in peace."

"Did you kidnap John Warren?"

"Of course not," she said.

"Did he die because you poisoned him?"

"What kind of question is that? I loved him. I'd never do anything to hurt him."

"Do you know there's a warrant for your arrest in Oklahoma?"

"That's a bunch of hooey. I've done nothing wrong, and there's no warrant for my arrest anywhere."

"If not, then why did the police have you in handcuffs? What are you guilty of?"

"Nothing, I've already told you."

"Did you spirit Mr. Warren away from Tulsa and then demand a ransom from his son?"

Suddenly overwhelmed, Attie began to sob. Big Al leaped up on the hood of the car beside her.

"You people got this story all wrong. John ran away from home because his son would put him in an old folks' home. Attie picked him up in a snowstorm on an icy Tulsa street. It kept him from freezing to death. She's a hero, and you could take a life lesson from her."

"If you're innocent, will you stand trial in Oklahoma?" someone yelled from the crowd.

It was more than Hulk could take. "Leave her alone. She has more love and compassion in her little finger than any of you ghouls. Go away and let her grieve in peace."

Hulk's words failed to dissipate the crowd, and the insistent storyseekers began pushing and shoving. Big Al jumped off the hood and helped Attie down. Norma opened the door and pulled her inside.

"Get in here, girl," she said.

"We have to do something," Lillie Mae said

Big Al shoved his way through the crowd, standing beside Mike, Hulk, and Scooter as people rocked the car. The reporters were egging things on. If they couldn't get an interview, they'd be there to cover a near riot.

The wail of sirens sounded in the distance, and the headlights of three police cars appeared down the hilly road, the sirens not stopping until they'd driven right up to Mike's Cadillac, scattering the crowd in the process. It was Sheriff Simpson and his men.

"You folks okay?"

Attie stuck her head out the window. "Scared to death, but otherwise unharmed."

"We'll set up a roadblock and detain this posse for you."

"Thanks, Sheriff," Mike said, opening the Caddie's door and sliding in. "The van and camper are with us."

"We'll let them through. Good luck, Attie."

Sheriff Simpson motioned the police vehicle driver. He backed up, letting Mike's Cadillac, Scooter's van and Hulk's camper drive past. They were alone again on the dark road, Attie giving directions.

"Better tell Scooter and Hulk to hang close. The turnoff from the blacktop to my house is so well hidden, sometimes I even miss it."

Chapter 30

H ulk barely had time to shut the gate, barring the road to Attie's house, and relock it before a spring rainstorm began drenching the hillside.

"We'll have to run for the porch," Attie said. "I don't have covered parking."

Though barely twenty feet from the driveway to the porch, they were soaked when they arrived. They waited, dripping, as she fumbled with her keys. Big Al produced a flashlight.

"Never know when you'll need one of these things."

"Thank goodness for a planner," Attie said, rushing inside and opening windows to expel must and warm air.

"Your house is beautiful," Norma said after her eyes had adjusted to the light.

"Native stone and wood. My husband Roland designed and built it."

"Husband?" Mike said.

"My deceased husband."

"Sorry."

"It's okay. He's been gone a long time. We planned on having a large family. It's just me in this large house with too many empty bedrooms, though tonight, it's perfect for guests."

"We don't want to impose," Sue said.

"Nonsense! You can get your bags when the rain lets up. I was planning to turn the house into a bed and breakfast. You can tell by the ramp outside that it's handicap friendly."

Scooter was grinning when Attie showed him and Sue their room. "You weren't kidding," he said. "This is better than most hotels."

"Roland and I intended to turn it into a bed and bath someday. I even bought guest robes and pajamas. Get out of those wet clothes and try them. I know how tired you all must be. I think I'll stay up awhile."

Already late, nobody felt like arguing. When the rain finally eased to a steady drizzle, they retrieved their bags from their vehicles. Although it was late, nobody wanted to go to bed just yet. They all wandered back to Attie's spacious den, gathering with her in front of the stone fireplace.

"I made hot chocolate and coffee. There's also plenty of Choc left over from John's stash."

The rain finally stopped, leaving only a cool breeze blowing through the open windows, flickering the candles Attie had lit. Norma, Sue, and Lillie Mae soon embraced Attie and shared her sadness. Attie allowed herself to have a good cry for the first time that night.

"We're so sorry, honey," Norma said.

"John's not dead," Attie said. Norma gave Mike and Big Al a look. "He's not, is he?"

Everyone looked away, and no one answered. When Attie began to cry, Norma, Sue, and Lillie Mae hugged her.

"We don't know for sure," Lillie Mae said. "It was the talk on the street."

Lillie Mae sobbed and said, "We came as soon as we heard."

"You got here just in time. I don't know what I'd have done if I'd been all alone."

"I miss John already. He was the closest person to a dad I ever had," Hulk said.

"Though I only knew him for one night, he was as dear as any friend I have," Scooter said.

"He always knew how to say just the right thing to make you feel good," Mike said.

Big Al broke the tension, and everyone laughed when he added, "Well, he wasn't much of an auto mechanic."

Attie's smile didn't last long. Norma noticed. So did Sue and Lillie Mae.

"I know, honey. It hurts for us, too. I can imagine how you feel right about now."

"It's more than that. I feel so helpless."

"There was nothing you could do," Lillie Mae said.

"That's not it."

"What then? Tell us. Maybe we can help."

Attie crossed her arms and legs and shook her head. "I made John a promise. Now I can't keep it."

"What promise?" Hulk asked.

"John wanted to be buried on an Arkansas hillside, near here, his grave facing west. I promised him I would see to it. Now, I know it's never going to happen."

"But it's what he wanted. Who . . ."

Mike grabbed Norma's wrist, looked into her eyes, and shook his head.

"Maybe John's son will come to his senses," Lillie Mae said. "He can't deny his father's dying wish."

"Who'd have thought he'd have hounded him all the way to Arkansas? He's a different breed of cat," Scooter said.

Attie glanced at the big grandfather clock. "It's late. Please, everyone, go to bed. We'll talk more tomorrow."

"You too," Norma said.

Attie shook her head. "I'm going to stay up for a while longer, and I need to be alone. Please."

Feeling the pain in her voice, everyone went to their rooms, leaving her alone on the couch.

ᏋᏨᎩᏨᏏ

The group awoke the following morning to the aroma of bacon and eggs cooking in the kitchen in

Attie's old cast-iron skillet. Unlike the previous night, she had a smile on her face. The sound of popping grease, crackling bacon, and the song she was singing reassured everyone that she was okay.

"Give me the keys, Ms. Attie. Me and Mike will drive down and retrieve your RV."

"Thanks, Big Al," Attie said, retrieving the keys from a bowl on a kitchen cabinet. "I was wondering what I was going to do about it."

"Mind if I tag along?" Scooter asked. "I didn't get a chance to see much scenery coming in last night."

"You bet," Mike said. "We'll load your wheelchair in the trunk."

Big Al grinned. "I hope Attie doesn't make us leave before we have a bite to eat."

"Wouldn't think of it," she said. "I cooked enough for a log rolling. I'll bet there's enough for even you and Hulk."

Lillie Mae elbowed Hulk when he said, "Don't know about that. I'm mighty hungry."

After breakfast, Mike, Scooter, and Big Al left to retrieve Attie's RV.

"Lillie Mae, Norma, and I can take the van into town. Pick a few things up for dinner tonight," Sue said.

"Sounds like everyone's going somewhere except Hulk and me," Attie said.

"Good," Hulk said. "I got something to show you a little later. Meanwhile, it looks like the storm last night tore up a bunch of trees. I'll clean up the mess for you."

"You don't have to do that," Attie said.

"I don't have to do anything. I want to. Besides, I need the exercise."

Attie stared out the kitchen window, aimlessly polishing a glass as she watched Hulk dispose of the last tree limb that had fallen the previous night. When he entered the kitchen, her morning smile disappeared, replaced by a sullen expression. He didn't give her a chance to start reminiscing about John.

"I told you I have something to show you. Want to see?"

"Course I do. What is it?"

"Come on, and I'll show you."

Attie followed him out to his camper. When he opened the door, the cat bounded out.

Attie smiled. "I was wondering what happened to Charlie."

"Well, Charlie might not have been such a good name."

"Oh?"

Hulk reached into the camper, retrieving two squirming kittens. Charlie's a girl. She brought these two kittens to camp right after you and John left."

"Then John was right."

"About what?"

Attie smiled again. "He said Charlie was a calico and that all calicos are females."

"Charlie sure is. We named the two kittens Luna and Sol because Luna is black as night and Sol is orange. "Hopefully, they'll remind you of Lillie Mae, me, and how you and John changed our lives."

Attie embraced the big man and sobbed. They were both sobbing when Norma, Lillie Mae, and Sue returned from town with bags of groceries. Mike and Scooter arrived shortly after, followed by Big Al with the psychedelic RV.

"Got there just in time," Big Al said. "A truck already had her hooked up, ready to tow her away."

"Oh my! How did you stop them?"

"Turned out to be a cousin of mine. He showed me a shortcut here so I wouldn't cause so much attention. Whoever painted that thing up ought to be shot," he said, tongue-in-cheek.

"I like it," Attie said. "It grows on you."

Everyone piled into the kitchen, where Sue and Lillie Mae made sandwiches. Norma was showing them how to make gazpacho.

"Never thought I'd eat cold soup," Scooter said.

"Norma doesn't know how to pick a good man, but she sure knows how to cook," Big Al said.

Attie just grinned and shook her head. "I think she knows how to do both."

"Whatever, you girls aren't cooking tonight," Mike said. "Big Al's not the only one who has Arkansas relatives. My cousin Enzio owns the Limerock Hotel in downtown Eureka Springs. We're having a party in John's honor tonight, and Norma and I are footing the tab."

"Bull on that," Big Al said. "I'm chipping in."

"So are we," Lillie Mae said.

Attie was smiling again, and Norma noticed.

"You got a plan, don't you?"

Attie nodded. "I'm going to call John's son. Tell him his dad's last wish, and try to convince him to let me bury him here."

"And if he doesn't go for it?"

"At least I'll have tried."

Later that afternoon, as everyone was getting ready for the celebration, Attie called the Warren's house in Tulsa. Someone picked up on the third ring.

"Warren residence," the person said.

"May I speak with Dan Warren?"

"Who's calling?"

"Attie Johnson."

There was a pause before the person said, "I'm Billie, the housekeeper. Mr. and Mrs. Warren are in Arkansas. Can I take a message?".

"No," Attie said.

"Mrs. Warren checks in every day at noon," Billie said. "Want me to tell her you called?"

"It's Mr. Warren I need to speak to," Attie said.

"I can hear the pain in your voice," Billie said. "Mind if I offer some advice?"

"I'm at my wit's end and could use all the help I can get."

"Mr. Warren is acting like a fool and needs his butt paddled. Mrs. Warren has tried talking to him but hasn't caused him to budge."

"What's your advice, Billie?"

"Trish and Emily. They know old Mr. Warren better than either of their parents. They've followed the story since the night Mr. Warren disappeared. I've even caught them calling you grandma."

"What are you trying to tell me?" Attie asked.

"The twins are here with me in Tulsa. Get them to Arkansas and have them pull the right strings. Mr. Warren acts like a monster but is a softie at heart, just like the old man. If you get the twins to Arkansas, they'll change his mind about you."

"How will I do that?" Attie asked.

"Give me your number. I'll have Mrs. Warren call you. Believe me when I tell you that everyone, including her, is pulling for you and Mr. Warren."

"How will the twins get here?"

"Nothing I'd like better than to bring them myself," Billie said.

Attie's phone rang shortly after noon. The person on the line sounded distraught.

"Mrs. Johnson, I'm Cynthia, John Warren's daughter-in-law."

"Thanks for calling, Cynthia. Please call me Attie. You sound distressed. Where are you?"

"At a hospital payphone. Dan is in the ICU with his father," Cynthia said,

"Is he...?"

"The doctors are keeping him alive, even though he isn't lucid. Dan refuses to let him go and tried to arrange his transport to Tulsa."

"For what purpose?" Attie said.

209

"He's not thinking straight," Cynthia said. "Doesn't matter because the hospital is refusing to release Grandpa in his condition."

"Cynthia, can I level with you, woman to woman?"

"Of course you can."

"I only knew your father-in-law for a week, and I know this sounds farfetched, even to me, but I loved him, and he loved me."

"I believe you. What can I do?"

"John's last wish was to be buried on an Arkansas hillside, facing west, not far from where I live. I promised him I would see to it. I don't want anything else from you or your husband, and I'll pay for the burial."

"Dan is a stubborn man. I've tried everything to change his mind. Nothing has worked."

"Billie said the twins can change his mind," Attie said.

"She told you that?"

"Yes," Attie said.

"Attie, I love my husband, though when it comes to his father, he refuses to listen to reason."

"Billie's on our side, and she said she would drive them here," Attie said.

Attie waited through a long pause before Cynthia said, "Billie's more of a mother to Trish and Emily than I am."

"Billie told me you are a wonderful mother," Attie said.

"You're fibbing, but thank you for saying so," Cynthia said. "I can call Billie and have her bring the twins, though I don't see how that will change matters."

"Let me call her first," Attie said. "I have a plan."

Chapter 31

Cynthia had barely hung up with Attie when she dialed Robert Baker's phone. He answered on the first ring.

"Cyndi, what's up?"

"Robert, sorry to bother you on the weekend."

"I had my calls transferred to the club. Eight over par, I decided to call it a day and head to the clubhouse for a martini."

"You're so nice, you'd say that even if you'd just hit a hole in one."

"Only for you, Cyndi. Now, what's so important?"

"First, thank you for intervening with the Arkansas governor. Dan would have moved heaven and earth to return his father to Tulsa."

"My pleasure, although I wish Wild Bill could have reacted before Mrs. Johnson was arrested and publicly humiliated. Sorry about that."

"What you did was wonderful."

"I rue the day Dan finds out I was responsible. He's the firm's smartest lawyer, and I'd hate to see him go somewhere else."

"This story's gotten so blown out of proportion. Half the people think Attie Johnson is a heroine, the other half a murderess."

"It's a real media event, and Dan is the only person who can rectify the situation."

"Which brings me to the second reason I called you."

"I'm listening."

"I just talked with Attie Johnson. She told me Grandpa's last wish was to be buried on an Arkansas hillside. I told her I'd help."

"Excuse me! I hadn't heard that your father-in-law had passed," Robert said.

"Dan has refused to let the hospital take Grandpa off life support," Cynthia said.

Robert Baker paused before replying, and for a moment, she thought they'd been disconnected.

"Maybe Dan has his reasons," Robert said.

"Selfish reasons," Cynthia."

"Dan's not that way. Cyndi, Ms. Johnson has no legal rights in this matter."

"Dan is dead set on returning Grandpa to Oklahoma and burying him in the family cemetery."

"Next to his wife?"

It was Cynthia's turn to pause and think about her answer.

"Dan's mother was cremated, her ashes scattered across Lake Skiatook, where she and Granddad had a weekend home. Dan was against it, but Granddad acquiesced because it was her dying wish."

"Then why is Dan so determined to bury him in Oklahoma?"

"Because he's stubborn and a control freak. It kills him when he doesn't get his way."

Baker laughed. "The very traits that make him such an effective trial lawyer."

"Yes. and an absolute asshole to live with, sometimes."

"Cyndi, my group is waiting for me."

"Robert, I'm so sorry. I was just hoping you could pull some more strings and see that Granddad gets his last wish."

"I can't help you with this one. It's a civil matter. Dan is your father-in-law's next of kin. Mrs. Johnson, I'm afraid, has no legal recourse."

"But I promised her."

"You know I'd do anything for you. This one's out of my hands. No judge on earth will overrule Dan's wishes on this."

Cynthia hung up, suddenly aware that she had yet to call Billie. Billie was waiting for her call.

"I need your help, Billie, and I'm unsure what to tell you."

"Ms. Attie has a plan," Billie said. "I'll be in Eureka Springs with the twins in about four hours."

"What do you want me to do?" Cynthia asked.

"The Limerock is an old hotel in downtown Eureka Springs. There's a fancy restaurant called Amore's. Can you get Mr. Warren there about ten?"

"For what purpose?" Cynthia asked.

"Ms. Warren, I have to wake two sleepy twins from their nap, pack their clothes, navigate rush hour traffic, and drive through the heart of the Ozarks to get to Eureka in time to make this work. I have no time to explain, so please trust me."

"You got it, Billie. I'll get Dan there if I have to hogtie him."

Chapter 32

It was dark when Attie's group convoyed to Eureka Springs, parked in the small lot of the old Limerock Hotel, and entered through the back entrance. A smiling man who could have been Mike's twin brother greeted them in the lobby, pumping Attie's hand.

"I'm Enzio. Glad to meet you. You're the most famous person in town, you know?"

"Or infamous, depending on who you're talking to," Attie said. "I've eaten here before. Your food is wonderful. I had no idea you were Mike's cousin."

"Hell, all us Italians west of the Mississippi are cousins. Mike and me are real cousins. Our mothers were sisters."

"I'm glad to meet you, Enzio. Think you can handle this crowd?"

"You bet we can. Follow me."

Enzio led them down a flight of limestone stairs to a warmly lit basement, complete with a large table dressed in a white tablecloth, burning candles, jugs of Chianti, and antique crystal stemware. A scratchy Billie Holiday melody played softly in the background, and the delightful aroma of good food wafted from the kitchen. Before long, they were seated and feasting on steak and pasta, reminiscent of Mike's place in McAlester. Norma sat on Attie's right, with Lillie Mae to her left. After several bottles of wine, Attie stood and spoke.

"When I was a girl, I read every fairy tale, fantasy, and gothic romance I could get my hands on. I was convinced Prince Charming would one day come riding in on a white charger to whisk me away to a world of make-believe. You know, strangely enough, that's exactly what happened."

"Here, here," Scooter said, clinking his wine glass with a fork.

"John wasn't the only knight in shining armor I met. Until this past week, I never realized there were so many amazing people in the world."

"Here, here," Scooter said again.

"Scooter, you and Sue inspired John and me to stand up for our beliefs. Mike, you and Norma provided shelter, support, and love during our darkest hours. Lillie Mae, you and Hulk demonstrated what it means to love someone completely. Big Al, you were strong when we needed strength, brilliant when we needed a plan, and gentle when we needed someone to hold our hands. God bless you all."

When Attie sat back down, Norma grabbed her arm.

"You've been smiling all day. I'm so happy to see you feeling better."

"Being here with wonderful friends has raised my spirits."

"Look, honey, even if it doesn't work out for some reason, it's not your fault. You tried your best. Mike and I will take you to the funeral in Tulsa if it comes to that."

Attie shook her head. "John's not going back to Tulsa."

Big Al smiled. "I knew you'd come up with a plan. Tell us what it is."

"Not now," Norma said. "Attie can tell us when we return to her house."m

Enzio appeared from the kitchen. "None of you are returning to Attie's tonight," he said. "Mike and Attie have booked rooms for everyone at the hotel."

Mike's toothy grin indicated he knew something none of the others did. He stopped grinning when Norma gave him a dirty look.

"This better be good," she said.

"Got that right," Big Al said.

"Meet in our room after you get settled," Mike said. "I'll explain everything."

Someone knocked just as Vince finished giving directions to Cynthia Warren and hung up the phone. The kitchen faucet had developed a severe leak, which he had reported before work that morning. Thinking the person at the door was Clancy from maintenance, he flung open the door, wearing only a blue terrycloth towel. On his porch, smiling at him, stood Marla, holding a bottle of wine adorned with a colorful red bow. Seeing her, he nearly went into terminal shock.

"Peace," Marla said, thrusting the bottle toward him. "I want to apologize for what happened the other day." As he sucked in his gut, he nearly lost the towel wrapped around his waist, managing to grab it with his free hand before he embarrassed them both. "I also want to thank you for the beautiful red roses. I love flowers, and roses are my favorite."

Catching his breath and hoping she couldn't hear his pounding heart, he motioned his favorite leggy brunette inside.

"Please, sit down," he said, his voice an octave too high. "I'll put on some clothes."

Vince rushed into the bedroom, shutting the door behind him. As he hurriedly rummaged through the closet for something to wear, his heart raced so fast that it threatened to send him into hyperventilation. When he pulled too hard on the clothes rod, it collapsed, sending all his clothes onto the closet floor.

Hoping Marla hadn't heard the crash, Vince yanked a red sports shirt and khaki pants from the pile and hurriedly put them on. He stopped at the door, his hand on the knob. Rushing back to the bathroom mirror, he combed his hair. When he finally returned to the living room, Marla stood up and extended her hand.

"I'm Marla MacDonald. It was my fault we had such an unpleasant introduction the other day."

"Vincent Blakeman," he said. "The fault was mine, and I'd like to apologize for the whole affair."

Marla said, "No permanent damage done. My irises survived."

"I'm glad."

Realizing he was still holding Marla's hand, Vince quickly let go and gestured toward the couch. After he'd plopped down in his old recliner, Marla glanced at the bottle on his kitchen table.

"Hope you like it as much as I've enjoyed the roses you sent."

"I'm not much of a wine person," he said. "But I know I'll enjoy it. Like a glass now?"

"It's white," she said.

"Pardon me?"

"It's not chilled."

As Vince stood up, he bumped his shin on the coffee table and felt his face turn red while retrieving the bottle. He was clearing out space for it in the freezer between TV dinners when it occurred to him that Marla might not have intended to stay long enough for the wine to chill.

"This might take a while. Like a Moosehead until it's cold?"

"I love Moosehead. After tending to the garden in the heat, I always keep a few frozen mugs in my freezer for a cold drink."

Having no frozen mugs or any mugs, he grabbed two of his best cheap tumblers from the cabinet and placed them, along with two bottles of Moosehead, on the coffee table between them.

Marla said, "I'm a nurse. I work at General. What do you do, Vincent?"

"A detective with the Tulsa Police Department."

"Are you serious?"

"Ten years."

Squirming in her seat, she said, "You won't believe this. My two hobbies are gardening and reading murder mysteries."

"The hell you say."

"I read every new mystery novel as soon as it arrives at the library, along with every mystery magazine and police procedural I can get my hands on."

Stifling a precinct reply, he said, "Really?"

"I even have a police scanner in the bedroom. I've never met a real detective," she said, inching forward on the couch.

Vince filled the tumblers with Moosehead and raised his own in an impromptu toast. "Well, here's to you, Marla."

"And to you, Vincent," she said, tapping his glass. "Were you involved in the Riverside Strangler case?"

"I was there when they arrested him."

Marla fairly squealed. "You were? I don't believe it. Are you working on last night's homicide?" Remembering the gruesome remains of the hapless teenager in the morgue, he lowered his head and nodded. "It upset you. I can tell."

He could only nod again and hurry to the refrigerator. "Better check the wine. Don't want it exploding on us."

Marla touched Vince's hand across the coffee table when he returned to the chair.

"Sorry Vincent. Guess I've read too many cozies. I know it's not like that in the real world."

"You'd think I'd get used to it after ten years."

"I work in the emergency room at General."

"Then you probably see more gunshot wounds than I do."

"Too many, and most are victims of random crime. Surrounded by so much daily misery, it's a wonder I get so involved with fictional mysteries."

"Hey, I think I understand."

Leaning forward once more, Marla gazed thoughtfully into Vince's eyes. He noticed that her's were an unnerving shade of violet.

"When we both have lots of time, I'd like to hear about the Riverside Strangler. Even though I read newspaper accounts, having an actual detective on the case tell me the real story would be wonderful."

Vince felt his neck and face grow warm. Seeing Marla's nearly empty tumbler, he returned to the refrigerator for two fresh Mooseheads. His stomach gurgled as he filled the tumblers, and he remembered he hadn't had any food all day.

"Have you eaten?"

Marla shook her head and glanced at her watch. "No time. I'm on duty in an hour. Usually, I grab a snack when I take a break."

"I have two TV dinners in the fridge. Only take a minute to heat them in the microwave."

Without thinking about it, she smiled and said, "Sounds great."

Once more, Vince rummaged through the freezer. Remembering the wine, he took it out and set it on the kitchen counter, trying to recall if he had a corkscrew. He didn't, so he started searching cabinets and drawers for something to open it with.

"I have a corkscrew in my condo," she said, sensing his plight.

"No need. I have something."

Vince rummaged through the drawers of a cabinet by the front door until he found his red Swiss army knife. With an awkward twist, he uncorked the bottle without allowing too many shavings to fall into the wine. In a hurry, he placed the frozen dinners in the microwave. He didn't bother setting the kitchen table; instead, he dumped the well-heated contents onto two plates and served them on the coffee table. Remembering that he had no wine glasses, he discovered two oversized shot glasses in the cabinet by the sink.

"Not exactly the Ritz," he said,

"It's wonderful. I work such erratic hours that I miss most of my meals. I won't eat if I can't have something healthy."

Thinking about the chili dogs, tacos, and barbecue sandwiches that made up most of his meals, he sucked in his gut and sat up straighter in the chair.

"More wine?"

Marla had barely touched what he'd already poured her. She shook her head and said, "I need to stay sober for my shift, even if I'd sometimes rather be inebriated."

Corking the bottle, he pushed it aside. "Then I'll save it for later."

"You're nice. I can't believe I've lived next door to a real detective for the past year and never knew it."

Vince couldn't believe it either. Removing the dirty dishes and putting them in the sink, he wiped the coffee table and plopped back into the chair.

"If you'd like, I could give you a tour of the precinct sometime."

"Love it," she said, glancing again at her watch. "I only have ten more all-nighters before going on days for a month. Maybe I can return the favor and fix dinner for you."

"Sounds wonderful."

Vince couldn't quit smiling at her. Marla didn't notice as she reached across the table to take his hand.

"Now, I have to get ready for work."

Reluctantly, he released his grip and walked her to the door, mooning into her big violet eyes. Quite unexpectedly, she kissed him before reaching for the door handle.

"Thanks again for the roses," she said.

"Hey, the pleasure's all mine."

Chapter 33

The lights were dim at Amore's, with Attie sitting alone at a large table when Dan and Cynthia walked in. Dan frowned as Cynthia approached Attie and hugged her.

Dan's arms were crossed tightly against his chest when Cynthia said, "This is Attie Johnson."

"Why am I not surprised?" he said, not bothering to join them at the table. Enzio saved them, bringing a martini for Cynthia and a scotch for Dan.

Dan frowned, took the scotch, and said, "We didn't order drinks."

"On the house," Enzio said. "Attie told me you've had a rough day."

"Did she now?" Dan said.

Delightful aromas drifted from the kitchen, and Dan felt his stomach rumble.

"Please, sit," Enzio said.

Dan remained motionless. Everything shifted when Billie walked into the dimly lit restaurant with the twin girls, Trish and Emily. Spotting Attie and their mother at the large table, they ran over to Attie and embraced her.

"Grandma," they said. "Is it you?"

"It's me, babies," Attie said.

Trish and Emily rushed to their father and hugged his legs.

"Daddy," Trish said. "Why do you look so angry?"

Dan glared at Billie and didn't answer.

221

When Emily asked, "Where is Grandpa?" Dan shook his head.

Once again, Enzio and his wife relieved the tension by bringing steak and pasta for Dan, Cynthia, and Billie, along with special meals and colorful drinks for Trish and Emily.

"We're not hungry," Trish said.

"You may be after you see what Missy cooked specially for the two prettiest little girls in Eureka Springs," Enzio said.

Enzio placed the twins' plates topped with colorful ingredients on the table.

"What is it?" Emily asked.

"Mini-Margherita pizzas, Missy's kid-friendly Italian classic, and pasta arranged into smiley faces on the plate."

"What's to drink?" Trish asked.

"Italian cherry sodas," Missy said. "It's a combination of flavored cherry syrup, club soda, and a splash of whipped cream."

Intrigued, Trish and Emily sat down to sample the food. Billie and Cynthia smiled while Attie gave Missy and Enzio a thumbs-up. Unimpressed, Dan chose to stay seated alone across the dining area. Cynthia joined him after finishing her meal.

"What do you have to gain by acting like an asshole?" Cynthia said.

"That woman kidnapped my father," Dan said.

"She did no such thing," Cynthia said.

"Truth speaks louder than words," he said.

"What did she have to gain?" Cynthia said. "You said yourself he was penniless."

Cynthia's words struck Dan like an unexpected gut punch.

"I shared that information in confidence. I never expected you to turn on me," he said.

"I'm your wife, not your client," Cynthia said.

Their conversation was interrupted when Enzio returned with more drinks.

"We need a room for the night," Dan said. "Can you help us?"

"Afraid not, folks," Enzio said. "The town is a media circus. You'll probably have to drive to Bentonville to find a room."

When Enzio signaled Attie, she appeared at their table.

"I have a large house with lots of bedrooms. Your dad would want you to stay with me."

Dan glared at her, looked away, and said, "We'll sleep in the car before we stay with you."

"You can sleep in the car if you like," Cynthia said. "Billie, the girls, and I are staying with Attie."

"Fine," Dan said. "You can drop me off at the hospital. I'll stay with Dad."

The twins joined them, climbing into Dan's lap before Cynthia could reply. His frown melted away.

"Did you see the dessert that Missy made for us?"

"What did she make for you?" Cynthia asked.

"Fried dough balls dusted with powdered sugar with warm chocolate for dipping," Trish said.

"Sounds yummy," Cynthia said.

"Can we come back tomorrow?" Emily asked.

"We'll see," Dan said.

"We can eat here after seeing the buffaloes," Trish said.

Dan glanced at Cynthia before returning his gaze to the twins. "We aren't here to see the sights," he said.

"Please," Emily said, tugging on his shirt sleeve.

"Your dad is staying at the hospital tonight. We'll see how he feels tomorrow," Cynthia said.

"Why aren't you staying with us at Grandma Attie's house?" Trish asked.

Emily and Trish pouted when Dan said, "She's not your grandmother.

Cynthia was frowning and shaking her head when Dan glanced at her.

"We'll stay at the hospital with you and Grandpa," Emily said.

"Your grandfather isn't well, and I don't want you to see him like he is," Dan said.

Both girls began to weep. "We want to see him," Trish said.

"You're too little to understand the situation," Dan said.

"They aren't too little," Attie said.

"Excuse me," Dan said. "You have no say in what my kids do or don't do."

"Excluding children from the bedside of a dying family member can have unintended consequences," Attie said.

Cynthia glared at Dan when he said, "No one asked for your opinion."

Attie persisted and said, "Depriving children of the opportunity to share their loved one's final days isn't the mark of a loving parent. Like adults, **children benefit from having the chance to say goodbye.**"

"We're all going to see Grandpa," Cynthia said.

Dan pointed at Attie and said, "She's not."

Attie drove with Billie and the twins to the hospital, and Dan never asked why she wasn't in her own vehicle. He stopped her when they reached John's room.

"You aren't welcome," he said.

"Why are you being so cruel?" Cynthia asked.

"It's okay," Attie said. "I'll wait in the hall."

Billie, Cynthia, and the twins cried as they exited John's hospital room without Dan. Attie was also in tears, and they all embraced before stepping away from the door. Billie left her car in the hospital parking lot and drove to Attie's bucolic home with Cynthia. It was raining when they arrived, and lightning flashed in the distance.

"Be careful," Attie said. "Gets kind of slippery when it rains."

The back door led into the big rustic kitchen, with copper pots and cast iron skillets hanging from hooks.

"Oh, I love this kitchen," Cynthia said.

"Just don't expect I'm a wonderful cook because of it."

"I'll bet you're just saying that."

"I do have a few specialties," I'll cook one of them for you if you can talk Dan into staying awhile."

"Good luck on that one," Cynthia said.

"Let me show you and Billie your rooms," Attie said. "The girls can sleep in the loft. It's just their size."

"Your house is gorgeous," Cynthia said. "It's almost like a bed and breakfast."

"Believe me, I've thought about turning this place into one. It's so big and gets lonely here sometimes."

Trish and Emily were yawning. When Attie pointed Cynthia to the loft, she herded them upstairs.

"Mind if I tuck them in?" Attie asked.

"They'll love it," Cynthia said.

Even though it wasn't cold, Cynthia and Billie had started a fire in the living room's stone fireplace. When Attie came downstairs, she went to the kitchen and returned with a tray of hot chocolate. After Billie finished hers, she excused herself, leaving Cynthia and Attie alone. Outside, the rain continued to fall.

"I'm sorry Dan is acting so hateful," Cynthia said.

It's okay," Attie said.

"It's not okay," Cynthia said. "Dan had his father declared incompetent, sold his possessions, and planned to put him in a nursing home. When Grandpa ran away, Dan feared the world would discover how callous he'd been. That's why he's acted so horribly."

"John knew about the competency action," Attie said. "He told me the first night we met. He didn't intend to reclaim the property."

"Dan wasn't worried about his dad's intentions. He was worried about you," Cynthia said.

"John agreed to accompany a lonely old woman to Red Rock to play Indian bingo. He wanted to go to Hot Springs one last time, and I agreed to take him there. Somewhere along the way, we fell in love."

Eric Wilder

Cynthia clutched her hand and squeezed. "I believe you," she said.

"How can I ever change Dan's perception of me?"

"Seems to me Dan should be more worried about your perception of him," Cynthia said.

Chapter 34

Dan awoke with a start, his stiff neck protesting the hours spent slumped in an unyielding recliner. The rhythmic beeping of medical devices filled the dim hospital room, a constant reminder of his father's fragile state. John lay motionless beneath a thin white sheet, his face pale and his breathing mechanical. Nothing had changed. What lingered was the persistent memory of an unsettling dream Dan couldn't shake.

A nurse entered as the door creaked open, her soft footsteps whispering against the cold tile. Her dark auburn hair was neatly arranged in a bun, and discomfort overshadowed the kindness in her green eyes as she checked the monitors with the efficiency of someone who had performed this task countless times before. Dan noticed she was avoiding his gaze.

The resident doctor overseeing Dan's father's case walked in behind her, his crisp white coat and silver-rimmed glasses resting on the bridge of his long nose. The man in his late fifties was tall and lean, bearing the weary expression of a physician who had delivered bad news too many times. After glancing at the machines, his lips formed a thin line.

His voice was calm yet firm when he said, "I'm Doctor Morgan, Mr. Warren. Your father isn't going to recover. The machines are the only thing keeping him alive. It's time to think about letting him go."

Dan's jaw clenched, and anger flared in his chest. "Who made you God?"

"I'm not God, just your father's doctor. It's my job to inform you of his condition, and I won't sugarcoat it. Mr. Warren has very little chance of survival."

"Put a number on it," Dan demanded.

"Less than one percent," Doctor Morgan replied. "We've done everything we can. At this point, only divine intervention will save your father, and I'm not one to believe in miracles."

"Longshots happen, and I'm giving Dad every chance he needs to recover before I allow you to pull the plug," Dan said.

"Do you have a medical power of attorney?" the doctor asked.

Dan disliked the doctor's veiled threat and pressed his index finger against his breastbone.

"I don't know if you're aware, but I'm a trial attorney—and a damn good one. You will do whatever it takes to keep my father alive. If you pull the plug without my permission, I will take your license and ensure this entire hospital regrets it. Are you getting me?"

"Loud and clear," Doctor Morgan said as he stepped back from the room.

In the hallway, Cynthia stood with her twin daughters, holding their hands. The five-year-olds pressed against their mother's legs, their wide eyes absorbing the sterile surroundings. Beside them, Attie stood with her arms crossed over her chest, worry creasing her normally warm features.

Doctor Morgan paused, rubbing his temples before meeting Cynthia's gaze. "Your father-in-law is suffering and needs to be allowed to pass peacefully. Your husband refuses to accept this."

Cynthia exhaled sharply and said, "Please explain."

"He believes your father-in-law has a chance of surviving and is refusing to let us act in his best interest," Dr. Morgan said. "He threatened me and the hospital if we proceed with what's right."

Dan watched through the open doorway as Attie said, "Count me on Dan's side."

"You're not a family member and have no say in this matter," the doctor stated.

"There are dozens of cameras and microphones outside the hospital, just waiting. You'll understand how much I matter when I give them an interview."

"Fine," Dr. Morgan said, raising his hands in exasperation before walking away.

Inside, they found Dan with his shirt rumpled and shadows beneath his eyes. He looked up as they entered, his gaze flicking from Cynthia to Attie to the girls. For a moment, no one spoke; the beeping of the machines filled the silence. His mood lightened when Cynthia and the girls embraced him.

"Billie packed a suitcase, and we brought you a change of clothes," Cynthia said.

Dan took the clothes and asked, "Where is Billie?"

"Returning to Tulsa to check on the dog. We're lucky to have her."

Trish and Emily crawled onto the bed with their grandfather. Looking morose, Attie draped herself over John's chest. Dan said nothing as he headed to the bathroom to change clothes. When he returned, Attie glanced at him as he touched her shoulder.

"Do you believe in miracles, Mrs. Johnson?" he asked.

"Everything I've experienced in the past week has been a miracle. And Dan, call me Attie."

Outside the hospital, the media frenzy continued, with reporters vying for position and asking difficult questions while film crews documented the crowds gathered to witness and partake in the spectacle. Attie, Dan, Cynthia, and the twins headed to the black Mercedes in the parking lot. Attie sat in the back, flanked by the two twins, who had their arms draped around her neck as if they couldn't bear to lose another loved one. Cynthia noticed this, and so did Dan.

They headed down the hilly road from the hospital to the highway outside town. Dan looked much more relaxed, dressed in jeans and a western shirt. Attie provided directions and described local landmarks. They soon reached the outskirts of Eureka Springs.

"I've never seen so many motels," Cynthia remarked.

"It's a tourist town, for sure," Attie said.

"How can there be no rooms when there are so many places to stay?" Dan asked.

Neither Cynthia nor Attie answered his question.

The weather was mild, so Dan rolled down all the windows as they drove slowly through the old Victorian-era town nestled against the rounded bluffs of the Ozark Mountains.

"It's like a fairy village," Trish said.

"Yes," Cynthia said. "All the buildings are built right up against the mountain cut."

"It's probably the only place on Earth where you can access three stories, all on the ground floor," Attie said.

"There are so many people," Trish remarked.

"Tourists, baby," Attie replied.

Happy shoppers, wearing shorts and t-shirts while carrying shopping bags filled with souvenirs and knickknacks, filled the sidewalks and storefronts.

"What do people do for a living?" Cynthia asked.

"Eureka is an artist's colony," Attie said. "Visitors come from all over to explore the shops, savor the local cuisine, and enjoy a variety of musicians. It's probably the most eclectic town in America."

"Just don't get caught smoking pot," Dan said.

"Dan . . ."

Attie chuckled. "He's right. Arkansas doesn't tolerate drug use. It's almost lunch hour, and you look hungry. Find a parking spot, and I'll treat you to lunch."

"We aren't hungry, Grandma," Trish said.

"We want to see the buffalo," Emily said.

"Your dad's hungry," Cynthia said. "We can see them after lunch."

"I can wait," Dan said. "Which way?"

"There are only two ways out of town, and you're heading in the right direction," Attie said.

Both girls were thrilled as they left the small town and took a winding road into the countryside. The narrow blacktop ran along a ridgeline near the summit of the rounded mountain range, dropping steeply on either side. Dan slowed the car when an armadillo lumbered out of the ditch and crossed the road in front of them. Cynthia still wore a frown, her arms crossed tightly, and her knees pointed toward the door. Attie pretended not to see. The road finally leveled off, with pastures on both sides and a tall fence enclosing them.

"Oh, look at those big animals. Stop, Dad!"

When Dan pulled over and parked, Attie, Cynthia, and the girls got out. Trish and Emily dashed to the fence.

"What are they?" Trish asked.

"They're called bison, which are somewhat like large wild cows. A local rancher keeps a sizable herd here."

Cynthia and Attie turned to look when a semi-truck passed on the highway and honked its horn. Turning back, they saw Trish and Emily running toward the bison herd. They had discovered a small hole in the fence and squeezed through.

"Oh, my God!" Attie said.

"Trish, Emily! Come back here this second," Cynthia screamed.

Neither girl noticed. Both were carrying handfuls of grass, focused on feeding the large animals. Attie climbed the fence, leaping to the ground just as the herd noticed Trish and Emily. A female with a calf began pawing the earth and moving toward them.

231

Dan scaled the fence in a single bound when he saw what was happening. He landed on the other side just as Attie caught up with the girls, scooped them off the ground, and ran back toward the fence. The female bison snorted and trotted after them. When Dan's path crossed Attie's, she attempted to hand the little girls over to him.

"Take them. I'll stop the creature."

"No, you won't," he said. "Get them over the fence. Hurry."

Without time to argue, Attie sprinted toward the fence with the two frightened little girls. Dan stood his ground against the female bison charging him, planted his feet, and clapped his hands.

"Hah, go back! Hah, you stop right there."

Confused, the bison stopped, nearly nose-to-nose with Dan. Attie had pushed the crying girls back through the hole in the fence and turned to assist Dan. Hearing her approach, he shook his head and waved his hand.

"Get over the fence! I know what I'm doing."

Seeing that the intruder wasn't intimidated by her bluster, the female bison turned and rejoined the herd. Dan began to back up slowly until he reached the fence, then scaled it like a person possessed. Cynthia and the girls, all crying and nearly hysterical, grabbed him when he hit the ground.

When everyone finally settled down, Attie said, "Those animals are far from tame. That mama bison weighs over a ton. For the life of me, I can't figure out how you managed to back her down."

Dan dusted his jeans as Cynthia and the girls looked on with admiring smiles.

"When I was a kid, I saw Dad confront a bull that had cornered my cousin and me. I just tried to mimic what he did."

When everyone calmed down, Attie said, "That little episode whetted my appetite. Let's return to Eureka."

No one protested as Dan followed the road back to town and found a parking place. A boy dressed in shorts and no shirt guided a skateboard down the middle of the steep street, weaving in and out of cars and pedestrians.

Cynthia and the girls were soon gazing into the windows of the town's many eclectic businesses. After browsing several shops, Cynthia had purchased several sacks of tee shirts, postcards, and Ozark souvenirs. Trish and Emily loved every minute of it. Dan frowned, tapping his toes as he waited for Cynthia to try on an Arkansas peasant dress.

Seeing his discomfort, Attie said, "The Limerock is just up the street. There's a little bar inside, and we can get a treat for the girls and cold beers."

He grabbed Cynthia's hand with a nod when she returned from the dressing room in her new dress.

"You look great," Dan said. "Pay the man, and let's go. Attie tells me there's a cool bar near here, and I need a beer."

"But they have so much neat stuff here."

"We can come back later."

Cynthia frowned and paid for her purchases. They soon returned to the sidewalk, heading toward the multi-story Limerock Hotel. As the name suggested, the hotel they had visited the previous night was built of old glass and native rock. The sign on the window read ESTD 1888. A large cat lounged on the front desk.

"Oh! Look at the beautiful cat," Emily said, rushing up to the counter.

Enzio, Limerock's owner, smiled from behind the counter.

"His name is Bourbon," Enzio said. "He's a Maine Coon."

"Is he really a coon?" Trish asked.

"He's all cat with the coloration of a raccoon."

Seeing Attie with Dan, Cynthia, and the twins, Enzio winked and said, "I guess your plan worked."

Eric Wilder

"Better than I could ever have imagined," Attie
said.

Chapter 35

Attie shrugged and smiled when Dan glanced at her. "Trish and Emily want something to drink. Dan, Cynthia, and I need a cold beer."

"Follow me," Enzio said, leading them to a dark bar. "I'll be right back."

He returned with chocolate sodas for Trish and Emily, iced tea for Cynthia, and large draws for Attie and Dan.

"This is good," Dan said after taking a sip. "What is it?"

"Choc," Enzio said. "I brew it for my special customers. It was your father's favorite."

"How does he know so much about Dad?" he asked once Enzio had left.

"Seems everyone who met John had lots of stories about him. He was that kind of person. It would take six months for me to tell you all of mine."

"Good," Trish said. "I love this place."

"Me too," Emily said.

"Me three," Cynthia added.

Enzio soon satisfied their appetites with more beer and barbecue sandwiches. Trish and Emily received special souvenir cups filled with colorful gelato. As the twins finished their desserts and Attie and Dan sipped their beer, they noticed a group at another table pointing and whispering. Perturbed, Dan crossed his arms and stared at one of the men until he turned away, embarrassed.

"Sorry," Enzio said. "I'll boot them if they're bothering you."

Attie shook her head. "Forget it, Enzio."

When they exited the hotel, a young woman, backed by a film crew, thrust a microphone in Attie's face.

"Everyone in the world wants to hear your reaction to the news from the hospital?"

"What news?" Dan asked.

"You haven't heard?"

"Tell us," Attie said.

"John's alive. The doctors and staff are calling it a miracle," the reporter said.

"Alive?" Dan said.

"He's sitting up in bed, cracking jokes with the hospital staff. Everyone's calling him Miracle John."

Attie pushed through the gathering crowd, with the girls following her. Cynthia and Dan were close behind, moving through the crowd as their smiles told the story better than an interview. They returned to the Mercedes, and Dan hurriedly drove to the hospital along the main highway.

The crowd at the hospital had only increased when Attie and the crew arrived. Sheriff Simpson and his men were there and escorted them through the crowd and into the hospital. Attie saw Hulk's head poking above the crowd. When she smiled and waved, he lifted Lillie Mae onto his shoulders. From Attie's vantage, it was hard to tell if she was laughing or crying. Attie blew her a kiss and continued into the hospital.

John's smiling face was the first thing they saw when they entered his room. When Trish and Emily piled on the bed, he welcomed them with open arms. Attie stood by the bed, tears streaming down her face. Attie and the entire family were soon in a group hug that would have continued if the nurse hadn't shooed them off the bed.

"Oh, John," Attie said. "I thought I'd lost you."

"You almost did," he said. "My mind was awake, but I couldn't move except my eyelid. I wasn't sure if Dan saw me blink. He did, and it even frightened me when he read the Riot Act to my doctor. My body needed a few more hours to recover, and he provided that extra time. Trish and Emily, your dad saved my life."

The nurse heard the story, and it quickly spread through the crowd. The doctors weren't allowing any further visitors but let Hulk, Attie Mae, and the rest of the Oklahoma contingent peek in the door and wave.

"Call us," Norma said.

"When John feels better, I'm inviting you all back to spend some time with us," Attie said.

After the nurse had shut the door, John said, "I can't believe they came to Eureka Springs just to see me."

"You don't know the half of it," Attie said.

Epilog

Six months passed before John recuperated enough to have the party Attie had planned. It took place at the Limerock Hotel in Eureka Springs. Lillie Mae was pregnant, and she and Hulk were ecstatic. Mike, Norma, and Big Al drove from Oklahoma. Scooter and Sue were also there, along with Dan, Cynthia, the twins, and Billie. Everyone stayed with Attie and John for the weekend. Billie and the Warrens remained at the house on the bluff for the entire week.

Two kittens raced around the corner as the black Mercedes vanished down the hill, skidding between her ankles. She scooped them up, pressed them to her chest, and looked at the darkening sky.

When John said, "I'm going to miss everyone," Attie turned with a smile and joined him on the porch swing as large raindrops began falling.

"Not for long," she said. "We're meeting Scooter and Sue to play Indian bingo in April. We'll stop in McAlester and see Norma, Mike, and Big Al."

"Hulk and Lillie Mae are determined to have us present when their baby is born," John said.

Attie squeezed his hand. "We are responsible for the pregnancy."

"Right about that. I still miss Trish and Emily."

"They've visited at least six times since you left the hospital. Tulsa is only a few hours away, and now that we have a reliable car, we can see them whenever we want." John chuckled when she said, "How did I let you convince me to buy a red two-seater convertible."

"I've always wanted a Miata," John said.

"Well, now you have one," Attie said. "I still can't believe you're alive and with me."

"Me either," John said. "I thought I was a goner until that first night and the angel appeared."

"Angel?" Attie said. "I didn't see an angel."

"Dressed like a nurse. She was an angel."

"You were on heavy painkillers," Attie said.

"I was floating above the bed, ready to meet my maker, when the angel told you I needed your help. She had you touch me," John said. "When you did, my spirit rejoined my body."

"I remember someone telling me to touch you," Attie said.

"You asked the angel if I was going to survive. Do you remember what she said?"

Attie nodded and said, "How deep is your love."

"Guess it's pretty damn deep," John said.

A hawk with a beak that reminded Attie of John's nose swooped almost to the ground before floating upward, parting the clouds to reveal the sun for the first time in a week. Squirming from her grasp, the two kittens ran around the house to chase the peacocks.

"The woman was a nurse," Attie said.

"Angels come in lots of packages," John said. "Doesn't matter. The sun's finally out. Let's put the top down on the car and go for a ride. I feel like stretching my legs."

Attie laughed and said, "Old man, you're insufferable, but I love you."

"Love you too," he said. "Let's go before the rain starts again."

"We can't stop the rain, my dear," Attie said. "Doesn't matter because right now, the sun is absolutely magnificent."

End

Book Notes

After reading a 1990s newspaper article about an old man who disappeared from his son's house during a brutal Oklahoma winter, I penned the original version of *Of Love and Magic* I titled *Prairie Sunset*. Though I searched for updates on the story, I never learned what happened to the man.

I had only written one novel then and was still working as a geologist. Following the oil bust of the 1980s, which cratered the state's economy for almost two decades, times were still difficult in Oklahoma. I'd made an unsuccessful sales trip to Tulsa and decided to take a scenic route on my return to Oklahoma City.

A late winter snowstorm was beginning to cede its grip on the weather reluctantly, and warmer temperatures and welcome signs of spring greeted me as I drove through the rural Oklahoma town of Red Rock. The town was the home of a bingo casino that gave away thousands of dollars weekly to gamblers from surrounding states. The saga of John and Attie began taking shape during my unplanned excursion.

There were no Vegas-style casinos in Oklahoma during the 90s, and Remington Park, the first world-class parimutuel racing facility in Oklahoma, had only opened in 1988. The newly beginning gambling era in Oklahoma, the Bible Belt of America, set the stage for the Bonnie and Clyde-like adventure of an old man 'escaping' from his son's house in a raging snowstorm to avoid spending his remaining years in a nursing home.

Years have passed, and I was mostly happy with the novel, but I never liked the ending. The recent passing of my wife, Marilyn, prompted me to revisit *Of Love and Magic*. While events in life are irreversible, fictional endings aren't.

I hope you enjoyed reading *Of Love and Magic*, which has an alternate ending from the original book. I know it would have made Marilyn happy, and that realization makes me happy.

Since penning *Of Love and Magic*, I've written three series and another standalone novel. My *French Quarter Mystery Series* features moody private detective Wyatt Thomas.

You might also like my *Paranormal Cowboy Series*, which features Buck McDivit, my modern-day cowboy detective who likes horses, cowgirls, and Australian sheepdogs.

Hopefully, you're already a fan of the *Oyster Bay Mystery Series*, set on a Louisiana island near New Orleans. For those who haven't read it, I've included a three-chapter teaser of the first book in the novel in hopes it will catch your fantasy.

Thanks for being a fan. My stories would be little more than morning fog wafting across a forgotten lawn without beautiful readers like you. Thank you.

About the Author

Eric Wilder is an American author known for his gripping mystery novels set in New Orleans. He was born and raised in Louisiana, where he discovered his love for storytelling at a young age. After completing his education, Wilder spent several years in the oil and gas industry before pursuing a career as a writer.

Wilder's breakthrough came with the publication of Big Easy, which introduced readers to his signature blend of suspense, action, and local color. The book instantly succeeded, drawing critical acclaim and a devoted following. Wilder followed up with a collection of thrillers set in the heart of New Orleans.

Wilder's writing is characterized by his deep knowledge of the city and its unique culture and his skillful use of suspense and plot twists to keep readers on the edge of their seats. His books have been praised for their authenticity, vivid descriptions, and compelling characters.

Today, Eric Wilder is a respected author with a loyal fan base and a reputation for delivering top-notch thrillers that transport readers to the heart of New Orleans.

Wilder is the author of twenty-three novels, several cookbooks, many short stories, and Murder Etouffee, a book that defies classification. His series features characters who often find themselves involved in the paranormal.

Eric lives in Oklahoma near historic Route 66 with his wife, Marilyn, and their two dogs, Moe and Buddy.